MW01034773

Three Floods is a captivating story th
and forgiveness. Matt draws inspir
and emotions to reveal a grace filled understanding of the heart of God
toward the human condition.

You will be invited on a journey of self-discovery and spiritual
reflection, encouraging you to open your heart to grace, love, and hope
despite the overwhelming circumstances you may face.

If you enjoy books that blend fiction with spiritual and emotional
depth, *Three Floods* will be a meaningful and thought-provoking read.
This story will become a part of you and leave a lasting impact.

Trish Beckenham
Greater Things International
www.greaterthingsinternational.com

Matt Beckenham has given us the greatest gift in allowing us to return
once more into the biblical narrative with the Designer Himself. *Three
Floods* reads to me as an instant classic and appears to take us deeper
than we have gone before into some of the most challenging stories of
the Bible. We are given a new access point into the life of Noah and the
coming flood. The way we journey and explore this well-known story
with this unique approach feels like we are excavating a historical gold
mine.

This book is trailblazing; Matt is tapping into the world of parables
that allows us to grab a hold of long-held beliefs and experience the love
of God in such a way we are not the same again. These moments with the
Designer will transform you and leave you wanting more.

Jessie DeCorsey
Artist
jessiedecorsey.com

Once again, my friend Matt has been able to capture the heartbeat of our beautiful Father in these pages. Fictional, yes; but each character and every emotion lines up with the yearning of a God who longs to know His creation intimately. From the opening chapter and the words **"... I have never stopped inviting people to sit with me ..."** to the very last chapter, **"For it to be real, love must be chosen,"** the absolute love of the Father is evident on every page. Matt has a way of inviting his readers in through a door of culture and historical contexts balanced with real human emotion and a contagious desire to just stop and sit with the Father, for no other reason than love. I can't wait for part two!

Mandy Woodhouse
www.mandywoodhouse.com
YouTube: MandyWoodhouse2023
The Outrageous Hope Podcast

So many times, it is difficult for me to put myself in the narrative of the Bible. To feel what it must have been like or to know what questions people had, beyond the Biblical account, is often difficult to imagine. What I love about *Three Floods*, is the way Matt has invited us into conversations with the Designer. I found throughout reading this book that my questions blossomed. Quickly, I was able to find a place in the story of Noah. My curiosity and imagination came bubbling to the surface, and I was able to explore this story in more depth. The dialogue happening between the characters soon became a dialogue I was having with the Lord. With deep love and appreciation for the word of God, Matt has added his own imagination as an invitation to sit around a campfire with the Designer. This book had me running back to my Bible with fresh eyes for the stories we've read a thousand times. It had me snuggled up next to the Lord, asking Him to tell me more.

Matt Beckenham is a person who is leading the way back to intimacy with God. To know Matt is to see a person whose desire is to know what the Lord is thinking and to encourage others to saturate themselves in His presence. He is truly a friend of God.

Jade Schultz

Matt takes the art of storytelling to another level in *Three Floods*. There is great beauty in the invitation to open the pages, step into his craftsmanship, and experience the tangible real love of Yahweh. Like Noah listening to Eagle, I felt like I was engaging with a story that had been shared with me many times over, ever since I was a little girl. That feeling of familiarity is best described as 'coming home'. It's a sound that is deep and full of life and love. It's a resonance that our spirits know, and our hearts desire and it comes alive within us through the power of remembrance.

At one point Eagle says to Noah, "There is no one else in all of creation like you." I am so thankful that there is no one else in all of creation like Matt. He is one-of-a-kind, and he authors divinely inspired dialogues that are authentic, vulnerable, and liberating. It is always a joy and a revelation to read his works.

Kerri-Ann Luketic

I have never met anyone who reveals the heart of the Father as easily, beautifully, powerfully and personally as Matt does. *Three Floods* is an outpouring of this deep well of encounter, revelation and wisdom that Matt so naturally imparts from his own life, experience and love for others. Through one of the most unique literary expressions of prophetic fiction this modern day parable brings to life a famous biblical story and fills it with description, detail, imagination, inspiration and characters that enable us to connect in a brand new way with such a familiar narrative, while simultaneously discovering a life transforming revelation of how the Father sees us, knows us, created us and continually woos us, awakening every reader to the voice of the Father and uniting closer to the heart of love and indescribable grace of God himself.

Natalie Fuller
nataliefuller.co

As you read this book, *Three Floods* by my friend Matt Beckenham, you will be drawn into a beautiful parable, a stunning piece of fiction that is filled with such creativity, inspiration, imagination, and revelation. You will be drawn into the Father's heart and surrounded by His love through Matt's experiences and writing. Matt has such a gift in how he writes and shares that draws people into encounter with the Father's heart at deeper and deeper levels, that leaves them marked afresh by the kindness, freedom, and love of the Lord that far surpasses our understanding, and I know as you journey through this stunning parable you will be marked afresh by the love of the Father and how deeply He knows you and draws you into unprecedented depths of intimacy with Him and revelation of His nature.

Lana Vawser
lanavawser.com

So good to fly further into the narrative of God's word with Eagle, who seems to me to be becoming a friend I want to journey with. I find myself longing for the moments in the story when Eagle is sat with the creator, eagerly waiting to see what He will say next, knowing that whenever He speaks, He will speak with love and life.

This is a view of God that I know Matt longs for others to have – a God who is relational, loving, kind, and just – A God that we long to be in the presence of and to hear from.

My hope is that as you continue on in this story, you will have such a longing to know God as intimately as Eagle does – that's the invitation of John 10, and that, I know, is the heart of the author of these stories.

Rev'd Carl Smith
Church of England Vicar and Writer, UK

THREE FLOODS

THE SHIPBUILDER OF ENOCH

MATT BECKENHAM

Illustrated by Jessie DeCorsey

Published by Greater Things International
Sydney, New South Wales, Australia
www.greaterthingsinternational.com

First published 2023

Copyright © Matt Beckenham 2023

THREE FLOODS: The Shipbuilder of Enoch

 A catalogue record for this
book is available from the
National Library of Australia

ISBN: 978 0 6457868 3 5 (Paperback)
ISBN: 978 0 6457868 4 2 (Hardback)
ISBN: 978 0 6457868 5 9 (ePub)

Cover design and illustrations by Jessie DeCorsey
Typeset by Helen Christie
Printed by Ingram Spark

To Trish,

My Wisdom and my Eve.
Slowly we have learned to build a beautiful marriage
that would take us across troubled waters and into
new lands and adventures.

ACKNOWLEDGMENTS

Trish Beckenham, Jade Schultz, Frances Kreamer, and Jessie DeCorsey, thank you for all the reading, correcting, rereading, correcting, rereading, and correcting you have done for me.

Jessie DeCorsey, once again, you have brought this story to life through your brilliant illustrations. Each picture speaks so much of the story into being and allows the reader to easily picture themselves in it. Thank you.

Winifred (Winnie) DeCorsey, thank you for brilliantly illustrating Eagle and Wisdom. May we forever be blessed by your creativity and joy.

Zoey Engelbrecht, your artwork has always been such an expression of God's love. We love you and are so thankful your artwork is in this book.

Willow Gamble, thank you for sharing your art with the world. You have such a gift and it's such an honor to include it in this story.

Michael Henderson, thank you so much for being willing to write the foreword. Your heart, life, and work have inspired me to step beyond where I could imagine and believe in myself.

Emma Bollom, thank you for helping me be able to explain the wonders of childbirth in a way only you can. When I got to this part of the book, I knew it was your experiences and wisdom I wanted to add to the story.

Lastly, thank you to all who call me "friend." Your willingness to listen to all my stories and still want to have coffee with me will never be forgotten.

FOREWORD

by Michael Henderson

To read Matt Beckenham's writing is to listen to his heart. It is to listen in on his own personal conversation between him and God, and with the people in his life. I have known him for many years, and I hear his voice in this story. That is not a comment on grammar or style. It is to say that I hear his compassion and grace. I can hear him speaking with people and paying attention to them, noticing how unique and beautiful and complex they are. His writing reveals how deeply he listens to these people, and how he does it with such empathy and compassion and love, and how deeply he searches them, hunting for the gold he knows is in each one of us. It is a voice that causes me to remember God's voice, and as I read *Three Floods* I found it hard to tell the difference.

Some retell the old stories like we still live back there. Others throw out the old stories. And some, like Matt, embody a humility when they listen to these old stories that they can reveal their timeless truths so we can connect to them today. This is *Three Floods*.

There is as much wrestle and tenderness in the dialogue between Designer and Wisdom and Eagle, as there is when it is extended to Noah and all the others contained in this story.

I found the interaction between Noah and Designer so profound. In particular, there is a scene where they have a direct and honest conversation where Noah remembers his grandfather. He recalls a time when he harvested a field of grain too early, and was overcome with such fear of punishment that he hid. As his grandfather searched for him, he was forced to listen and wait until he was eventually discovered. However, instead of the expected punishment, Noah was met with love. In the conversation with the Designer, this recalled event moves Noah to laugh, then to joy, and that joy breaks a stronghold that allows him to speak freely and openly once again. The Designer rounds out this conversation with a comment that Noah will learn much more of love in the years ahead. This is what I mean when I say I can hear both Matt and God's voice in the story of *Three Floods*.

In the context of this old story of Noah and floods, there are big and complex themes, loaded with lament and confusion, and here infused with hope and compassion and a depth of seeing actual people. What comes out is that even in the most tumultuous of times, our God is always present with us.

This is a story for our moment, born out of Matt's connection with the people he meets and does life with, framed into a story of redemption and hope and grace, with each word revealed in story.

Is this story fiction, as Matt says? Is it a pastor using his words to reveal the truths of our God? Is it prophecy? Whatever it is, I believe stories can remake the world. This story is one of them. And our world needs a little remaking at the moment, a little infusion of hope in what can be tumultuous times. *Three Floods* gives me hope that we can do this.

Michael Henderson
Artist and Writer
www.michaeljameshenderson.com.au

LIST OF CHARACTERS

(In order of appearance)

The Designer – God

Eagle – He is an eternal eagle and the narrator of the story
Wisdom – She is an eternal eagle and Eagle's Eve*

Adam – The first man
Eve – The first woman
Cain – son of Adam and Eve
Abel – Son of Adam and Eve
Miriam – Abel's Eve
Seth – Son of Adam and Eve
Michael – Angel
Gabriel – Angel

Enosh – Son of Seth
Kenan – Son of Enosh
Mahaallel – Son of Kenan
Jared – Son of Mahalalel
Enoch – Son of Jared
Methuselah - Son of Enoch
Hadar – Methuselah's Eve

---

*   In referring to marriage, I have used the words "Adam" and "Eve"
(i.e., Wisdom is Eagle's Eve, and Eagle is Wisdom's Adam)

Lamech – Son of Methuselah

Rebekah – Lamech's Eve

Noah – Son of Lamech and Rebekah

Caleb – Lifelong friend to Noah

Ben – Lifelong friend to Noah

Cain – Descendant of Cain, son of Adam

Nashah – Cain's first daughter and Noah's Eve

Deborah – Cain's second daughter and Ben's Eve

Nacham – Cain's son

Baht – Housekeeper for Cain

Lucifer – Satan

Banay – Master shipbuilder

Abishai – Son of Ben and Deborah

Shem – Son of Noah and Nashah

PREFACE

Jesus would often teach about the Kingdom of God using parables, which are short stories/allegories of fiction that would help the listener understand a greater understanding or revelation. This story, like its predecessor, *Three Trees*, is a parable. *Three Floods: The Shipbuilder of Enoch* is the series' second book. I pray that this will help you get curious about the familiar stories people have learned for generations and see more of what a relationship with God can look like.

MAP

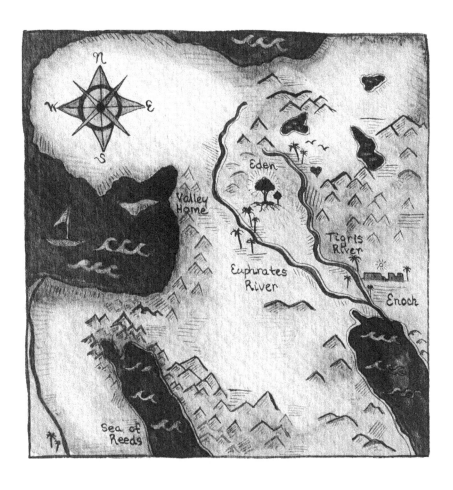

"Grace is found by those who search for it, and when discovered, it is seen in everything."

"Three Floods, but only one is eternal."

PROLOGUE

My name is Eagle, and I was created to soar the heavens and watch over the Designer's creation. I am an eagle, but my years have far surpassed those that also were created as eagles. They would live for many years, but few would live as long as I have lived. I have soared across His creation and seen wonders that few can believe. There are other eagles like me, but the one I cherish above all others is my Eve, Wisdom; together, we are one. As her name suggests, she holds the understandings of the Designer within her. She is His calming voice, as much as she is His powerful voice. She has the ability to see events of the future and has told me of stories I cannot even imagine. But the story she loves to tell is the great love story the Designer began before the foundations of the world. Long before Cain murdered his brother Abel, or the first woman, Eve, took a bite of the fruit from the *Tree of Knowledge of Good and Bad*, the Designer sang His great love story into being. This song includes the stars in the skies above and the animals that live deep within the ground. It is a story I know as much about as the length of my years, but I have yet to hear its ending. Even though

I do not know the end, I was there when it all began. Much has changed in the story, but the one who has not changed continues to love as He always did.

Many years have passed since my charge was to watch over Adam and Eve, who have now died and joined Abel and Cain.

From the ground, they were made, and to the ground, they returned. But the glow they contained could not be buried. Their spirits lived on and never tasted death.

Their youngest son, Seth, carried the glow of Adam's family, for he also loved walking in the cool evening with the Designer. He had a presence about him that showed he was confident and happy with who he was created to be.

Like Abel, he loved people well, and, like Cain, he knew how to work the soil. Even though he had grown up without either, Seth carried the best of both his older brothers. Abel had died before he was born, and Cain had moved away to build the city of Enoch. Late in Cain's life, he returned and spent time with Seth. But by then, Seth was a grown man and had become a leader whom people would follow.

Cain's return was beautiful and complex. I was with him when he stopped at the place where he killed his brother. So many tears flowed from him into the ground. The blood had long since disappeared into the soil, but the memories were as clear as if it had just happened. With his hands in the ground already, the Designer had been waiting there for Cain. The events of the past could not be changed, but Cain's heart could continue to heal.

The day of Abel's death continues to occupy my thoughts as if it had happened yesterday. So much occurred in a brief space of time.

It was the day the brothers were to bring a gift of their produce to the Designer. Abel had given Him the whitest lamb I had ever seen; the Designer was so happy to receive it. Cain's gift, if he had had his way, did not possess the same purity. I remember so clearly when Enoch, Cain's son, defied his father and brought the best gift possible from Cain's harvest. Cain had told him to take from the mildewed and rat-infested grain, but Enoch would not present that gift to the Designer. Cain learned that day the Designer knew when he was lying. I find myself shaking my head when I remember Cain's shock and then seeing his son carry the glow of the Designer. The events of that day would scar us all. It was the day Cain allowed his anger to be a louder voice than the Designer's.

When I close my eyes, I can still imagine Abel's blood on the ground with Cain's digging tool lying in the glistening red pool. I can remember the screams of Miriam and Eve as they realized what happened. Then Adam's rage at discovering what Cain had done. Talking snakes seemed to be everywhere I looked. Remembering them hiss out their lies still inspires anger in me.

Long after Abel's death, I often found Eve sitting on the ground where his body had laid. She would be there for hours, and no one dared disturb her. Sometimes she would return home with tears in her eyes, and at other times, she would return to tell anyone who would listen all the things Abel achieved. Eve ensured his memory never faded. Abel's wife, Miriam, had his son, and he looked every bit like his father.

I will never forget finding Cain wandering in the desert; he was near death and far from home. He expected to be judged and known forever as a murderer. But that was not what the Designer had in mind for him. It is not the Designer's character to destroy. He did what no one expected: He marked Cain with his mercy, a mark he carried for the rest of his life. Cain went on and built the magnificent city of Enoch, named after his son. It was a place where he could, once again, apply his ingenuity. Cain and his family thrived in that land.

People were drawn to the city of Enoch for many reasons. It was prosperous, and many traveled long distances to trade there. The city became renowned for the tools its tradespeople would make. It also became famous for the master artisans who created instruments, particularly harps and flutes. The sounds that flowed from these instruments they called music, and they were sounds that moved my spirit. I could have sat and listened to them play until the end of my days.

But it was the many conversations with the tradespeople that excited Cain. He would sit with them for hours, locking minds around fixing a problem. Invariably, after a long night of wrestling, they would emerge with a solution and a tool to help them.

But the primary reason people would travel to Enoch was to see the Designer's mark on Cain. The story of one brother killing the other had traveled to places near and far. It was a pain Cain carried with him throughout his life. The Designer's mark, however, took people's breath away. The glow he carried became the mark of the Designer on him, and they would often leave with the same glow. I would hear many stories of people being healed or changed by Cain's presence.

Adam and Eve would often make the trip to the city of Enoch to see their son. Their first trip was challenging, as it was the first time they had seen Cain since he fled. The Designer joined and walked with them. I remember He invited the three of them to sit with Him on the ground and to place their hands into the soil. He invited them to reach past the pain and feel the love flowing into and through them all. They shed many tears on that trip. As each subsequent trip came and went, it became less challenging, but I wonder if it ever became easy. Some wounds take a lifetime to heal.

Miriam and Abel's baby was born a few months after Abel's death, and he was a fine young boy. His mother gave him the name of his father. Abel means His Breath; it is a beautiful name to hear spoken. Hearing Miriam call him was like listening to the Designer speak Adam into existence all those years ago. Abel was breathed into again and grew to be a shepherd, like his father. The lessons his father had taught his apprentices were now passed to his son, and he was a fast learner.

Once Adam and Eve had died, the Designer charged me to watch over their youngest son, Seth. Generations of faithful people would come from Seth. But it was to his son, Enosh, that the Designer would reveal one of His names. I had only ever known Him as "the Designer" or called Him "my Lord." To discover He had a name shocked me at first. But when he spoke it, it was like I had known it all along: He became known as Yahweh, which means He brings into existence whatever exists. To even think His name brings peace and joy to my spirit.

The atmosphere would shift whenever someone spoke Yahweh. It was a powerful name that inspired awe. The Designer loved His name and shared His presence and love with His people. What started with Adam and Eve walking in the cool of the evening with Him became a crowd of their family gathering by the banks of the Tigris River each evening. It was a beautiful time for everyone there. They would wait on every word that He spoke. They would sit and feel the powerful love that holds everything together, flowing through the ground.

Over time, though, the people spoke His name less and less. Some claimed it was too awe-inspiring to come from the lips of people who had given up Eden. One day when I asked the Designer about this, I saw His countenance change.

He said, "They are beginning to believe more in my name than in who I am." He was silent for a time before He continued, "My name is indeed all they have described, but it is who I am that I long for them to see and connect with. It is not a word that merely defines me; it is a word that invites me. I have never stopped inviting people to sit with me. They would sit with me as Adam and Eve once did when they accepted my invitation. You have seen this many times, Eagle. You were there when they would walk home glowing after being with me. They had been permitted to understand the mysteries of my kingdom. They called me 'friend,' just like I have called you 'friend.' The glow you saw in them was not because I favor or love them any more than anyone else in my creation. They are the ones who have learned that I love to walk with them. I would walk with any of the people I have created, but I will not force them to walk with me. In this, Eagle is the essence of the invitation of my name."

That was many years ago, and I have had many charges to watch over. I would watch the Designer love them as He loved all of His creation. His character remained as true as His love. He gave each the freedom to choose Him or leave Him. It was a choice He would always allow, even when it hurt Him terribly. He knew if He withdrew their choice, He would have already withdrawn His love from them.

The Designer commissioned me to watch over this generational line. And now, my charge had changed again.

CHAPTER 1

Generations had come and gone. From Seth would come Enosh. From Enosh would come, Kenan. From Kenan would come Mahalael. From Mahalael would come Jared, and from Jared would come Enoch. This was not Cain's son, Enoch. That Enoch had long ago joined his father in death. This was another Enoch, and he would not taste a physical death.

Each generation had its own expression of relationship with the Designer. Since Seth and Enosh, few had carried the same intensity of glow, and rarely would I find people walking with the Designer in the cool of the evening. They would occasionally come, and difficult seasons usually marked these times. When there was not enough rain, they would go back to the banks of the Tigris and wait to meet with the Designer and ask for rain. Once the rains returned, people would find other things to do rather than walk in the cool of the evening with Him.

That was until Enoch came along. He was at the river every evening and always glowed with the Designer's presence. It was not need that drew him to His presence; it was the Designer's love.

I often wondered if it was reciprocal and if Enoch's love drew the Designer to him.

He loved to spend all of his time with the Designer. People would often make jests about him. They continually mocked him, calling him 'The Designer's favorite,' but it never bothered Enoch. It baffled him why everyone was not at the river each evening. I have not met a person more curious than him. His father, Jared, could not answer all his questions and often became frustrated that he would not follow him in becoming a shepherd. Enoch even had a way with animals that reminded me of Abel and Seth, but it was not animals that caught his imagination; it was the Designer.

Wisdom loved spending time with Enoch and would often be found talking with him long into the night. They would share the most wondrous stories of things I had never seen or heard of, about the future, and of angels I had never met. He had the most glorious visions and monumental dreams. Sometimes he would share what he saw with me, but it was beyond my imagination to grasp all the realms and angelic forces he described. Maybe I would in the future, but when he spoke of great battles yet to happen, it often made me wonder if he meant the spiritual realm or here in creation. The stories fascinated me, and I always longed for more.

There was much more to him than the stories he told or the visions he had. Enoch had a love that could not be hidden. Often people would bring their sick loved ones to him, and I watched them heal just by being in the presence of his love. He was never too busy for anyone. To each one, he would stop, listen, and love them. There was even a time when I watched him bring a dead person back to life. I watched as he placed one hand in the dirt and another on the man's chest. The love and glow that flowed from Enoch into the man restored his life.

Enoch lived within sight of Eden for three hundred years and was always close to the Designer's heart. It was a rare moment if the Designer arrived and Enoch was not already there. He would often have the fire roaring and a list of questions ready. When they were together, everyone could see where they were, for the glow that flowed from them both was like the moon at night. Days, weeks, months, and years were spent in each other's presence.

But then, on one of those days, of one of those weeks, of one of those years, Enoch disappeared. People looked for him everywhere, but no one could find him. Some said he became a wanderer like Cain and just walked off, but I did not believe that. The day he disappeared, I was out soaring and looking for him when Wisdom flew right up to me. She came up so fast that I got a surprise. She was laughing at catching me off guard. Few can, but Wisdom could always do that.

She said, "Eagle, what are you doing out here?"

"I'm looking for Enoch," I said. "The Designer commissioned me to watch over him, and I have lost him."

At that, she laughed, "Eagle, you will not find him out here."

"Wisdom," I replied, "If you know where he is, you must tell me."

Still, she laughed, "Where did you see him last?"

"He was with the Designer on the banks of the Tigris River," I said.

"Yes, he was Eagle," she replied. "You didn't see him return home, did you?"

"Of course, he must be still with the Designer," I exclaimed.

"In a way, Eagle," she said.

"In a way? What do you mean, Wisdom? Please stop talking in riddles. You sound like the Designer," I exclaimed.

That caused her to laugh again, which caused me to get frustrated.

"Eagle," she said, "The Designer took him back to Eden."

It took me a moment to understand what she said. Then when it did make sense, I went from shock to confusion, and then I did not know what to do. I was too shocked to form words and nearly forgot I was flying.

Finally, I blurted out, "He took him to Eden?"

"Yes, Eagle, The Designer took him to Eden, and Enoch ate from the *Tree of Life*."

"Wisdom, no one has done that since Adam and Eve. The Designer placed angels to prevent anyone from doing that." My voice became a screech, "Wisdom, are you certain of this?"

I could not comprehend what I was being told. Those angels had been placed so no one could access that *tree*. Why would the Designer let him do this? I flew in silence as I pondered this, and slowly it all began making sense to me. Enoch's glow was so strong, and it was the same glow I saw when Abel's spirit left his body. Enoch must have become one with the Designer. I continued to fly in silence as memories of my time with Enoch flooded back. As they did, tears also flooded.

"I would have loved the opportunity to say farewell to Enoch," I sniffled.

"He is gone, Eagle. The Designer walked so closely with him, and their bond was so strong. Death had and has no power over Enoch." She continued, "Other events happened yesterday, but in this, the Designer simply asked if he wanted to go to Eden, and Enoch took one look over his shoulder as if farewelling us all and said 'yes, my Lord.' At that, they walked into Eden and only stopped to eat from the *Tree of Life*."

I could feel Wisdom's joy, but for me, there was sadness, maybe even grief. He was my charge, and I was supposed to be watching over him, and for over three hundred years, I had. But in one moment, all that changed, and I missed it.

I knew flying to Enoch's home would not be the same. Someone, without equal, had been taken from creation. Usually, I would have been soaring and taking in the magnificence of the sunset, but that night, the colors were not looking as bright.

I wondered who would replace Enoch. He had children, but none had the same desire to meet with the Designer. But it was too soon to be thinking such thoughts. That night I sat by myself feeling lost; the Designer had not told me of His plan for Enoch's departure, and a part of me felt hurt not to know.

The last light of the day faded, and the deep dark of the night grew, but still, I sat. The stars that night were a sight to behold as they stretched across the night sky, and again, usually, I would have been in awe, but I could not even feel the cold; I was numb.

Only when the sky started to lighten did I stir. There were still so many unanswered questions. I knew the Designer would want to see me, and although I did not want to think about it, soon I would discover my next charge.

CHAPTER 2

I left Wisdom to her soaring the next day as I needed time to think about everything I had witnessed. There was a high mountain where I liked to do this. It was one of the highest mountains in the area, and very few animals could ascend to its heights. If I ever wanted solitude, this was the place where I would be alone with my thoughts. Even the flight there was enough to bring peace to every part of my spirit. The joy of finding the powerful winds deflecting off the mountains was intoxicating. Each one would take me higher, and then I would find another and go higher again. I could feel the temperature drop as I climbed, and I knew the summit drew closer.

The only sound I could hear was the wind and the cries I shouted. I loved to listen to them as they bounced off the cliffs. The sound scared me the first time I did this, as I thought another eagle must be up here. I was soon to learn what an echo was, and once I did, it brought me joy to hear my own voice.

The colors of the mountains changed as I climbed. The rocks at the base of the mountains could not be seen because of all the mighty trees surrounding it. There were all manner of trees in the forests. Enormous oak trees grew in the valleys, and tall pine trees grew further up the mountains. As I flew higher, the trees gave way to great grey rocks and deep brown soil. The stunning sheer cliff faces would prevent anyone from climbing these mountains everywhere I looked. Climbing higher, the plants also changed, with low-growing plants often covering the rocks. The summit was my destination, and I loved it above them all. It was here the snow had fallen amongst the rocks, and its bright white starkly contrasted with the heavy grey of the granite. There were some plants up here, but they were tiny. Some even had flowers; these, too, were small. But the purple, yellow, and white colors they carried were stunning, and they continued to declare the Designer's most perfect design.

Every part of the flight up was awe-inspiring. However, when I arrived, I found I was not alone. The Designer was waiting for me, and it looked like He had much on His mind. He was not shocked to see me but I was to see Him. Yet, I could tell something weighed heavy on his spirit. He greeted me with half a smile and silence. I knew He was here to talk with me, so I waited.

As I sat beside Him, I let my spirit settle and take in my surroundings. It was impossible to sit beside Him and not be affected by Him. His presence brought vibrancy to everything around Him. Every one of my senses heightened, colors appeared brighter, and my eyes could see further. As hard as the ground was, I sunk my talons into the soil and waited for the Designer to speak.

From this mountain, I could see the horizon in every direction. I could see the Tigris and Euphrates Rivers snaking their way through the ground in the east. I could nearly see the city of Enoch. It was cold up here on the mountain, and the longer I sat, the more I began to feel the chill. But one of the beautiful parts of my design is that I was created to bear this. As I sat, a memory seeped back into my mind of Abel climbing this very mountain and complaining he was not designed for such cold. He had climbed from the south, avoiding the sheer cliffs surrounding the mountain. I smiled to myself as I remembered how He would bring clothes made from the wool of his sheep. He boasted that they would keep him warmer than any other clothing he knew, but up here was a cold his clothes could not keep out.

I was shaken out of my memories when the Designer spoke. I could feel heaviness in His spirit and even grief in His words. I had expected to hear of how He had taken Enoch to Eden to eat from the *Tree of Life*, but His voice had no celebration.

"Wisdom told you I took Enoch to Eden, and it is true. However, I did not take him there to celebrate him but to protect him." The Designer's words hung heavy in the air. I did not know what to say, so I waited.

"Eagle, what do you see of my creation?"

"My Lord, I see your presence in all of creation. Just to take in everything I see here would take me years to describe, as it is beautiful beyond words," I replied.

"Yes, Eagle, I can see it all as well. It is indeed beautiful, and it is indeed good." A long silence followed, but I felt He was preparing to tell me more, so I waited.

"Eagle, you are more than one who watches for me; you are a see-er for me. What do you see when you look upon the ones created in my image?"

I was beginning to understand what He was asking. My task was to be His eyes for Seth and the generations that followed him, but many other eagles were tasked to watch over other families. Their tales differed vastly from mine, and they were troubling. When we gathered, I would hear stories of pain, grief, and death. I heard tales of the spirits that had entered lizards, snakes, and vultures that had now entered those created in the Designer's image. I heard stories that gifts given to the Designer had become

15

known as sacrifices, and those sacrifices were even children. These stories horrified me, and I think, in those early days, I chose not to believe them.

I had learned a new word, 'evil.' It was a word I would never speak out loud. When my fellow eagles spoke it, I felt the atmosphere get heavier. I had heard other descriptions of it, such as 'destroyer,' 'abyss,' 'adversity,' and 'distress.' Words I did not want to learn. The Designer formed none of these, but I knew where they had come from.

Very few of my eagle friends reported seeing the glow or the mark like Enoch had carried. Instead, they spoke of darkness and how they could no longer communicate with their charges. Some even wondered why they were watching over people who did not want to spend time with the Designer.

A heaviness had been spreading over the land. Even in the family I had been charged to watch over, there were fewer people who would meet with Him to experience His presence. Enoch was the exception, and his son, Methuselah, also carried the glow, but I had always found his name troubling.

When Methuselah was born, everyone was shocked by the name Enoch had given him. It literally means 'his death shall bring forth.' No one could understand why Enoch had given him such a name. They would ask, "What was his death going to bring? What did that even look like? Would Methuselah be another Cain?"

To my eyes, Methuselah was another Enoch. He loved following his father down the river and meeting with the Designer. He, too, had so many questions that even I thought the Designer would tire of listening to him. But the Designer never did; instead, it brought Him much joy to hear all that was happening within the young boy.

So, to me, his name was a contradiction, but then again, I knew Enoch had foresight, and I knew he had conversations with the Designer about this name. I learned this from Wisdom's foresight;

not everything was as I had perceived. She told me that foresight is like looking through a curtain, sometimes it's clear, and other times it is not.

But what had Enoch seen to give his son this name? That would become clearer in time, but back then, I was sitting on a mountain with the Designer who had much on His mind.

"Eagle," He said. "I am sorry I even made these people in my image." A long pause followed this before He continued, "Can you see how far these people have drifted from me? Can you see what they have become capable of doing? Even the stories of them sacrificing their children are true." And again, He said, "I am sorry that I have even made them."

His words hung so heavily in the air I felt I could have reached out and grabbed them; He said them with such feeling and pain. Then I heard a sound from Him I had never heard before; a deep groan. His heart was breaking, and I did not know what words to say.

"The children, Eagle," He said. "Their blood cries out to me like Abel's blood all those years ago," he continued, "The depravity of these people is beyond comprehension, and there is no love found among them. Love has left these lands, Eagle."

At that, the Designer's tears flowed, and His tears brought me to tears. All I could do was sit beside Him and let them roll from my eyes. I had never felt so helpless and even hopeless at that moment.

After many moments, I asked, "My Lord, can I say something?"

"Yes, Eagle, you are my friend; you always have permission to speak to me."

"My Lord, how can love leave these lands when everything is held together by the love you have poured into them? If you stopped loving, we would all cease to exist."

He paused, exhaled deeply, and said, "You are correct, Eagle. My love is still there, but my creation is killing itself. Eagle, I know you can also feel what I speak of in the animals. Many of them are no longer behaving as I created them to, they are turning on each other, and death has become a part of their lives."

The Designer was right; I had felt all He had said. Even some eagles were not behaving as they were created. This 'evil' was leaving its own mark, but this mark was not drawing people to it. This mark was causing people to live in fear. All who carried it dominated and controlled others by it. Truly, the Designer's design had been horribly compromised.

I asked the Designer, "My Lord, is evil winning?"

He sighed deeply again and said, "No, it is not winning." Then, His shoulders dropped a little before He continued, "No, it is not winning, but it hurts Eagle, it hurts."

"My Lord, is now the time for the seed to be sown into the ground?"

"No, Eagle, not yet, but I cannot keep letting this magnitude of evil go unchecked. The daughters of Eve have forgotten the strength of their heel and how to destroy those talking snakes. They have not only listened to them again but also welcomed them in, and now my words are being replaced with lies."

We sat in the quiet for so long that the day had turned to night. I was always so comfortable sitting in His presence; He was never in a rush to get to where He was going next. But I could see Him wrestling with what He wanted to say to me. He would open His mouth to speak, close it just as fast, and think some more. But I was prepared to wait for as long as it took for Him to speak; I would never miss the opportunity to feel the love in His voice. Even when His voice was so heavy, such love was still in it.

Finally, He said, "Methuselah's death will bring about a moment that my creation has not yet seen. Eagle, do you know the meaning of his name?"

"Yes, my Lord, it means, 'his death shall bring'."

"That is true, but until now, you have not known what it means and what it will bring. Eagle, it will bring my judgment on the evil my creation has been infected with. But because my creation has welcomed this evil, it will also feel the weight of what is about to happen."

A long silence followed before He said, "Methuselah has born a son named Lamech. Lamech will then have a son named Noah, and if the ones created in my image will not turn back to me, then this judgment will happen in Noah's days."

I did not know what to say. Hearing Him speak of judgment on His creation sent a shiver down my spine. Death was not in His character, and I had only known Him as the source of life, not the bringer of death.

"Eagle, this is still many years away. Until then, I will continue inviting these people to meet with me in the cool evening, as I have always done. I will not hide from them. There is still time for them to turn around. If more than one carries my mark, then I will change my mind."

The weight of His words was so heavy that I cried. I could not help the tears that fell from my eyes and onto my feathers before they landed in the snow beneath me. I could not comprehend what He meant, and His very words were enough to cause my heart to break. It was as if I was grieving already, but I could not understand what I was losing. He spoke of regret for even creating these people, and I even wondered if He regretted making me.

Reading my thoughts, He placed His hand on me and said, "My dear Eagle, I would never regret creating one who carries such love as you."

His touch and words soothed my spirit, but these words of the future still troubled me. I knew this was still many years into the future, and not before Methuselah and Lamech's spirits would join Adam's.

CHAPTER 3

When the Designer took Enoch from creation, He left only two men who carried the mark of His grace and mercy, Methuselah and Lamech. The Designer's words rang in my ears, 'If there is more than one who carries my mark.'

Well, there were three. Not only did Methuselah and Lamech carry the mark, so did Methuselah's Eve, Hadar. She would hardly be separated from Methuselah, and they joyfully carried the Designer's mark so easily that people saw them as one. She was a woman of uncommon beauty and carried such compassion in her spirit. She had time for everyone and loved to cook. The aromas that floated over the valley when she cooked drew everyone working in the fields to Methuselah's home in the evening. The smell of roasting onions, garlic, and freshly picked mushrooms became irresistible to us all and was an invitation to eat with her family.

She loved Methuselah, and he loved her. They had met when they were both young, and from that age, they walked together in life and love. They had more children than just Lamech, and she poured love equally on them all. To be a child in their home was the envy of many. They all knew they were loved, and they all knew they were trusted. I would watch over them as they would disappear into the valleys to explore. Each time, they would return with a bump or a bruise, but they all carried stories of the adventures they got themselves into.

I remember a day when Lamech came bursting in through the door, telling his parents of the enormous animals he had seen in a valley far to the north. He spoke of the horns on their heads and a tale resembling a club. No one initially believed him, and I watched as the joy of his discovery was robbed. A few days later, that animal walked into the valley, and everyone could see that Lamech had been telling the truth.

Hadar was much shorter than Methuselah, but what she lacked in height, she carried in her love for the Designer and Methuselah. Her hair was jet black, darker than anyone I had ever seen, and it made her stand out in a crowd. Every evening she would join Methuselah and meet with the Designer; she would often linger with Him long after Methuselah had gone home. The darkness of her hair framed the glow she carried, and they combined to make people stop on the road to gaze upon her. Women would come from all around to learn from her and listen to the wisdom she carried. She was not as old as Methuselah but had outlived many other women her age.

Methuselah lived so long people thought his name was a jest and he would never be brought to or taste death. He had lived for hundreds of years and did not look like joining his ancestors anytime soon. Some joked that he was not good enough to be taken to Eden like his father. Others joked that the Designer had given him long life as a punishment for all his mistakes. But, like his father, he loved to spend time with the Designer, and when his son, Lamech, was born, he would join his parents most evenings.

After many years, Lamech found an Eve of his own. Her name was Rebekah, and as her name suggests, she was captivating. She and Lamech had a son they called Noah. Again, his name intrigued me, for it meant 'rest.' When I thought about his grandfather's name, I felt like puzzle pieces were slowly coming together; 'his death shall bring rest.' Even so, I could not fit Lamech's name into this. His name means 'poor, or made low.' At that, I decided I needed to find the Designer again.

It was never hard to find Him, as He always seemed to be where my heart desired Him to be. That day my heart desired to meet with Wisdom as well, and when I found her, I found Him. They were sitting beside the mighty Euphrates River. This river is an incredible part of the Designer's creation. All manner of fish live in this river, and that day, Wisdom and the Designer were watching the fish swim upstream. This always intrigued me, and because He was watching them, I found another question I wanted to ask Him.

"My Lord, why do these fish swim upstream?"

"They do this to reproduce," He replied.

"But why do they have to swim upstream to do this?" I asked again.

"Eagle, look closely at these fish. Can you see the powerful tale they have been created with?"

"Yes, my Lord, I do."

"They need this when swimming upstream to move faster than the current going downstream. The strongest ones can make it to the areas of the river to reproduce safely. This way, the fish that come from them are the strongest," He said.

Even after all these years, His design and ways continue to amaze me. There is so much more of His creation I know nothing about, but a few minutes with the Designer opens my mind to things I could have never imagined.

"My Lord, can I ask you another question?"

He smiled at me and said, "Of course."

"I have just come from the birth of Lamech's son; they called him Noah." I continued, "Noah means 'rest.' My question is, if I combine his grandfather's name with his, I get, 'his death shall bring rest.' Has the time come for rest, my Lord?"

My question made the Designer sit very still. He nodded, looked into my eyes, and said, "It is not long now, Eagle, and the time will come when only one is left that carries my mark."

"But what of Lamech's name? I still do not understand why he was called this."

He replied, "Lamech's story and his choices are his own. He has been created with such a humble heart, but he still has not understood this and does not know who he is."

"Will you tell him, my Lord?"

"Eagle, do you remember when Cain would meet with me after his family left Eden?"

"Yes, my Lord, I do. It was like he knew he had to do that instead of desiring to do it."

"Lamech is similar. The difference is that he has learned not to listen to talking snakes. He has learned that my love flows through all things, including him. He longs for what his father has, and he will envy what his son will have. But do not fear, he will discover who he is through it all and before he joins his ancestors in the ground."

"So, it has nothing to do with his father's or son's names?"

"It has everything to do with them, Eagle. If those I created in my image fail to return to my love, they will be brought low, as his name suggests. They think they are rich, but without my love, they are poor. But rest is coming one way or another, and Noah will usher it in."

I looked at Wisdom, but she had her head bowed, and I could not see her eyes. Nothing about her made me feel that this rest would be good for many of those created in His image.

CHAPTER 4

Lamech and Rebekah had many other sons and daughters, but Noah captivated me. He was born with the mark the Designer had placed on Cain, and it was impossible to hide. Everyone who saw Noah could see the Designer's presence within him.

Lamech was proud of Noah but often had trouble telling him. It was not always obvious, as I often saw Noah on his shoulders as they walked in the cool evening with the Designer. But there were times I could see Noah's desire to hear his father praise him, but Lamech could not find the words. I would watch as Noah walked away, wondering what he needed to do to please him.

Then there were also times I would see Noah on the Designer's shoulders. There was such joy when the three generations would sit with Him. Methuselah was a wonderful grandfather; he took such care to show Noah all the plants of creation, and he was a willing student. From the moment he learned to talk, his grandfather taught him the words that would identify the plants and all the plants would do.

As a grandfather, he spoiled Noah; nothing was withheld

from the young boy. If Noah was hungry, Methuselah would feed him. When Noah wanted to play, he would always entertain him. I would often hear Rebekah telling Lamech to speak to his father and stop him from spoiling Noah. These were the first moments I saw Lamech's discomfort with his father. Maybe it was jealousy, or perhaps it was regret, but Lamech would never talk to me about it, so all I could do was watch.

Methuselah often credited his long life to the way he would combine the plants. People would travel far and wide to listen to how the combinations of these plants would bring healing. I would never tire of seeing this as I marveled at his wisdom and creativity. When he was with the plants, the Designer's glow would grow within him, and more often than not, another ailment would be healed.

As Methuselah was with the plants, Lamech was with the animals. He reminded me so much of how Abel would care for and tend to the sheep. He knew them all by name; he knew when they were hungry, and he could feel when something was wrong with them. It was through the animals Lamech first noticed something in the atmosphere had changed. Where once there was such peace, now there was growing unrest. Initially, he thought it must be what they were eating, but soon he realized something evil was at play. It was here he learned to deal with talking snakes; he noticed animals acting in ways that contradicted their design, and he could hear it in their voices.

One afternoon, I was sitting in a tree watching over Lamech and Noah when I heard one of those now-familiar voices. By this stage, I no longer needed to wonder who the voice belonged to. It did not matter if it was a strange lizard, a talking snake, a mocking vulture, or a crude person; the voice belonged to the enemy of all that is good.

It was not Lamech's first time hearing the talking snake, but it was Noah's. Lamech, being the father he was, allowed Noah's curiosity to find his voice. Lamech could have trodden on the snake, but he wanted Noah to learn how to discern these evil voices.

So I sat and watched Noah. He was only five years old, and everything caught his attention. Lamech watched closely over him, but a strange thing happened when Noah approached the talking snake. Every part of me was ready to swoop down and get rid of the snake if it even looked like it would strike Noah. But as I watched, I saw the snake whimpering as Noah approached it. I had only seen this once before, and that was when I took a talking snake to the Designer. As Noah got closer to it, the voice was silenced. It was as if the snake had become mute. And then, shockingly, he picked it up. He picked it up as if it was a plaything. The snake calmed even more and went to sleep in Noah's arms. It was then I felt a rush of wind fly past me, and I heard an evil screeching voice say, "I will return."

It was only the Designer I had seen this in. He did not need to yell at the snake or the spirit; he simply invited the snake into his arms. But what stunned me was Noah was only five, and he handled the snake as if the evil spirit was not even there.

Lamech simply reached down and put his arm around Noah's shoulders. He was perplexed but still said, "Well done, my son." He was still cautious of the snake, and I could see him observing its every move, but Noah was untouched by his father's concern for him.

As I watched this event happen, I was struck by a memory of the Designer speaking to Cain when He marked him. The Designer had told Cain the mark he received would protect him, and no one could take his life. Here, right in front of me, it felt as if I was watching this happen. Noah carried the mark the Designer had placed on Cain, and no one, not even a talking snake, could take his life.

Both Lamech and Methuselah knew of the coming rest Noah was named for, but I was unsure if they knew exactly what that meant. The promised rest, the Designer had previously described to me, sounded more like a promised judgment. But both the men knew it was tied to Methuselah's death. They both knew Noah carried the promise the Designer had placed within him from the day of his birth. They had discussed this many times with the Designer, and just as often, they left with unanswered or even more questions. Their curiosity then peaked when the Designer tasked them to train Noah in the ways of plants and animals.

As the years went by, those talking snakes would often appear. Noah would go to the snake each time as if rescuing it from the torment the spirit had caused. Rebekah, though, had taken to the ways of Eve and learned the weight of her heel was all that was necessary to stop the snake from talking in its vile voice. One day, Noah found three dead snakes hanging on a post behind their home. He was shocked to see these beautiful creatures displayed like this and ran into the house, demanding who did such a thing. Only to be met with his mother smiling at him.

She said, "Noah, I do not have your heart for these creatures, but the Designer has given me a heel for them, and that is what I will use."

Noah had learned early that there was no arguing with Rebekah when she had made up her mind. She was a woman of great courage, and when she had made her mind up, no one would change it. She loved Lamech and her children with such passion. The lion within her would come out if anything threatened her children, and she wouldn't let anything harm them.

I watched Noah grow in wisdom and stature. Methuselah, Hadar, Lamech, and Rebekah were so proud of him. The curious boy was becoming a man right in front of their eyes. His wisdom had increased so much that he began noticing things in creation that his father and grandfather did not. Methuselah found this intriguing, and I would often watch the older man learn from a young man, but I did not see Lamech doing the same. Much was changing for Noah.

Eventually, it was not just how Lamech's animals behaved that gave evidence of the changing atmosphere in creation. More and more stories were coming to them of horrifying atrocities happening in towns and settlements far from them. The world that Noah was born into was quickly becoming less and less safe to live within. Like his father, Noah felt this change in the atmosphere and saw it in the animals and plants. He would use all of his knowledge to find solutions and healing, but they often felt just out of reach. These were the moments he would be found with the Designer.

CHAPTER 5

One day, Noah came to Methuselah and Lamech and told them he wanted to travel to the city of Enoch and learn to use the tools of those who work with timber. He spoke of a conversation with the Designer about the need to learn this trade in the days ahead. He was not sure what that entailed, but he knew Cain's people had become famous for the tools they made.

Now Cain had long ago died, but his legacy lived on through the generations that followed him. Nobody alive made better tools than those trained in that city. Methuselah and Lamech could use those tools, but they both knew the training Noah could gain in Enoch would far surpass their rudimentary understanding and skill. But still, they both knew Enoch was not a safe place to be, and they feared for Noah.

That evening, the three men were already waiting for the Designer. They did not need to be found by Him; they were ready for a conversation. They had already built the fire the Designer would usually create himself, and when He arrived, He looked disappointed that He was not the one to make it.

"My Lord," Methuselah started. "Noah wants to travel to Enoch to train with the ones that build with timber."

The Designer smiled and replied, "That is a wise thing to do. I wish I had thought of that." He laughed before continuing, "I agree, Noah, you should go to Enoch."

Before Noah could open his mouth, Lamech quickly responded, "But, my Lord, the stories that come from Enoch are evil. In every way, they are evil; nothing good can come of this, and Noah may be in grave danger."

Noah did not appear eager to join the conversation. It was another feature of his character; even though he was still so young, he was a very patient man, and he listened well. Methuselah was less so, and he wholeheartedly backed up what Lamech had spoken.

"My Lord, surely you, too, have seen the depravity of these people. Cain died many years ago, and they do not remember or carry the mark you placed upon him."

The Designer stayed quiet through all of this. He was happy to listen and have them get all their concerns out first.

Lamech continued, "Forgive us, my Lord, but we fear what would become of Noah if he traveled to Enoch. To learn what he is seeking will take years, and surely the people of Enoch would seek to take advantage of him or even kill him."

Again, the Designer stayed silent.

To break the silence, Methuselah added, "My Lord, everything rests in Noah; you know this. For years, you have spoken to Lamech and me of all that is to come. We have sought to guide and protect him, but we cannot do that out there." He continued, "I have lived many years and seen many things. The wonder of your creation continues to inspire me, and our time together has brought me so much life." Methuselah paused, but we all saw that more was coming. "I have been faithful with everything you have placed in my hands, from the smallest seed to my son

Lamech and my grandson, Noah. I have carried a name that no one understands, and many people mock me for it. But I know my name is what you gave to Enoch, and I know my death will fulfill your words, so I have carried this name you gave me willingly."

Methuselah kept going, "I have often wondered if you have given me so many years because you do not want to bring your words into fulfillment. I think you have withheld my death because of your mercy to all people. I have watched you give mercy when many would give none. I have watched you faithfully care for your creation when much of your creation has not been faithful to you. Great love continues to flow from you, but so little love flows back into you. You have held on to the hope that these people will eventually rediscover your love. I asked myself, 'Is this a fool's hope?' It is as if you are withholding this coming rest hoping your people will turn to you." Then he finally said, "You are telling Noah it is good to go to the city of Enoch, but my Lord, it is a city of talking vipers. This, you know." Then Methuselah went quiet; everyone was silent.

Eventually, the Designer stirred and cleared His voice, "Methuselah, there is much truth in everything you say except for one thing, I do not carry a 'fool's hope.' I might be considered foolish to continue to love when there is no love in return, but if I stopped, I would no longer be who I am. Yes, Methuselah, I have given you many years, and there are still many more to come. And yes, I am waiting for my lost people to return." I could feel the sadness in the Designer, as could everyone who surrounded him. After a long silence, He stirred again and said, "Methuselah, after all these years, have you ever gone without?"

"No, my Lord, you have caused the ground to yield much to us all. We have prospered by the power of the love that flows through our lands." Methuselah answered.

The Designer continued, "Have you lacked protection from those who would steal from you through any of those years?"

This time, Lamech answered Him, "No, my Lord, we have not. There have always been rumors of bandits roaming the hills and fields, but we have not even lost one lamb to them."

"So, why do you worry about Noah's safety?" The Designer asked. The silence that followed was evidence of the conviction in their hearts. I wondered if they wrestled with the simple truth that Noah would be so far away from them and so far away from their protection. The Designer's voice broke their thoughts, "I will protect Noah as I have protected you. There is much for Noah to learn there, but this is not the sole reason for him to go to Enoch."

This got all three men's attention and mine. "You three are not the only ones to carry my mark upon you; there is another. Methuselah, you spoke of no one carrying the mark of Cain in Enoch, but there is one there, and she feels forgotten. Her name is Nashah." Then looking at Noah, He said, "She is your Eve."

Noah's eyes went wide at this. He was of the age when men looked for a partner, but there was no one so far. My eyes went straight to his father and grandfather, and they both stifled a yelp within them. It was Methuselah who spoke first. "My Lord, this can not be. Surely there is one amongst us who can be the Eve for Noah?"

Lamech added, "What good person could come out of Enoch?"

Methuselah motioned to agree with Lamech but saw the Designer was about to speak. Whatever words were about to come from him, we would never know.

"My friends, you have not heard what I have said; you have merely heard what you wanted to hear. You did not hear that my mark was on a woman in Enoch. Instead, you heard that Noah was to become one with a family you no longer see worthy of being connected to yours."

From their reactions, I could see that the Designer spoke the truth. Both Methuselah and Lamech stayed quiet. This talk about Eve, partners, love, and connection made me think about Wisdom.

I had not seen her for a long time, for she had left for Enoch; the Designer had given her a charge to watch over. I wondered where she was and what she was doing when the Designer interrupted my thoughts.

"The eagle, I call Wisdom, is in the city of Enoch, and she is watching over Nashah." At that, He looked up at me, and with a smile, He winked at me. No one there would have understood the smile and wink, but I always loved it when the Designer could see me like this.

"Noah, I want you to bring Nashah back when you return home. There are children for you to have before this time of rest occurs." The Designer's voice trailed off with these last words, and under His breath, I heard Him whisper, "When this rest occurs."

Then stirring out of His thoughts, he continued, "Nashah is of Cain's line. By bringing her to your home, you will restore Cain's line into the lineage of Adam. It has long been my desire to do this."

I found it intriguing that the Designer spoke His thoughts this way. Things were now happening to bring about all the Designer was planning. I could also feel a growing sense the Designer was losing hope in the ones created in His image. He wanted them to rediscover His love, but all we heard was the discovery they made of the evil moving across the land.

Finally, the Designer said to Noah, "I will never make you do anything. You are free to choose what you will do. You are free to stay here and free to go to the city of Enoch. You are free to take Nashah as your Eve, and you are free to say 'no'."

Noah never rushed a decision, and this decision had become more significant than just going to Enoch to learn a trade. His father and grandfather looked intently at him, and I could feel their confusion. Fear and love were contesting their thoughts, but I knew they would respect whatever Noah decided.

"My Lord, I need time to think," Noah replied.

CHAPTER 6

Noah was my friend and often sought me out when he had decisions to make; this time was no different. As he got up from the Designer and his family, he invited me to come with him. He walked long into the night. His favorite place to think was when he was in sight of Eden. He would often ask me to speak of my experiences there and would listen intently for as long as I would talk. He loved hearing about the *two trees*, Abel's hidden tomb, and the stories of creation. He would repeat them to me to ensure he had heard them right. I knew they would become stories he would speak to his children.

By the time he arrived at his favorite spot by the great Euphrates River, the sky had lightened. The night sky's deep black canvas, littered with more stars than could be counted, slowly dissolved into a deep pink that folded into a deeper red. Watching it was inspiring, and I have never tired of seeing it. Soon, the chill in the air would be replaced with the growing warmth of the sun as it rose. Everything about this time of day made me come alive. It was a time when I loved to soar. Before all the other birds would take flight, I would be up there by myself, enjoying the great expanse of the sunrise.

This time, though, was different. The longer Noah had walked, the heavier his steps had become, and I could tell the Designer's invitation was weighing heavily upon him. Usually, Noah would have all but run to the river, but this night, he took his time and kept his thoughts to himself.

He sat by the river and watched the power of it flow past him. I had often marveled at how much water flowed down the Euphrates and Tigris Rivers and wondered where all the water had come from. It was never-ending, and it was mesmerizing to watch. Sitting there that day reminded me of Cain and how he could divert the Euphrates River to irrigate his farming lands. He was the definition of a problem-solver. There was only one problem Cain could not find a solution to, and the memory of it brought tears back to my eyes. I had never forgotten the image of seeing Abel lying in a pool of his own blood, with Cain's digging tool abandoned beside him.

Noah had been watching the river for quite some time before raising his head and calling for me to come. I had been waiting in a nearby tree, and as soon as he motioned, I flew and sat beside him on the bank of the river.

"Eagle," he started, "You have been here since before Adam walked this earth."

I smiled at the memory of this. It was truly a wonder that revealed the brilliance of the Designer's handiwork.

"Yes," I said. "I was there when the Designer formed Adam from the dust."

"Eagle, tell me again of the story when Eve chose the fruit that grew on the *Tree of Knowledge of Good and Bad*."

I do not know how often I told him this one story, but it always challenged him. I told him of my conversation with Wisdom about the two greatest forces created by the Designer: choice and love. He always seemed to grasp the force of love, but it was the force of choice that intrigued him.

"Eagle," he started again, "The Designer has given me choice. I can go, and I can stay. I can find this woman who feels she has been forgotten, or I can walk past her." He paused momentarily and continued, "What will happen if I choose to go and not find this woman?"

"I could not tell you, Noah. You are asking me to look into the future based on choices that you may or may not make. I know the Designer's creation is reaching a critical point in its history, and He is committed to ensuring your safety and your family line. But I also know the Designer will not make you do anything, and He will never take your choice from you."

"He must trust us a lot to give us such freedom to choose like this," Noah replied.

"Yes, Noah, He does. I have found that His trust is not based on your ability, choices, or behavior. It is founded in His immense love for you."

"But how does He know I will succeed? How does He know I have what it takes?" He asked.

"Because He made you, Noah. He knows everything about you and designed you to be you, and there is no one else in all of creation like you."

At that, Noah went silent and gave himself over to his own thoughts. His gaze was on the water, and he was watching the way the water flowed. I could see him studying the rocks beneath the surface and how the water was forced to find other channels around those rocks.

After what seemed an age, he stirred from his thinking and said, "Eagle, could you imagine if the Euphrates and Tigris Rivers burst their banks and flooded this land?"

I had never thought of this, and these thoughts seemed ridiculous. I had never seen this in all my years, but the thought struck me of the destruction that would come to all the creation that surrounded these great rivers.

"Noah, this is not something I would want to imagine," I replied.

Noah seemed happy with my answer, and it felt like a passing thought, but it was not really what he had been pondering. He got up, dusted himself off, and said, "Come Eagle, I know what I will do."

At that, Noah set off back the way he came. This time, he broke into a run, and I could sense joy and hope flooding back through him. Whatever he had decided to do, it brought him joy.

I took to the skies and followed him home.

CHAPTER 7

Noah asked me to gather his father and grandfather to meet with the Designer that evening. With the speed he was running, I was sure he would beat everyone back to the place where they would all meet with the Designer.

As expected, I found Methuselah in his garden; it was the place that made him happy. His hands were always dirty, for they always worked with the soil. He loved the smell of the soil as he plowed and turned it. He did not seem to mind when the birds would fly down, looking for worms and bugs unearthed as he tilled the soil. It was only when they stole the seed he sowed that angered him. The joy he worked with could be seen in his garden's abundance. I only found him happier when Noah was in the garden with him.

I landed in a tree near him, and as I did, he looked up at me, smiled, and said, "How is my grandson?"

"He is well," I replied. "He is on his way to the meeting place with the Designer and has sent me to ask you to meet with him."

At that, he got up from the ground, clapped his hands together to break off the dirt, then took a step back to take in all he had accomplished in the day. I watched as he took a deep breath in and said, "Well, Eagle, I guess today we will see what will be."

Before he left his garden, he approached me and asked me the most peculiar question, "Eagle, have I been a good grandfather to Noah?"

"Methuselah, I have seen all of your ancestors, from Adam to you. I have watched a man care for his family as the Designer cares for his creation. You have been a very good grandfather."

"I have tried my very best, Eagle, but I fear I should have done better," he replied.

At that, I said, "Should?"

It always made me smile when I heard anyone using the word 'should.' It reminded me of Wisdom, correcting me for using it. I repeated her words to Methuselah and added, "Methuselah, 'should' is not a word friends use, nor is it a word grandfathers use. You have loved Noah well, and he knows this."

Methuselah laughed and said, "You have been talking to Wisdom." Then he continued, "Yes, I love Noah very much, Eagle. I have tried to give him a good example of who a man is, but my father, Enoch, was a hard example to live up to. Do you remember when he argued with the Designer about my name? My father did not want to call me Methuselah. He would have preferred anything else other than that. He did not believe I would be the one who would bring death forth." There was a long silence before he spoke again. "Eagle, have I brought death to my family? I wanted to be more like my father."

"You are the grandfather Noah has needed," I replied.

Methuselah was speaking as if he was Noah's father, not Lamech. I had long seen how Methuselah watched over Noah. Sometimes, I felt he was even doing what the Designer had asked me to do. But then again, I know the Designer had told Methuselah many things about the future and his hopes and design for Noah, and some of those things were very troubling.

When Enoch left us and returned to Eden, no one was more shocked than Methuselah. He grieved this like Eve grieved Abel's death, and, like Eve, he did not get a chance to farewell him. Enoch was everything to him, and he loved him with everything he had. But losing him, as he did, caused a wound that is yet to fully heal. It seeded a fear deep within him that others would be taken from him. His own fathering of Lamech often showed the fear he would lose him or that Lamech would die before he did. He always liked to have his family close to him.

"Methuselah, I have seen you with the Designer when he invited you to put your hands into the soil. What did you feel?" I asked.

Methuselah smiled and gave a half laugh as if the memory of this was something he could easily find himself in again. "There have been many times, Eagle. The first time I felt the pain of losing my father, and it was too much for me to bear." A silence followed before he continued, "It was not just the loss of my father the Designer had me there for. There were other reasons, Eagle."

I waited to see if he would continue talking, and when he did not, I asked another question.

"Can I ask you a question, Methuselah?"

"Of course, you can, Eagle, but not about the ground," he replied.

"What kind of father is Lamech to Noah?" I asked.

Methuselah stopped to ponder this question. As he did, the sadness on his face lifted, and a warm smile slowly stretched across his friendly face. "He is the father to Noah, that I should have been to him," he replied.

"There's that word 'should' again," I replied. "He is a good father because you have been a good father to him. Everything he knows, he has learned from you. But Lamech carries his own disappointments in parenting, as you do."

"But has that been enough, Eagle?" He replied. "Lamech is a good father, but there were many things he should have done better."

I smiled and said, "This word 'should' is often used when we have judged ourselves to be less." Before he could argue the point, I continued, "You were the one who introduced him to the Designer. You were the one who gave him his very first lamb. Do you remember Lamech's joy when you gave it to him?"

Methuselah laughed again, saying, "He did not know what to do with it. I thought we would have roast lamb for dinner." Methuselah was laughing again at this precious memory. It was good to see him happy.

"If I can say one final thing, Methuselah?" I asked. He simply nodded, so I continued, "These three generations, from you to Noah, have been marked with the Designer's love; this you already know. It has always been the case in the generations of your family, but it has not been so with you. In your shortened years with Enoch, you discovered a lifetime's worth of understanding of creation with him. It was through him you learned the power of the Designer's love. You were with him when you first felt this love in the ground. You felt the Designer's life flowing through all things; it is the same with His love. You know you experienced His healing there as well. Somewhere in that journey, you realized you no longer needed your father to be there for those moments. They were now part of your story, and they flowed naturally from your relationship with the Designer. Now you have passed these things on to your son and grandson, the greatest of all inheritances. Because of this, both Lamech and Noah have found a safe place to grow."

I continued, "They are now men and explorers, which, at times, has given you much heartache when you did not know where they were, but they always came back. They came back because your love drew them back. Methuselah, I hope you understand what

I am saying; your love drew them back. They knew they were free to explore and roam from this loving place; they grew to trust it. The stories they have returned with have blessed and inspired you. They have become men to be proud of. When they took greater risks than you would take, and even when they chose poorly, they knew they could return to their father and grandfather without fear of punishment or judgment. Yes, Methuselah, you have been a good father and grandfather."

I could see a tear in the old man's eye. His whole life had come to this one moment in time. At that, he simply nodded and went to clean himself up to be ready to meet with Noah and the Designer.

Then I was off to find Lamech.

CHAPTER 8

I found Lamech in his shed, frantically packing a wagon full of supplies. All kinds of tools, provisions, tents, water, and food were being loaded onto it. He was barking orders to an apprentice about getting harnesses prepared for the horse and ensuring it would be ready when needed.

I flew straight into the shed and landed on one of the stalls that would typically house a horse. If the horse had been there, it might have even kicked me. My entrance startled Lamech enough, and he said, "Eagle, why aren't you with Noah?"

"I have come from Noah, and he has asked if you and Methuselah would meet with him and the Designer this evening," I replied.

"Good," he said before continuing, "I am glad he decided quickly. Sometimes he frustrates me with how long he takes to decide." He paused and said quietly, "Then, when he makes his mind up, no one can change it. Sometimes I wished he listened more to me and not his grandfather." In a louder voice, he said, "What has he decided to do?"

"I do not know, my lord. I was with him when he made the decision, but he did not share it with me," I replied.

"That sounds like Noah."

"My lord, what are you doing?" I asked.

Lamech looked over the cart and said, "I am getting ready to go with Noah."

"I did not hear the Designer ask you to go, Lamech," I replied.

"I know, Eagle, but Noah is young and will need me to be there for him."

"Will you meet Noah with the Designer and your father this evening?" I asked.

"Yes, Eagle, I will be there." As I prepared to fly, Lamech turned and asked me, "Have you already been to see my father?"

"Yes, Lamech, he is making his way there now."

"What did my father ask you?" he wondered.

"He asked if he was a good enough grandfather," I replied.

Lamech grunted, and under his breath, he said, "When I was Noah's age, I longed for his approval. My whole life, I tried to get his attention. I worked so hard just to get one word of encouragement, but, to me, they were rare. I always felt I had done something wrong or was not the son he wanted."

At that, he ended the conversation and headed back to his cart, and I took to the sky. The afternoon was nearly gone, and the cool of the evening would soon be upon us. Lamech had his own story of what a parent should be, but unlike his father, he was not thinking about what kind of father he was to Noah.

CHAPTER 9

It was a strange afternoon of questions, insecurities, and honesty. The meeting ahead would be life-changing for these men. Methuselah and Lamech were self-reflecting and wondering if they had done enough for Noah. Both thought he was too young, but I wondered if it was simply the feeling of wanting more time with Noah before he left. To me, Methuselah looked as if he would apologize for not being enough. Lamech looked like he would make up for his shortcomings by going with Noah. And with both of them, I did not think they would get their opportunity to do either.

As I soared overhead, thinking through all of these conversations, I spotted the Designer walking along the bank of the river. He looked up at me and called to me. I will never tire of hearing him call my name and invite me to spend time with him.

"Eagle, what have you seen?" He asked.

"Much, my Lord," I replied.

The Designer smiled, laughed, and said, "Well? Are you going to tell me? Or do you hold secrets now from your friend?"

When he called me 'friend,' I felt like my heart would burst with the love that flowed from his voice.

"My Lord, there are no secrets between us. As always, there are questions," I replied.

He laughed again, saying, "Maybe I should have called you 'curious' instead of Eagle."

"Friends do not use the word 'should,' my Lord."

Laughter peeled through the trees at that, and He said, "Eagle, you've been talking to Wisdom, haven't you?"

"Yes, my Lord, but not for a long time. In truth, I miss her terribly. Will I see her again soon?"

"That all depends on the meeting we are about to have," He replied. "What about these questions of yours?"

"Do you remember the first time you asked Methuselah to put his hands into the ground?"

"I do," He replied.

"He told me there were more things to heal than his broken heart," I said.

"Yes, there is more yet for him to heal from. He resented me for taking Enoch from him."

And as the Designer said this, I could feel the pain in his own voice. Enoch's leaving was not received well by everyone.

He continued, "Methuselah has forgiven me for Enoch's leaving, but he does not understand I did not take him."

"But, my Lord, surely you gave him the choice?" Came tumbling out of my mouth.

"Yes, Eagle, I did. Just like I did with you when you returned to see Abel's final resting place," He replied.

"Could I have stayed?" I blurted out the words.

"You could have asked," He said with a wink and a smile.

"My Lord, if Methuselah has forgiven you for taking his father, why does he still hold resentment in his heart?"

"Enoch has been gone many years now, and time and my presence have combined to be a healer that has softened Methuselah's heart. Back then, he had so many questions and not a lot of patience. Now, he loves to spend time with me, walk with me, laugh with me, and he still asks me questions. But he will often resist when I ask him to place his hands into the ground again to heal from this. The time will come when this changes, and then it will be the right time. There is still much for Methuselah to learn and see before he joins his ancestors."

He walked on in silence. The evening was upon us, and creation was doing what it was designed to do. The shadows between the trees were growing, and soon it would be impossible for me to fly through them. Even my eyes were not good enough to see in complete darkness. Animals were always curious when the Designer walked among the trees, and His love would draw them to Him. He would always stop to care and speak to them. Above us, the sky's brilliant blue slowly changed through the most beautiful sunsets. Each of them is different in its own way, and each would take an age to describe the pallet of colors the Designer would use to create it. But tonight, it felt like the sunset was being pulled across the sky to reveal all of the stars. Without a cloud in the sky, I felt as if I could hold every one of them in my sight and spirit.

"Can you feel the cool in the air, Eagle?" He asked.

"Yes, my Lord, I can."

"Have I ever told you this is my favorite time of the day?" He said with a laugh.

"Once or twice," I said with a laugh of my own.

"Come Eagle; now we will see what will be."

CHAPTER 10

When the Designer and I arrived, it surprised me to see Lamech waiting for us. I had expected Noah to be there long before we arrived, but there was Lamech, and he looked lost in his thoughts and impatient. He was pacing the ground, and our arrival surprised him, and he said, "Oh, it's you."

The Designer smiled and said, "Who were you expecting, Lamech?" Lamech struggled to answer or even look at the Designer. So, the Designer answered his own question, "You were hoping we were, Noah."

Lamech was old enough to know there was no hiding his thoughts from the Designer. The slumping of Lamech's shoulders showed the Designer had spoken the truth. He replied, "Yes, my Lord, it is true. Forgive me."

The Designer kept going as if he had not heard him. "Lamech, I know your love for Noah, and I know you desire for him to be safe. A good father would do as you have done, but this journey is for Noah to choose or not choose."

"Yes, my Lord," Lamech responded. "I named him Noah, not just because it means rest; it was more than that." A silence followed that the Designer would not break. I am sure He knew what was coming, but He wanted Lamech to own the words he was thinking. The moment's awkwardness was eventually filled by Lamech spilling out the words, "I called him Noah, in the hope his life would bring rest to the land you cursed. And now you are sending him away. The land will never be at rest."

Still, the Designer was silent. He was listening and watching Lamech intently. "You are sending him into a lion's den. To do what?" He exclaimed and then continued, "To find a woman who comes from Enoch, of all places. There are many women here who would be more suitable."

"More suitable," The Designer repeated softly to Lamech. I could see Lamech's heart was breaking, and the Designer's peaceful response had diffused some of Lamech's anger. "Where is the talking snake, Lamech?"

Lamech's eyes flicked at the question. I could tell he was caught in a question he did not want to answer. I had sensed it myself; I knew it was close, and I knew the Designer knew exactly where it was. But, again, he wanted Lamech to own his words and his actions.

"It hides," Lamech confessed. "I don't know where it is, but I know its voice. I have heard it many times in the past, and each time I was able to ignore it. But this time, it was different; it was saying what I wanted it to say. You have told me many times of all that is coming, and although I still cannot see it clearly, I know you have great plans for Noah. Forgive me, my Lord."

Lamech slumped to the ground. He was tired, and his heart was breaking. The Designer was sending Noah to where he could not go, and he was holding onto hope that he could.

The Designer made his way to Lamech. He stopped briefly and reached behind a rock, and pulled out the snake. Initially, the snake writhed in His grip, but He simply whispered to it, and the snake calmed. He then returned it and continued to Lamech. All of this was done so simply and seamlessly that Lamech did not even notice. I could see that shame had caused Lamech to drop his head, but as the Designer returned the snake, it was like the words on Lamech's mind were lifted. He stood and embraced the Designer, and tears flowed unashamedly, and he wept.

The Designer held him for a time. Eventually, releasing him, He looked directly into his eyes and said, "You have named Noah well, Lamech; it is also the name I gave him. He will bring rest to the land, but it will not be as you have hoped. Much depends on what Noah is about to tell me and if he chooses to go to Enoch. This promised rest will not happen until your body is dust and your spirit has joined with me and all your ancestors. You no longer need to listen to the talking snake, my friend. You know my voice. There is only one voice to cling to, and it is the one you feel life in, not death. Trust me, Lamech."

Lamech clung to Him again. The strength of the embrace spoke to me of his shame for doubting but even more so of his love for the Designer. "Forgive me, my Lord," he whispered.

"Lamech, you are my friend, and you are a good father. When your father named you, he did so because I asked him to call you Lamech, for you have carried so much. Now I ask you to carry my words, for they are life to all who hear them. Soon, Noah will need to hear them from you, his father." Then the Designer continued, "There are many words a man will hear in his lifetime, but certain words are designed to come from his father alone. These are the words I have given to you. You know who Noah is; he needs you to tell him who you see. You need to tell him he is strong and you trust him. No one alive can speak these words to him more powerfully than you; not even your father can speak these words to him."

Lamech looked at Him and said, "I have not been the father I could have been, my Lord. If he chooses to go to Enoch, please allow me to go with him, and I will be the father he needs me to be there." They were then interrupted by the people we could hear walking through the trees.

The Designer simply said, "Ah, our friends have arrived."

CHAPTER 11

The Designer greeted Methuselah and Noah warmly. If I did not know the magnitude of the meeting about to happen, I would have thought this to be a normal gathering. The Designer loved to love, and in these three men, there was a lot of love for Him.

As per usual, the Designer took the time to make a fire. If He was desperate to receive Noah's answer, it did not appear so. He was meticulous when He lit a fire. Everything had to be just right, and He loved it when the sparks flew from the flint and the tinder crackled into flame. It reminded me of when He breathed life into Adam as He breathed over the small flame. It was a memory I will never forget. I had watched the Designer spend all day crafting Adam out of the ground. At first, I did not know what He was doing, but before long, I could see He was molding a form that looked similar to Himself. Like with building a fire, everything had to be perfect. Then, once He was satisfied with the form He created, He breathed into its mouth. He then sat back and waited. Then after a few more moments, He leaned forward and breathed stronger than He had. At that, the most extraordinary thing happened, Adam opened his eyes and then exhaled the breath the Designer had breathed into him. Then he kept breathing and did not stop until his final breath. Such a precious memory to me.

Once the fire was lit, He sat back and watched it grow and spread across all the firewood. He looked proud of the fire, then turned to them all and warmly invited them to sit with Him. Once they were settled, He looked at Noah with a smile that showed nothing more than His love for him.

"Noah, do you have an answer for us?" He asked.

"Yes, my Lord, I do," he replied and then continued. "I will go to the city of Enoch to train as one who works with timber. I know they call these people carpenters in Enoch, and I will be gone for as long as it takes to learn this trade." The Designer simply nodded at Noah, and the smile had not left his face. He exhaled deeply, but remained silent. He then returned to the fire and, pulling a stick from it, prodded the fire more into flame.

Lamech broke the silence, "Are you certain, my son?"

"Yes, father, I have never been more certain of anything in my life. I can feel a drawing of my spirit to Enoch, and ignoring it seems to be the wrong thing." Noah replied. The conversation paused at that, and the only thing to be heard was the Designer poking at the fire. Everything else was still. Even the forest animals were silent as if they were waiting to hear more.

This time it was Methuselah who broke the silence and asked the question they all wanted to know the answer for. "And what of Nashah? Will you find her and bring her home?"

Noah remained silent for a time. It looked as if he was trying to find the right words to say. I believed it was this woman who made Noah leave last night's meeting to seek a place to think. His heart was already in Enoch to learn everything he could, but the woman was not a part of his heart, nor did he want a distraction from learning.

Eventually, he said, "I will find Nashah."

Lamech let out what could only be called a groan; it was obvious this was not what he wanted Noah to say. Methuselah remained silent; his face was impossible to read whether or not he was pleased. The Designer had still not looked up from the fire and was busying himself by stoking the fire again.

Lamech's immediate response had cut short what Noah was about to say, and it wasn't until the Designer looked up at Noah that he continued. Saying again, "I will find Nashah, and I will ask her if she would be willing to return with me to these lands. I will not force or demand she come; I will simply invite her. I believe I will be there for many years. During that time, I will discover who she is and allow her to see who I am. If she is my Eve, I will await the unity that Adam and Eve had."

At that, the Designer beamed. He was so happy to hear this answer. It was as if the Designer was speaking through Noah. It was an answer He would have surely given. The Designer got up from the fire and went to find more firewood, leaving the three men together. Once He was gone, it was Lamech who spoke first. "My son, are you certain of all of this? You do not have to go there, and you do not have to bring this woman back."

"Father, you both have given me a great many things. One of those things is the desire to be who the Designer created me to be. Grandfather, you have taught me all there is to know of the plants, and father, you have taught me all you know about the animals, but there is something more here. I can feel it in my spirit. The name you gave me was for a reason beyond my understanding, but I believe I will discover it. Father, I know you have longed to be who you are created to be, but you have often second-guessed yourself. There is nothing here for me to second-guess. The Designer asked to go, and go I will. If He has asked me to go, I know He will protect me, as He did with Cain all those years ago." Noah replied.

Methuselah then spoke, "My son, the Designer spoke of Nashah as well. Do you also believe this must happen too?"

"In my heart, yes, grandfather, I do," he replied. "But in truth, it was not something I was looking for, and I believed the woman for me would come from our own lands."

"And she could still yet," exclaimed Lamech.

"Yes, father, she could. But the same feeling I have about going to Enoch is now the same feeling I have about Nashah. Last night I did not feel this, and I needed time to think through all the Designer spoke to us," he replied.

Methuselah had felt this feeling before. Even though it still caused him pain, he knew his father would leave these lands long before his time. He sensed it in his spirit but found it difficult to express what he was feeling. No one had ever left these lands like his father, but I could tell the feeling was very familiar. He said, "The Designer can be trusted in this Lamech."

Noah replied, "Yes, grandfather, He can be, and I will. There is more to this trip than I can understand, but I believe all these events will bring our land to rest and bring our family to unity."

We could all hear the Designer coming through the forest with an armload of firewood, and we could see he carried enough to last the entire night. When they saw how much the Designer carried, they all looked at each other and knew this would be a long night. The Designer wanted to talk. "My friends, after hearing Noah's responses, there are now a few things you will need to know for the days to come. Some of these will occur soon, and some many years from now. Unless the people of this world turn from evil, my words will be fulfilled after Methuselah and Lamech have joined their ancestor's spirits, and their bodies are dust."

He continued, "You have heard stories but are unaware of how quickly evil is spreading across creation. What was once a voice from a strange lizard has now become the same voices spoken by those made in my image. The ones who carry these evil voices also carry fierce strength and have become mighty warriors who have fed the wars that have broken out between cities. They pride themselves on how many people they have killed. Victories are being won by the ones who inflict the most death. All of my creation is groaning with this pain of death and suffering."

"Families are in ruin because of this. You already know the stories that some are sacrificing their children, thinking they will please me. Because of this, fear is spreading out in every direction. Their imaginations are entirely evil, and the atrocities they imagine, they do."

"Men have become tyrants and lord their authority over many, demanding people do what they say. Their own wives are nothing more than playthings or vessels to create more children to fight their wars. They have enslaved people, taking their freedoms away."

"My creation is being destroyed to fuel their wars and corrupt everyone and every animal they encounter. Nothing is off limits to these tyrants, and they only seek to build their kingdoms, caring nothing for people. These same tyrants also fear everyone around them, and they fear that they, too, will be murdered or enslaved. They have become victims of their own doing."

"Still, they demand from me the ground to produce its crops, the rains to come at the right times, and the animals to reproduce more rapidly for their insatiable appetites. I have become a gift-giver they plead with or complain about. They even have priests who have created laws and rules about me, thinking they are doing what I want, but none of them will sit with me for a moment. They would rather assume my thinking than talk to me. In their pride, they have taken my role. Instead of people coming to me, they tell them to come to them. Some of these leaders once sat with me and listened to me. Now they rely on the things we spoke of many years ago and think what I would say now would be no different. The longer they spend away from me, the more the evil has spread. I will not be found in their temples or places of worship, for they merely worship what they have imagined and what they have made."

I could see the pain etched throughout the Designer's body as he shared what He had seen, smelt, heard, and felt. His heart was breaking right in front of us, and with words I had heard before, He whispered into the fire, "I am sorry I ever made them."

There was stunned silence among the three men. Even though the Designer had whispered it into the fire, they all heard the magnitude of what He said. I had seen this in Him on the mountain, and now these men could see it in every fiber of His body. I could feel tears begin to form. The first time I heard Him say these words, I felt shock; now it was immense sadness. These were the times I longed for Wisdom to appear beside me and offer me some of the hope she carried, but this night, as the tears began to fall, I sat on the branch alone. Beneath me were three generations of men who did not know what to say.

CHAPTER 12

I sat there in that tree and pondered all I had heard, and I allowed my thoughts to travel back in time and process all I had seen. The phrase 'life contained by a fragile body' kept running through my thoughts. Abel's body gave up his spirit after one fatal blow to his head by a digging tool. Now weapons are being made with the sole purpose of taking life in one blow. How easily these fragile bodies are exposed to death. Bodies made of flesh were not designed to withstand this kind of force. Why did the Designer make them so fragile?

For generations, my eyes were opened to see the Designer's plans and ways. Some of them still confounded me, and others I understood. The ones that confounded me usually began when I had expected an outcome, and then He would do something entirely different. I will never forget when He sat with Cain and took all of Cain's pain into Himself. I had expected Cain to be punished, but I saw Cain being loved.

One thing I was beginning to understand, though, was the importance the Designer placed on the spirit of people. In those early days, I was captivated by the wonder of His physical creation. These days, I marvel even more at the realm our physical eyes cannot comprehend. From the day I watched Abel's spirit become one with the Designer's, I knew there was more to see and understand. I knew I was no longer watching; the Designer had opened my eyes to see.

Sitting in front of me were three men. Each had a spirit that digging tools and weapons could not harm. I was looking at three mortal people carrying three immortal spirits. The spirit is where their character is found. In Methuselah, I see resilience, and I see great courage. In Lamech, I see a practical man always looking beneath the surface to discover more. In Noah, I see a man who knows the power of love and will trust where others will not.

Three immortal spirits living in fragile bodies that would one day expire. As I pondered this, I felt like a light came on within me. These bodies were only made for a season, not for an eternity. They were a gift for a time, but not forever. No eye had even seen a body like this before the Designer had created them. In creating Adam, He was doing a new thing. Creating him in a fragile body told me they were not made for war; they were made to love. But more than this, they were not made to last forever.

This last thought struck me like a thunderbolt. These three spirits were temporary visitors to this creation. He made them to live and thrive in this creation, but it was only ever to be for a season, again, not for an eternity. Giving us choice gave us the ability to live in this creation the way we wanted and not necessarily the way we were designed. What I heard from the Designer was the design had been corrupted. This meant the spirits of those created in His image were in danger of eternally living outside His presence. Once they died, they would no longer know where Eden was or who to return to. They would be lost and wander for all of eternity. The very thing Cain had feared was now playing out in my imagination. They had corrupted their design to the point they had forgotten eternity and lived only for the days they were in.

The sorrow and regret I could see in the Designer now made sense to me. He would never force anyone to choose Him; He would only ever invite them. For love to remain, love, their choice could never be taken from them. Even though he had created their very spirits, He relinquished His control of them.

I sat with these thoughts flooding my mind, and the more I thought, the more the tears fell from my eyes. Wisdom was right, this is the greatest love story of all time, but it was also the most painful love story of all time. Such fragile bodies that carried such treasure and wonder of His doing. He withheld nothing from them and continues to provide for them, even though they are so far from Him. They were not made for hatred and war but for love and unity.

He regretted making them because the loss He was grieving was an eternal loss. Every single one of them carried Him; they were created in His image. Every single one of them. No two of them are the same; they are all unique and all loved. How does one comprehend such love and loss at the same time? How does He save them from the eternity they are choosing? Their eternal spirits are unaware of the choices they are making in such fragile bodies.

The Designer's heart broke right before us, and three eternal spirits could not comprehend what they were experiencing. All three of them knew of the fragile bodies they possessed. They knew tiredness, sickness, and despair. I could see Lamech was acutely aware of Noah's fragility and did not want him to go to Enoch. Methuselah was measuring his life by the years spent and weighing it against the meaning of his name. Noah was young and had a long life ahead of him, but did he fully understand the magnitude of what the Designer was sharing?

Things were changing. In Eden, the Designer had given very few rules. They were to tend to the garden that surrounded them. They were not to eat the fruit from the *Tree of Knowledge of Good and Bad*. Other than these, they were free to do whatever they chose. They loved as He loved them. They were invited to do relationship with His creation, Him, and each other. I sat and wondered about the rules He gave them outside of Eden. He had given them complete freedom to choose, and again, nothing was withheld from them other than access to the *Tree of Life*. But somehow, they kept coming back and wanting to eat from the *Tree of Knowledge of Good and Bad*. These evil people had craved the very fruit Eve had first eaten.

It was then I felt another thunderbolt of revelation go through me; it was never about the fruit on that specific *tree*. It was not even about the *tree*; it was about freedom and choice. Choosing to let go of His words and love would move them further and further from His heart and their design. So, even though they were not in Eden, they were still eating from the *tree* that caused Adam and Eve such heartache.

These thoughts rocked me to my core. All I could do was concentrate on breathing deeply and holding onto the branch I was sitting on. I focused my eyes on the fire the Designer was poking at; He had not stopped doing this. I took several deep breaths, and as I lifted my eyes, I could see the Designer looking straight into my spirit. He knew what I had been thinking; it was He who opened my mind to it all. Once again, my tears and His tears muddied the ground beneath us.

Time passed, and no one spoke. I felt the cool of the evening turn to the cold of the night, and still, no one barely moved. Each one was lost in their thoughts of what the Designer had shared with them. My spirit eventually calmed, and as it did, another thought grew within me: Would the Designer take the life of these fragile bodies to save the life of their eternal spirits? The very thought of this made me shudder. I could not comprehend the Designer willingly taking life; it was not His design to do so. Then I remembered my animal friends who died in Eden to clothe Adam and Eve. The Designer had chosen to kill them to cover Adam and Eve's shame.

I look back now, and I know my friend's spirits still lived within Him, but the shock became a scar on my own spirit. Death rarely creates a healthy conversation that people want to talk about; rather, I have noticed we all avoid it at all costs. But where will this lead us if no one will talk about it?

It is not love we avoid at all costs; it is death. People will run to those who love them, but they will flee from those who hurt them. A cycle had started in creation that would require a great cost to heal it. Long ago, it cost two of my animal friends their lives to cover the same of Adam and Eve. Now, the Designer no longer wanted to cover their shame; He wanted to heal it.

What would be this cost, and who would count it? Would He choose death again?

CHAPTER 13

As the evening wore on, both Methuselah and Lamech excused themselves and headed for their homes. Neither had spoken throughout this time, such was the heaviness of what the Designer shared and the grief He expressed. Noah remained, as did the Designer.

After the older two departed, it was Noah who spoke first. "My Lord, when would you have me leave?"

"You are free to go whenever you choose, Noah," the Designer replied. A silence followed this exchange. It was obvious this was not the question Noah wished to ask. They both sat staring into the fire. Now and then, one of them would stand to put another log on it. Neither of them was ready to leave yet.

Finally, the Designer spoke, "Noah, you are wondering about this coming rest or judgment, and you are worrying about standing alone without your father and grandfather."

"Yes, my Lord. It hardly seems worthwhile learning a new trade as this judgment approaches," Noah replied.

The Designer nodded to show He understood and then said,

"Noah, no one can yet tell what will be. It is still many years till this time, and much can happen in that time. I could even change my mind."

Noah raised his head and said, "Change your mind? I do not understand. What do you mean 'change your mind'?"

The Designer smiled at him and said, "Noah, you are young and have much to learn of love. Love is the most powerful force my creation knows; it flows through every single thing. Look around you, Noah; everything you see teems with my love. This fire in front of you is of my design; the wood, the heat, and the flame are all my gifts to you. They are my gifts to everyone. My love is so great that even the greatest rejection of my love will not stop me from loving." He paused to see if Noah would respond. When he did not, he continued, "One act of love can drive fear away from you. One act of love can restore people back into unity; surely you have seen this?"

"Yes, my Lord, I have seen this. I have seen this in my home when I argue with my brothers. I have seen it between my parents and grandparents. But what you are talking about is far greater than me forgiving any one of them."

"I remember a time when you harvested an entire field of your grandfather's wheat too early." At this, the Designer started laughing, and soon both He and Noah were roaring their laughter. Once the Designer regained His breath, He said, "Do you remember how scared you were of your grandfather?" This made the Designer laugh again. Although this was many years ago, Noah could very well remember this memory as if it had happened yesterday, and what I remember was Noah was not laughing at all back then; they had paid dearly for this mistake. "What did your grandfather do?"

Another question from the Designer ... The Designer knew the answer; it was another time He wanted to know if Noah knew it. "He went and found me, my Lord," replied Noah.

"Yes, you were scared of your grandfather's punishment, but when he found you, he simply wanted to love you. You felt the fear of punishment flee as your grandfather wrapped his arms around you. This is a small example of how powerful my love is."

"He was shocked, my Lord, this you know. And I am certain the words that initially came from him were not friendly. But you are right; when he discovered it was me, he simply used it as a lesson." Noah smiled and broke into laughter, and said, "A lesson that meant we did not have bread for a few weeks." As they laughed, I could feel all the tension lift from the small clearing. It was as if their joy broke something oppressive over them, and they could speak freely again.

"Noah, you will learn much of love in the days, weeks, months, and years ahead of you. Always love others as I have loved you. Much in the world will compete for this love and my place in your life. You will come across many who profess to know me, but you will be able to know if I am in them by the love they carry. Never forget this. But there is even more for you to know about this love; the more you search for it, the more you will find it. You will discover a greater love for all things and also a love for yourself."

"What do you mean, 'love for myself'?"

"To love others well, you must first learn to love yourself well. This means to have compassion for yourself when you make mistakes. When you harvested the wheat early, you felt shame. That shame would have been enforced and grown if your grandfather had punished you and not loved you. Shame can often lead to self-loathing, becoming like the clothing you wear. It is what people see first when they meet you. Adam and Eve wore this clothing, and when people saw them, they were reminded of the loss in Eden. On the days when you fail or make mistakes, people will see you, and you will think that they see your failure and not your true identity. So, when you make mistakes, forgive yourself quickly and learn from them. Do not hold on to the failure at the expense of who you are. I will remind you of these things in the days to come."

"Is this love truly the same mark you placed on Cain?" Noah asked.

"Each one who loves me is marked by me, Noah. Each is unique, but my love will draw you to others who carry my mark. Nashah carries such a mark. You will not need to look for her, for she will be drawn to you, and you will be drawn to her," He said.

"Will you come with me, my Lord?" Noah asked.

"Yes, Noah, I am always with you. I will also send Eagle with you. He will be your companion; you can trust him as you trust me. You will also find Wisdom in Enoch. She has been there for quite some time, watching over Nashah, and she will be most happy to see you both." At that, the Designer looked at me and said with a chuckle, "Maybe you more so, Eagle." These words caused my heart to soar, and everything within me would have soared if I did not want to hear the conversation between them. "Noah, the cool of the evening is still the time we can meet."

Noah exhaled deeply; he was obviously relieved to hear the Designer speak those words. This would be the first time Noah would be away from home for this length of time. He would often camp out in the woods for a few days and even weeks. But this was the first time he was farewelling his family, knowing it would probably be years before he returned.

"Noah, there is much yet for me to tell you, but the night is nearly done, and you need time to rest and then plan your trip. Your grandfather wants to join you on this journey, but he will not speak these words, for he fears you will reject him. This is not a journey I wish for him to take. But I withhold nothing from you, and even if you choose to take him along, I will not remove my presence from you." The Designer paused to ensure Noah had understood what He was saying, and then He continued. "Lamech also wants to join you on this journey; he has already prepared a wagon full of supplies. He will voice his desire to accompany you, but again, it is my hope you will deny his request. There is much I will require of them to do here while you are gone. Do you understand, Noah?"

"Yes, my Lord, I do, and I agree. I have known for some time this was an adventure I would be undertaking alone, and it is only now I feel free to make it."

I could just see the dark of the dawn give way to the most beautiful red, gold, and orange sunrise. Each sunrise is a treasured memory I tuck away in my heart, and this day was no different. It was like the Designer was drawing the veil on the stars and releasing Noah to go. The red hues spoke to me of the Designer's love, the gold of His glory, and the orange of the new season Noah was walking into. It was so beautiful to behold.

"My Lord, when should I leave?" Noah asked.

The response he received came from the Designer's smiling face. "Any time you wish, Noah. But first, farewell your grandparents, and then go to your parents and thank your father for the cart of supplies he prepared for you." The Designer started to laugh as he said this. He already imagined Lamech's face when he realized he had stocked that cart for Noah.

As the sun rose, Noah left the small clearing. The fire was now dwindling, and the warmth of the day would soon be felt. The Designer looked up at me and, once again, smiled with a smile that filled my heart with His love. "It has begun," He said.

CHAPTER 14

"Eagle, what have you seen today?" The Designer gently asked.

"My Lord, it is not just what I have seen; it's what I have heard as well," I replied. The Designer simply smiled and waited for me to continue. "This judgment or rest you speak of is beyond anything I can see or even imagine. It is also very hard for me to understand creation and your place in it, my Lord, when all I hear of is evil, death, and destruction. It troubles my spirit greatly."

"As it does mine, Eagle, as it does mine. But what else have you seen?"

"My Lord, what I have seen today is a family stretching. There were three agendas, maybe four if I included yours, playing out right in front of me. In you, I felt enormous grief and even regret of the kind I felt on the mountain with you. If I could describe it, it felt like one of my wings would no longer work as I tried to fly."

"You see clearly, Eagle. You see my design corrupted by the very fear that love is designed to drive away. Many now believe fear is stronger than love. They are unwilling to work through what needs to heal for love to be seen in their lives. Instead, they run from their pain and what they fear. They have become experts at hiding. No longer do they sow together fig leaves to hide. Now they build walls and armies to prevent people from seeing who they are and protecting what they have from those who would steal. Yes, Eagle, you see clearly. Creation is crying out for a solution, but it is not a solution most will like."

"Eagle, what do you see in Methuselah?"

"Much has changed in him, my Lord. He used to be so impatient, but today he was different. He can see what you have spoken, and he knows of the stories you speak of, and I believe he now knows what his name means," I replied.

"What do you mean, Eagle?" He asked.

"Tonight, I believe he realized you have placed within him the time frame of the future events you spoke of. I think he also realized when he lays down his life, everything changes. He knows now how much you trust him, and he knows that life will once again be reborn through his death."

"This is true, Eagle. He and I have had many conversations about this, and also Noah. At first, he pleaded with me to send him and not Noah. He repeatedly told me that Noah was too young and could not survive. He tried to convince me of this more times than you can imagine. In truth, he could have gone in Noah's place. Maybe Noah, even now, is asking him to go with him. But it is Noah who carries the name of rest, and my creation needs Noah to be who he is created to be."

"My Lord, can I ask a question?"

"Of course, Eagle."

"What of Lamech? To me, he is the hardest one to see. There are many emotions in him, and often confuse me, and I can only imagine what that does to him."

"Yes, Eagle. In this, you see truly. There are many conflicting thoughts flowing through him. It has been this way all of his life. He is still searching for who he is. He believes if he goes with Noah, he will find this and be the father he needs to be. He does not yet know he must first find who he is. We will soon see if tonight has changed anything for him. When we spoke to him before Noah arrived, I gave him a way to help Noah discover who he is; and maybe, just maybe, he will see himself while doing it."

I thought about all the Designer had shared with me. It was all true. Methuselah and Lamech were father and son and yet so different from each other. I wondered whether the revelations of tonight's meeting would have caused either of them to think differently.

After a while, I said, "My Lord, I have one more question." He smiled again and nodded for me to continue. "Why Noah?"

"Why not, Noah?" He said while laughing to himself.

Then He continued, "Noah does not fear me; he loves me with a purity I have not seen since Enoch or as far back as Abel. Nothing separates him from me, and he trusts me, Eagle. Surely you have seen and sensed this?"

"I have, my Lord. At times, so strongly, I dare not intrude upon your conversation. It is truly sacred and beautiful to behold, and I can see the same glow in him that Abel carried."

"I have been waiting for one, Eagle, who carries the same glow. Yes, Enoch carried that glow, and I can see it again in Methuselah, Lamech, and now finally, Noah. If Methuselah had not chosen to carry it, my plans would have been offered to Enoch and not Noah."

He paused before continuing, "Love has, does, and can change everything. As I have already said, it has the power to drive fear away. It has the power to heal, and it has the power to restore. Noah carries love in proportions like I have not seen for generations. It is a love that will build nations and will spread all around the world. It is a love that knows no bounds, and it is a love that cannot be silenced or killed." There was silence between us for a time. His words weighed heavy on me, and I knew He was again speaking of who He is.

"Eagle, it is not hate nor fear that can overcome love. No force in all of my creation can. Fear and hatred will always be temporary, and neither of them has the power to be eternal. It is only choice that will prevent love from doing what it is designed to do." He said, and then repeated, "Only choice." Once again, the Designer went silent for a time before he whispered, "And it is my love that will never take their choice from them." At that, the Designer got up and walked from the clearing, saying, "Come, Eagle, let us see who will be going to Enoch."

CHAPTER 15

When we arrived at Lamech's home, the scene that greeted us was one of frustration, even anger. Lamech and Noah were arguing beside the cart Lamech had loaded the day before. Everyone was keeping their distance from them. Methuselah and Hadar were also there, but they were merely observers. All that could be heard was Lamech yelling, "You do not understand how dangerous this is."

Noah had seen his father do this many times before, but he did not respond with the same anger; he simply kept repeating, "Father, please hear me."

Lamech's anger was not directed at Noah; more so, it seemed to be an overflow of his frustration that Noah would not agree with him. Lamech would often begin discussions with his opinion, and if the person he was talking to did not agree, then he would escalate in volume and, eventually, in anger. Then, no one would dare go near him; the only exceptions were Rebekah, Noah, and the Designer. "Lamech," The Designer declared, "What is the meaning of this?"

Lamech was startled by the Designer. He had not seen us come up from behind him. He spun around to confront the one who would summon him like this, only to find he was face-to-face with the Designer. Lamech was a tall man, but he still needed to look up at this close distance to see the Designer's face. Once again, the Designer said, "Lamech, what is the meaning of this?"

It took a moment, but the realization of this commanding voice belonging to the Designer finally dawned on him. His head dropped, and he said, "Forgive me, my Lord."

"Lamech, it is not me you have directed your anger at; it is your son. If you are not careful with your anger, it will lead you to make choices you will regret." Then, in a whisper that only could be heard by Lamech and my own ears, He said, "That same son we spoke of earlier. Lamech, do you remember the conversation we had? Do not let these words be the last he hears from you before he leaves. Make a choice to be who I have created you to be. You are a son, and you are a father. Noah is a son who needs you to be his father. You have been created in my image and my image alone; it is time you discovered this for yourself and for your son. Trust me, Lamech. You need to trust me."

As the Designer finished speaking these words to Lamech, Noah walked from the cart towards us and said, "It is fine, my Lord. My father wishes to come to Enoch, but I have said 'no' to him. He loves me and wants to ensure I come to no harm."

The Designer looked from the son to the father and could see such maturity in the son. I could also see the sadness the Designer felt for Lamech, and Lamech felt it, too. I watched as his anger drained away. Often, this would take days, and the silence of Lamech would mark those days. Over the years, I discovered Lamech hated his anger and would end up in shame each time it surfaced. His shame caused him to close down. It reminded me of Adam and Eve trying to hide from the Designer all those years ago. They thought sewing fig leaves would hide them; all it did was make them look even more foolish. Lamech, like them, often resisted the Designer's requests to heal from the shame. He did not know his silence was not only hurting him it was also hurting his family. The greater the length of silence would usually indicate, the greater the level of shame he carried. Eventually, the silence would break, and Lamech would speak again, but often, he would not address the reason he became so angry. It was like he hoped everyone had forgotten about the scene he had made and the damage he caused.

This time, though, was different. Rebekah had come out of her home and went straight to Lamech. I could tell she had been crying, and this break in the argument had been her opportunity to reach out to her husband. She could see the wrestle inside of him. He had allowed his anger to be seen, and she did not want her son to leave with his anger ringing in his ears. She embraced him and spoke words so softly I could not hear them, but they affected Lamech and drew his own tears from him. Lamech sighed deeply and turned to Noah, and said, "I am sorry, my son. You have deserved so much better than this. Please forgive me."

Noah replied, "Please, father, I understand. This is a journey I must make on my own. I cannot fully understand why I know this, but I know it is so. Please, give me your blessing to leave." Noah's kindness and love for his father completely broke Lamech's anger and heart, and he took hold of his son in a bear-like embrace. Both of them allowed their tears to fall, and once again, I was privileged to watch a moment where the mingling of tears and love bound a father and son together.

The Designer leaned across to me and whispered, "This is what love can do."

Lamech eventually released his grip on Noah and said, "My son, I am scared for you; that is true. The way I have expressed this has been poor, and again, I am sorry. You have needed me to be a better father, and I have fallen short. I can see you have become a man, but I wanted to be more of a father to you. I long to be your protector, but I see now my job is complete. You are strong and courageous, but more than this, you are the very image of the Designer. You carry his heart, you carry his love, and today you carry my pride. Forgive me for my anger."

With Rebekah holding his hand, he turned to everyone watching and loudly declared, "This is my beloved son; in him, I am well pleased. Today he leaves with my blessing, my heart, and my love." Lamech then went into his home and soon returned with his cloak. "If I cannot come with you, please take this. All who see it will know whose family you are from. May it also provide you warmth when the weather turns cold, and may it remind you of the love of your family." Noah proudly took the cloak from his father and then hugged him again with the same bear-like grip as before. It grieved him to let Noah go, but he could not have been more proud.

Rebekah, likewise, then grasped her son tightly. She had not stopped crying. She loved him dearly, and Noah loved his mother with the same depth. To my eyes, the embrace from her was as if she would not see her son again. It was hard to explain, but something about this moment was more than just a farewell for the journey; Rebekah was farewelling him in life.

Methuselah and Hadar then came forward holding seeds from their garden. Methuselah said, "Noah, plant these where you settle, and may they bring a harvest I will be proud of. And when you eat from the harvest, may the food remind you of the love of your family."

Noah, likewise, took the gift and embraced his grandparents, but this embrace was tender and demonstrated a gentle love that flowed between them. As Methuselah held his grandson, I could hear him speak the Designer's words over him, "I mark each one who loves me." As he spoke those words, we all could see the growing glow that came from within them. Their spirits were alive and connected by the love they shared.

Eventually, Methuselah and Hadar released him from the moment they both encountered him. Methuselah stepped back from him, looked him up and down, and said, "I am proud to be your grandfather, Noah. Go with the blessing of our family, and may the Designer be ever-present with you, and may His goodness and mercy follow you each day."

Noah thanked both his parents and grandparents, then came to the Designer and said, "Will they still be alive when I return?"

"Much will happen between this day and the day you return. Each of your parents and grandparents has already lived long lives, but they still have much to do while you are away. Leave them with me, Noah. It is I who will look after them."

I do not know if that was the answer Noah was looking for, but it was the one the Designer gave him.

The rest of the morning was filled with gathering all of the items Noah wanted to take with him. The Designer had told him to go home and plan his trip, but he had obviously decided that the planning had been done and he was ready to go.

He then climbed onto the cart his father had carefully prepared. Two of Noah's friends would also make the journey with him: Caleb and Ben. They had all grown up together and had not known a day when they were not planning another adventure. Noah then took the reins, and with a gentle motion, he got the horse moving. The loaded cart started its journey to Enoch.

CHAPTER 16

After Noah had disappeared from their sight, the Designer called Methuselah, Hadar, Lamech, and Rebekah to Him. Noah's departure visibly affected each of them, but they all knew being with the Designer would soothe their pain and grief. For Lamech, it took everything within him to tear his stare away from the horizon and of the last sight of his son.

Once again, The Designer built a fire and invited them to sit with Him. There was always something healing about sitting at a fire with Him. Branches of trees that no longer held life were being gathered for a fire that would draw people to Him, and somehow this seemed to impart life to those gathered around it. Was it the warmth of the fire, the fire itself, or was it simply the Designer; Maybe it was all three.

Many times I have seen this family gather around a fire just like this one. Long before Noah was born, it was just the four of them; they would sit and talk for hours. Then I would watch as life flowed into each of them, including the Designer. Once Noah was born, he would often join them at the fire. From a young age, his curiosity for life shone through him. He would ask question, after question, after question, and the Designer would answer every one of them.

As the fire caught hold, much of the stress and anxiety of the day seemed to ebb away. All of Lamech's angry words now seemed irrelevant as they sat, but I am sure Lamech still regretted his actions. He was such a deep thinker, and often his own thoughts were his worst enemy. But the longer he sat here, the more he seemed to relax, receive the warmth the fire provided, and share the love his father and the Designer were easily sharing.

The Designer would never remind Lamech of the angry words he spoke over his son this day. It was not in His character to remind anyone of their mistakes. To watch the Designer with him, no one would even think He had corrected Lamech earlier in the day. He would always encourage Lamech and help him to see himself as He had created him; He loved him.

"Thank you, my Lord," Lamech said to the Designer. "I did not want my final words to Noah to be in anger, and I love him very much."

The Designer smiled at him and said, "I know, Lamech."

Finally, when He was happy with the fire, He said, "Noah will be gone for many years, this you all know. You will need to trust me with him. He is strong and capable, but he has much to learn." These words were not soothing to their hearts, in particular, Lamech's. He had just relinquished the role of protector, and now the Designer was telling him how unprepared Noah was for the adventure. But the Designer continued, "Each of you has done everything I have asked of you for his preparation." Then directing his attention at Methuselah and Lamech, He said, "I know you both wanted to be with him on this journey, but I need you here, for there is much yet to be done."

This surprised them both, and in the same motion, they looked directly at each other and then back at the Designer. They must have thought they were just going to be waiting for Noah to return, and each year of his absence brought them another year closer to His plans being fulfilled. Purpose is what both men live for, and to do something for the Designer was all the motivation they needed to listen to all that was required of them.

"I need you both to plant a forest of cypress trees," the Designer said. By the shock on their faces, whatever it was, these two men assumed the Designer was going to ask them; it was not that.

Methuselah said, "My Lord, it will take many years to grow a forest of cypress trees."

"Many," said the Designer before continuing, "Noah will need timber from many trees. Ensure these trees grow straight and true. Where you can, plant them in rows so that access is easily provided around the base of the trees. Few cypress trees are growing in this area, so I have brought you seed to sow." At that, He handed the seeds to Methuselah, knowing he had such an extensive knowledge of growing things. Then He continued, "These trees grow best in wet and marshy land. You will find these areas further north along the Euphrates River."

Lamech then spoke, "Why cypress trees? As you have said, there are only a few of these trees in this area. Surely there are other trees that grow far more quickly than cypress, and we can grow them right here where we live. We will provide Noah with far more timber if we could plant pine trees."

However, before the Designer could answer, Methuselah asked the more relevant question, "What is Noah going to build?"

"It is enough for you to know that it is cypress timber he will need and a lot of it." The Designer paused before continuing, "This timber is highly resistant to water and rot; no other timber in my creation is like it."

Methuselah and Lamech still had shocked looks on their faces, and when they could think of no more questions, they looked at each other and shrugged their shoulders as if to say, "If that's what you want." The Designer was not finished, though. "Noah will also need vast amounts of tar, which can be made from the resin of the cypress timber. By mixing it with beeswax and wool, you will make the tar waterproof. Which also means you are going to find a lot of bees." He said with a laugh. He then turned to Methuselah, "When the time approaches, Noah will need seeds of every plant, many seeds of every plant."

Methuselah's eyes went wide at this request. "My Lord, such a request makes me think Noah will start your creation again. Is this true?"

"There is yet much to be revealed, Methuselah, and there are still many years and many choices made that will shape the events ahead of us. At this stage, I am simply asking you to prepare what you can for what I currently see ahead for Noah," the Designer replied. The silence grew as they sat by the fire. Now and then, a log would crack and spit from the fire. They were all lost in what they were hearing.

The silence that followed was only broken by the Designer, "Finally, Noah will need large stones. There is a quarry of granite to the west. You will stockpile all the rocks in that area. He will need many and also a way to move them. Lamech, I am giving this task to you."

Lamech nodded thoughtfully at the Designer and then asked, "Does Noah know what he is building, my Lord?"

"No, he does not, Lamech. All he knows is he is going to the city of Enoch to learn to be a carpenter and hopefully bring back a woman who carries the same mark he does. The task ahead is more than just what he will need to build; it is what he will need to learn and carry through this time abroad. He will learn far more than carpentry. He will learn to know my presence like never before. He will learn to know my love like never before. He will learn to love others like never before." The Designer paused momentarily as if He was weighing up what He was about to tell them. "If Noah chooses Nashah to be his Eve, then he will also learn more about parenting than he has learned before."

The four looked at each other and were lost for words as they attempted to understand what Noah was being asked to do. They could not imagine what he would become and what he would build. Did they even understand all the Designer had asked them to plant and gather? This would be a task not seen before, and Noah would also become a father.

This was not lost on Rebekah, who whispered, "I will be a grandmother."

The Designer replied, "Yes, Rebekah, you will be." And Rebekah wept.

CHAPTER 11

As everyone got up to leave the fire and return to their homes, the Designer reached out to Rebekah and gently said, "Please stay a little longer." She was still crying and obediently sat down beside the Designer.

"My Lord, would you like me to stay too?" Lamech asked.

"No, my friend, I need to speak with Rebekah." Lamech bowed his head, turned, and disappeared into the darkness of the night. The Designer allowed the silence of the night to envelop them.

"My Lord, what do you wish of me?" Rebekah asked.

"I wish nothing from you other than what you have already given me: you have given me your love, and I want nothing else."

"My Lord, do you want to say something to me?"

"Yes, Rebekah, I do. But first, I want to ask you a question. How do you feel?"

Tears were still falling from her eyes, and words seemed to have escaped her. Whatever the answer was going to be, I did not feel it would be good. "My Lord, I feel as if I am dying."

The Designer replied gently, "Soon, Rebekah, you will be joining me."

"I will never see Noah again," she whispered through her tears. The Designer reached out and drew her into His embrace. Her tears soon became a flood, and her cries were now painful to hear.

"You have lived many years, my daughter, and you have done all I could have wished for. You have been faithful in this life, and because of your faithfulness, you have equipped Noah with all he needs for his life."

"But what of Lamech? I love him but do not know how he will cope without me. He is a passionate man, but his passion has often spilled into anger. Only you, Noah, or I can speak to him when he is like this, and now Noah is gone, too."

"Trust me with him. Lamech needs to find his own path, and to do this; he needs to find himself. I will not abandon him; before the end, he will find himself."

Rebekah's head was buried in the Designer's chest. Her breathing was ragged, and her tears continued to fall. The Designer was in no rush; He allowed the warmth and glow of His Spirit to flow over her. All that could be heard was the fire crackling before us and the night animals scurrying, waking up, and looking for food. Then I heard the most beautiful of sounds; the Designer hummed a song. The vibrations of the song moved through the air, and I could feel the air moving around me. I had never heard Him do this before, and the sensations I felt were bringing life to every part of my body. I do not know how long He hummed, but when it ceased, I saw Rebekah sound asleep, with her head still buried in His chest. Her breathing had calmed, and her tears had stopped.

The night grew darker, and the fire faded, but the Designer was unmoved, and the warmth of His spirit had not lessened. I sat and watched all the stars come out above us. I did not know if it was His humming or the clear skies above, but the stars looked brighter than I had ever noticed before.

The Designer held her the entire night. Long after the fire had gone out, He remained unmoved. It was just as the dawn approached that Rebekah awoke. At first, she was surprised to have been in the Designer's arms, but her surprise gave way to the peace that blanketed the whole clearing. "My Lord, I am sorry I fell asleep."

"My daughter, there is no place for sorry here. It was the joy of my heart to hold you through this long night."

I could see the reality of last night's conversation fall back upon her as her tears fell again. "How many days do I have, my Lord?"

"Last night, I sang over you a song that added many days to your life. It is true you will not see Noah again, but I have added to your days, for Lamech's sake." Her tears became sobs, and the Designer's chest again became a pool of her tears. "The days ahead of you are becoming darker. I have said this to no one but you; A flood of evil is approaching. Your family is safe and will remain so, but these are the years of planning and preparation."

"My Lord, I am scared to die."

"Most people are, my daughter."

"What will happen to me?"

The Designer lifted her face so she could look directly into His eyes and said, "You have nothing to fear. Your love is as eternal as your spirit. I will be there with you when that day comes, as I am here with you today. And do not fear that you will not see Noah again, for you will have all of eternity to spend with him." At that, she rested her head back on His chest and watched the sun rise over Eden.

CHAPTER 18

"Eagle, fly ahead and go with Noah. I will be there soon," the Designer said to me.

Noah had not gone too far; he left the valley late in the afternoon and would have stopped for the night somewhere before the Euphrates River. Leaving the Designer and Rebekah to watch the sunrise, I spread my wings and headed for the heights. It would be easy to see where they were from where I would be soaring. My only regret was I would soar without Wisdom. It had now been years since I had seen her, and anytime we were separated, it felt like a large part of my spirit was missing. Other eagles who visited Enoch would often find me and speak of her beauty and power. To hear them encouraged me to know she was safe, and that is all I could hope for in the times we found ourselves in.

The sunrises I had witnessed over the past few days were another reminder of the wonder of the Designer. Where yesterday's was red, gold, and orange, today's was a beautiful deep red highlighted even more so because of the clouds on the eastern horizon. The sun rose behind them and gave a brilliant white outline to the tops of the clouds. It was the perfect time of the day, a time when the sun greets creation, providing its brilliant light and warmth. Such an exhilarating time to fly.

As I took flight, I did so with a wealth of thoughts, questions, and wonderings. It would take me no time to catch up with Noah, but before I did, I wanted to free myself from all the things plaguing my mind. I found no better way to do this than soaring on the winds. The power of my wings had me high in the sky so quickly, and soon I was searching for those powerful winds that would take me higher. I still do not know how the Designer made these winds happen, but as I get higher, the temperature gets colder, and with every shift, there is another strong wind that takes me higher again. I often found these around mountains, and there were plenty of mountains to the north. So, I flew towards the mountains with Noah not far to my east.

Once I felt those familiar winds beneath me, it was so easy to go higher and higher, way up beyond where most other birds flew. I loved the solitude in these moments, but I also loved the view I got from way up here. To the south is Eden and the mighty rivers that surround it. The *Tree of Life* can easily be seen from up here, and just a glimpse of it feels like an invitation to sit in its branches. It has stood tall and strong since the early days of creation, and my spirit fills with awe every time I see it. I have watched other trees go from acorns to the largest trees, but yet they still die. The *Tree of Life* has not followed this pattern; each year, it gets a little wider and a little higher. The other *tree*, the *Tree of Knowledge of Good and Bad,* is still there as well, but it cannot be seen from the air; the surrounding trees cover it, as does the *Tree of Life*. The last time I saw it, the trunk had grown wider, but it had not grown taller. The same fruit still hung from it, and there was a lot of fruit there. No one had touched it since the days of Eve, and everything about it made me think of that fateful day when Adam and Eve were last there.

Enoch is beyond Eden and further to the South and East, and even from this height, it is too far for me to see. It also has a voice in my mind that is drawing me toward it, and in my heart, I want that voice to be Wisdom. But, in my mind, I know there is much the Designer wants me to see in Enoch. It is a city of destiny and a city of peril for many.

Leaving Eden behind me, I search for another powerful wind to take me higher and towards the northern mountains. Each time I am up here, I can feel my heartbeat for what lies beyond what I can see. I love the adventure of seeing new things and places, and I long to experience everything the Designer has created.

I know further to the north, beyond the mountains, there is an enormous black sea, and it is beautiful. Its darkness strikes fear into some, but to me, it shows the Designer's handiwork. Further to the west is a sea far greater in size than that one. The life in that sea is abundant, and its magnificence draws me to it, and I want to discover what is on the other side of it. To the south-west, though, is a land that intrigues me. In my spirit, I know I will eventually call it home, and there is a longing within me that is too much for me to ignore. I have not explored far into the south, but it is a land that people describe as a "land flowing with milk and honey." I remember when I heard this phrase, I wanted to immediately find Wisdom and explore it at once. I know that one day I will, but this day my task is with Noah.

But not just yet ... first, I fly.

I never tire of soaring over these mountains. Because of the way the wind moves through them, I can be high in the sky, then plummet through the valleys, and then be back among the clouds in moments. All of it makes every sense of mine come alive. I can feel the changes in the temperature and variations in the wind. My sight and hearing are acutely aware of everything surrounding me. It is in these times I never want to return to the ground.

I had been up there soaring for most of the morning when another of my senses noticed something else; I could smell smoke. It was very faint at first, but as I turned and flew to the source, the smell of smoke grew, and soon it became all I could smell. In the distance, I could see a town burning.

As I flew closer, I could see people running in every direction. The sound of so many people screaming was all I could hear. I was looking for people who would put out the fires, but I found none. All I saw was more fires being lit and more homes being destroyed. Flames spread from building to building until all of the town was on fire.

I realized what was happening when I was close enough to hear the individual screams; this town had been attacked. I could see the dead lying in pools of blood where they had been killed. I could see mothers desperately searching for their children and loved ones. I saw more blood than I thought could be possible. The stench in the air of burning buildings and people made me ill. It was a scene of complete devastation, and I knew it would become a memory etched into my mind.

I was watching creation be destroyed. Nothing in front of me made any sense whatsoever – the loss of life, loved ones, homes, children, dignity, honor, and hope. Everything here was destroyed. Who would do this? Who could make sense of such death?

I found a tree, untouched by the flames but forever marked by the evil. I sat and looked across such hopelessness. As I watched, I saw a mother find her child among the dead. The sound from her broke my heart and, simultaneously, my hope for creation in front of me. Inside my spirit, I was screaming, "This can't be happening!" But it was happening, and there was nothing I could do to change it. Again, it took me straight back to Abel's lifeless body lying in his own blood. None of this made sense.

It was then I noticed snakes slithering out of the homes on fire. There were many of them, and all of them were contorted and making evil sounds. As soon as I saw them, I knew who they were and what was inside of them. One saw me, slithered toward me, and spat at me, "There's nothing you can do. They're all dying and will soon be dead. There is nothing but death here, Eagle."

I do not know how long I sat in that tree, but the afternoon was upon me, and soon, the cool of the evening would happen. I knew this was the Designer's favorite time, but I did not want him to see this. But as I thought this, I felt Him.

He was on the far side of the town. Even from this distance, I could see the grief He was carrying. He moved slowly between the wreckage of the town, but as He did, I noticed something very familiar happen. As He came to each life that was slain, He leaned over them and spoke words I could not hear, but the words released the spirit of the person. There was a glow in each one, it was very faint, but I could definitely see it. As the glow left the body, the Designer received it into His own body, just as I had seen with Abel all those years ago. I watched Him do this with more people until He came to one who was still alive. It was a woman, and she was covered in black soot. Her face was streaked by many tears that had fallen and splattered in blood. There was a wound in her side, her dress was stained with crimson, and the stain was slowly growing. She was holding one of her own children, who had not survived the attack. The Designer sat in the black soot with her and held her, and once again, I watched as the Designer's tears mix with the woman's tears he held; they cried over the lost life. Time passed, and the Designer whispered something into her ear, shocking her eyes wide open. She turned and said, "Yes, my Lord."

At that, the Designer held her again, and I watched as her spirit left her body and came into His. I had never seen this before. I had seen people die and join with the Designer like that, but never while the person still lived. Straight away, I was reminded of Enoch and wondered if this was what happened when the Designer took him back to Eden.

I watched the Designer through all of this. None of this gave him pleasure; His tears still flowed as if she was still alive, but I could sense a relief in Him as He felt her spirit join with His. This, again, was another moment where it felt as if everything slowed down for me. Maybe this sensation happens so I can comprehend what I am seeing, or it may be what happens when I see something for the very first time. Either way, what I saw became what I was now feeling; the Designer was sharing His mercy with her.

By the time the Designer had moved through everyone in the town, it was dark, and I could see how tired He was. He was sitting under a tree and looking over the whole town. A town that, hours ago, was a thriving center for people and families; now, it was a smoldering ruin.

I flew down and sat beside Him and said nothing. He acknowledged my presence, but still, it was silence we shared. What words could be shared in moments like these? I could feel anger within me growing, and again, I wanted to destroy all of the snakes I could find. The Designer could sense this in me, and the next thing I felt was His hand on me. I could feel His love and strength in that one act. It calmed my spirit and soothed my heart. It never ceases to amaze me how much His love changes what I feel.

"Eagle, now is not a time for anger, but it is a time for grief. There is no one left here who can grieve for these people. Soon this town will be forgotten, and the only ones to grieve them are us. Let us grieve them together." So we wept.

The evening turned to night, and we were still sitting under that same tree when the dawn started to break. Once again, streaks of red were painted across the sky, but this time they did not speak of love to me; they spoke of blood that was shed. It was as if the Designer was painting His grief across the skies. As the sun rose further, the Designer turned to me and said, "Eagle, what do you see?"

"I see meaningless death, my Lord. I see lives wasted, and I see a scar upon your creation."

"There is more here—more than you can know. To see what happened here, one must go back another day to discover its meaning. Let us be away from this place, and I will share that day with you."

He started walking east, and as He set off, I spread my wings and flew as I followed Him. All morning He walked without stopping. As the sun approached its peak, He finally stopped and rested under a tree. Looking up, He motioned for me to join Him.

"Eagle, when you arrived, you only saw a small portion of what happened. You saw the death and destruction of the women and children of the town, but where do you think the men were?"

"I do not know, my Lord. It had not even occurred to me that there were no men; all I could see was death."

"The men were all already dead but did not lay dead in that town." He said and then paused before continuing, "They died because they invaded their neighbor's town, intending to do the same thing to them."

If I thought I could no longer be shocked, then I was wrong. I lowered my head in disbelief. I could not even summon a tear; the shock made me numb. The Designer reached out His hand again and cradled me into Him.

"Eagle, before I came to this town, I had been to the neighbor's town. It was not a smoking ruin, but the smell of death was everywhere. Most of the men from this town we were just in are dead, and the rest had become slaves to the people of the town."

The Designer paused again before continuing, "Of all things, slavery, and child sacrifice I detest the most. Slavery takes all choice away and leaves nothing but oppression. This, you know, Eagle, is everything my creation is against. But child sacrifice is a different kind of evil. They have been told a lie that I would be pleased if they sacrificed children to me. Their greatest treasures were killed because they were convinced I would require this. Each of those children is safe with me now, and they will never again suffer at the hands of evil men. But this evil will not go unpunished."

I could now feel the Designer's own anger rise within Him. This was not something I often sensed, but when it did, I became fully aware of what one who created all things could do with this kind of power.

"My Lord?" I asked. My question broke the sense of anger I was feeling from Him and returned His thinking to me, so I said, "Did you see the snakes?"

"Yes, Eagle, I did, and as many as I could reach, I released from their torment," He replied.

"After seeing what has happened here, I am not sure I want to see the city of Enoch, my Lord."

The Designer sighed deeply and said, "It is true there is evil at work within Enoch, but there are still some there who remember me. The stories of Cain are still passed on, although some of them have become more of a myth than truth."

"Will Enoch suffer the same fate as this place?" I asked.

"There are many years in front of you, Eagle. This means there are many moments for people to turn back to me. You will see this, my friend. Not everything is lost, and it is never hopeless. It is the voice of evil who will try and convince you to doubt this. Soon you will meet the owner of this voice, and then you will have your own choices to make, my friend. Will you hold on to my words, or will you hold on to his?"

"My Lord, your words are life to me. I will never let them go."

"He can be convincing, my friend." The Designer replied.

"And only you are loving, my Lord," I replied.

"Well answered, Eagle. You bring me such joy," He replied.

CHAPTER 19

Later that afternoon, the Designer rose to His feet to leave. He took one last look back toward the burned city and then turned again to the East. "It is time you caught up with Noah, Eagle. He has already crossed the Euphrates River and will pass very close to Eden. I know you will want to soar above it once again."

The Designer's reminder of Eden made joy seep back into my spirit. But as I took flight, the smell of the putrid smoke from the town felt like it had stuck to my feathers. I wanted to fly as far from that place of death as possible. I was no longer thinking of soaring the winds; I had tasted death as I had never tasted before, and it was consuming my thoughts.

How could creation have gone so far wrong? Where were the ones who walked with the Designer in the cool of the evening? Had I truly believed Him when He said only Methuselah's family was left? What of Methuselah's and Lamech's other sons and daughters? Did none of them carry the same mark and glow as they did?

As I flew, I thought through each of them, and there were many. Each time I could barely remember a single time when they walked with their fathers when they met with the Designer. They occasionally did when they were very young, but that was long ago. Most of them had already left their father's home and were living in towns just like the one we left.

When I caught up to Noah, he was indeed past the Euphrates River and would soon be upon the Tigris River. To our right stood the mighty Garden of Eden. It is such a sight to behold, and every part of me wanted to dwell within Eden again. With my eyes, I could see the canopy of the *Tree of Life*, and it was magnificent. It towered above all the other trees, regardless of where it was viewed from. I could imagine the taste of the fruit it carried just by seeing it. I still marveled that the taste of the fruit would subtly change depending on what I was feeling.

Noah, though, was not thinking about Eden. His thoughts were on how they would cross the Tigris River, and I know he would have loved to have had my wings and just flown across. Crossing the Euphrates differed from crossing the Tigris. Much more water surged down the Tigris, and it was deep. They would have to go far to the north to cross the cart in a place shallow enough, but Noah did not want to add weeks to the journey. To cross it, they would have to build a raft.

Noah loved Ben and Caleb; they, too, wanted to learn all there was to know about building and working with timber. They were both very practical young men and saw each obstacle as a challenge needing to be solved. When I landed on the cart, I could see the three of them had a different design for a raft to build and a different place to put the raft into the river.

The night was nearly upon them, so they made camp and built a fire. The conversation about this raft's design continued into the evening. Each idea raised would be met with many challenges and difficulties. Progress was being made, but it was obvious that crossing this river was fraught with danger. Finally, by the time they were ready for sleep, they agreed on a raft design and a location to launch it from.

As they slept, I watched over them through the night. I slept in fits as memories of the burning town kept being replayed in my mind. I could still hear the evil voice in the snake as it spoke of a death that would come to all. So much death, and all of it was so pointless.

Somewhere in the darkest part of the night, I thought of sitting on the ground and allowing my talons to sink into the dirt. It had been a long time since I did this, and the idea quickly became an urgency within me. I could not get to the ground fast enough. Once there, I wondered why the thought had not come back to me in the town.

As I sat on the dirt, I allowed all of my senses to come together and be present in the very moment where I was. I had expected to immediately be back in the burning town, but instead, I was with Noah, Caleb, and Ben. I sat and listened to their breathing and Caleb's snoring. There was a rhythm to it all as I allowed my senses to come alive. The sound of the river was competing with the sounds of the sleeping men, but there was more I could hear. The night brings out many animals that cannot be seen in the day, and I could hear many in the bushes surrounding us. I could sense my breathing calm, and then I could feel my heartbeat slow. I let my talons feel through the dirt. As I did, my mind moved back to the burning town, and memories of pain, torment, and death flooded my thoughts. The pain of these feelings took all of my will to stay present and press deeper for the love that flows through all things, but there was more to feel. I felt hopelessness, despair, and fear. Each of these I have felt before, but here they were stronger than I had experienced. It was as if I was feeling the despair in all the people who had died or of the Designer himself. I knew the love had to be deeper, so deeper I went. But I sensed something else there, and it was new to me: I felt faithlessness.

As soon as I felt this, I knew what it was trying to do to me. It wanted me to cease believing in the Designer. As I sat in the feeling of faithlessness, I could feel the cries of many of the people as they cried out to the Designer for rescue. They had stopped believing in Him, and I could feel it, but now they were desperate for Him. There was so much pain in the land, but faithlessness drove the belief in the Designer from the land. Now I knew why the Designer felt so much grief there.

As I sat and felt this new sensation, a memory came back to me of feeling this with Cain. I did not know what it was back then; I had thought it was Cain's pride or indifference. But now knew the word to describe it. I also knew I had to go deeper into the ground; I could not stop at faithlessness.

And there, below it all, was love. Every part of my being was now centered in my talons as I felt love surge back through me. As it did, I could feel faithlessness peel away from me and disappear into nothingness. I sat and would not let go of what I had now discovered, and it fired my sight to understand the day and all I had seen.

Although my body stayed firmly on the ground, my mind soared into the heavens. I could see the great *Tree of Life* again, but this time I saw it in spirit. Instead of branches and limbs, I saw the pulsing power of the life that it released across creation. I could see into the ground how the Designer's love was the bedrock of everything that exists. Again, I could see the ground pulsing with the life that flowed through the *tree*. It was extraordinary to watch. It reached far beyond Eden. I could see it flowing under the ground where Noah, Ben, and Caleb slept. I could see it gently flowing into them.

I followed the pulsing love, and, in my mind, I was taken back to that awful scene of the town that was now ash, soot, and death.

At first, I recoiled from wanting to let my mind go there again, but as I watched, I saw the most peculiar thing. As the love flowed over those who lay dead, the ground beneath them opened up to receive their death, and in its place, new grass started growing. Nobody was left out for the vultures, and each returned to the dust that Adam was created from. It was then I saw Him; the Designer was there. He could sense I was close and called out to me, "Now you are truly seeing Eagle." He laughed at that, but I could feel no grief this time.

I watched as the love that came from the *Tree of Life* overwhelmed the town and the death it held. There was no scar on the ground and no talking snakes to be seen. The Designer had defeated death here, as He had poured out His life in its place. In my mind, I asked Him, "Where are all the people, my Lord?"

He smiled and said, "They are all with me, for they are all eternal. Death can neither harm nor steal from them, for they are safe within me. Eagle, there are no talking snakes in me."

It truly was like when I saw Abel return to Him. The fragile shells that would only ever last a lifetime had given up their eternal spirits, and now, where they were, death could not touch them. It had no sting, and it had no victory. The victory the talking snake thought it had won had quickly been reclaimed. I felt a surge of joy and love flood my body, and soon it overwhelmed me. I started to shake with the love I was feeling; it was more than I thought I could possibly hold.

When I opened my eyes, Noah held me and yelled something at me, but I could not understand what he said. He was looking down at me with a look of concern on his face that did not match the overwhelming peace I felt. "Eagle, you are here; you are alive," he said with relief in his voice. "I do not know what I would have said to the Designer if you died while with me."

"My lord, I am sorry to have caused you such distress, but I am perfectly fine. Even better than fine; I have never felt more alive than I do right now," I exclaimed. The shocked look on Noah's face said it all.

He said, "Eagle, we all woke up at once and could see you shaking. Your talons were in the ground, but we could not get them out. We did not know what to do." At that, I started to laugh. Seeing an eagle laughing must have looked so strange to these three young men. But I could not contain the joy and the love I was feeling. Never before had I felt such relief and love at the same moment.

"Eagle, what has happened?" Noah asked me.

I looked at him, smiled, and said, "Noah, to tell you that story, we will need every bit of time from here to Enoch, and I will tell it all. But first, you need to cross this mighty river, and I need to stretch my wings and soar."

CHAPTER 20

What had I just experienced? What had I just seen? What had I just felt? As I asked these questions, another voice came to me: the one I had waited years to hear. At first, I could not tell if I was imagining it or hearing it, but there was that voice again, it was her. It was Wisdom. She was soaring with me again. If there was ever a happier moment in my life than this very moment, I could not recall it. She was here with me, and I had so much to tell her. But when we got close, the only thing that tumbled out of my mouth was, "I love you."

She laughed and said back to me, "I know," and then flew off, and all I could do was follow her. She used to be able to hide from me, but that was a long time ago. I watched her every movement of her wings, every deviation she would take, and I felt I could sense where she was going before she went there. We were one again, and we were having fun.

Eventually, we landed on top of a mountain that looked down over the plains and off towards the Tigris River. In the distance, we could see Noah, Caleb, and Ben building their raft. For a few moments, we sat and stared at each other, and it was as if we were soaking in the presence that each of us carried. Finally, I said, "What are you doing here? I thought you were in Enoch and were not able to leave."

"Eagle, my task was to watch over Nashah; she is no longer in Enoch."

"Where is she? I must tell Noah where she is. She is one of the main reasons we are going to Enoch."

Wisdom laughed at me, "Eagle, in some ways, you have changed immensely, and in others, you are still the same. Slow down and look for yourself."

I was startled by Wisdom inviting me to look for myself, for if that was true, then Nashah was within my sight. I lifted my head out of my thoughts, and Wisdom was looking straight into my eyes, and again, she continued to laugh. This time, though, she did not stop laughing. Ever since I first met her, she surprised me, and she loved to do it, and this time was no different.

I looked past her and out beyond the Tigris River, and I could see way off in the distance, a small band of people approaching. At that, I looked back at her smiling face; it took everything in her not to start laughing again. "Yes, Eagle, she is there. Did the Designer tell you that Noah would not need to look for her? Did He not tell you she would be drawn to him?"

"Yes, He did, Wisdom," I exclaimed. "I just never imagined this is what He meant."

"Whether He imagined this or not, Eagle, that is a conversation you can have with Him. But, He would not make them choose what she or her family would do. There was something inside of her that knew she had to come. So here she is."

"What should we do, Wisdom? Should we let Noah know? Should we fly to Nashah and tell her?" I asked.

"There you go again with the shoulds, Eagle. I told you, friends do not use that word." She said, gently mocking. All I could do was smile. I was in the presence of Wisdom, and we were one again. "Eagle, we do not need to do anything. They have been drawn to each other by their love for the Designer. There is nothing for us to do other than watch and soar," she said.

At that, she took to the skies again. I felt no tiredness from all I had been through. All I felt was joy and love, so I took to the skies and followed her into the heavens. It was only yesterday I was doing this by myself and wanting Wisdom to soar with me. I recalled the ache in my spirit over this, and here today, I was soaring with her.

We found those powerful winds that flow through the mountains, and we ascended high above their peaks. So high that people looked smaller than ants on the ground. Then we tucked in our wings and feathers and swooped down quickly. We could cover long distances in such a short space of time. Through the valleys, we wove in and out of trees and along the rivers that flowed through them. We would stop only to eat or drink, and then we would be off to the heavens again.

It was a day I did not want to end, but at some point, we both decided we needed to get back to those we were charged with watching over. We had flown back to the mountain we had first sat at, and there we laughed and cried all over again before Wisdom flew east to the traveling band of people, and I would soon fly back to see how Noah was faring.

I watched Wisdom all the way back to Nashah, and I think I even saw her look back to see if I was watching her. I smiled at the thought and smiled again at the knowledge that it would only be a few days before we would see each other again. Spreading my wings, I allowed myself to fall and be caught by the wind and then used it to slowly make my way back.

When I returned to Noah, I could see the raft was nearly built, and it looked strong and sturdy. They had strapped large logs together with rope. They had worked hard all day to get to this point, and I could see the raft looked ready to begin its maiden voyage. They had decided the morning would be when they would do it, and all of their talk was about how to secure the horse and cart to the raft. By the look on the horse, it was already aware of what was in front of it. Its ears were flat on its neck, and its eyes were wide open. Noah attempted to calm the horse while they were discussing it all, but even so, the horse was in for an uncomfortable ride.

As I looked over all they had built, I marveled at their ingenuity and the work they had done. Tomorrow, they would see if it all worked. Noah secured the horse, approached me, and said, "Where have you been today? Was that you soaring with another eagle?"

At that, I smiled and said, "Yes, my lord, that was me, and that was another eagle."

"Who was the other eagle? She looked familiar, but I could not place her."

I replied, "Soon, you will meet her, and everything will be plain." I do not think my answer satisfied Noah. He waited for more information, but when he saw I was not offering any more, he shrugged and started making the fire to cook their meal.

CHAPTER 21

By the time the three men had all woken, I had already been off soaring the skies above, hoping to catch another glimpse of Wisdom. Like me, she loved to soar as the sun rose, but I could not see her. In the distance, I could see Nashah and the people she was traveling with. It would not take long to fly to them but to walk it; they were at least two days away.

As I soared, I thought back to conversations the Designer had with Noah about Nashah. So many pieces of the puzzle were coming together in front of my eyes. I had imagined this would be weeks of travel before we even saw Enoch, and then to try to find Nashah in a city of people was a challenge in itself. I did not know how many people lived in Enoch, but I had imagined many.

But now, here in front of me, the three men had no idea of the traveling band of people coming their way and who traveled with them. They were about to test the design of their raft and their theories about crossing this river. The raft looked sturdy enough, but even from above, this river looked dangerous to cross.

The waters raged past us, and one wrong move could have had them all swimming for their lives.

For these three, though, their time had come, and carefully, they loaded the horse and cart on the raft. Noah was leading the horse on, and the other two were doing all they could to keep the weight in the middle of the raft. Step by step, they pulled the hesitant horse forward. Its eyes were wide open, and its ears were pinned to its neck again; that horse did not want to be on that raft. Noah had a way with animals, and gently, he spoke to the horse in deep, soft, and reassuring tones. Eventually, the horse pulled the whole cart onto the raft, and everything was in perfect balance.

The three of them all exchanged glances, and slowly broad smiles were shared by them all. The smiles eventually became laughter, but it was also nervous laughter, as they all knew the next part would be the most challenging of all: untying the ropes that held them to the bank and pushing the raft out into the river.

Each of the men had long poles, and their plan was to use those poles to push out into the current and then use them to steer away from rocks projecting out of the river. They were aiming for a beach that was on a bend some distance downriver.

Once they were all ready, they untied the ropes and pushed out into the flow of the river. Quickly it became deep, and just as quickly, they were taken by the surging waters. The horse was terrified and no longer listened to what Noah was telling it. The raft lurched from side to side, but the width of the raft gave it some stability. Each man was completely focused on the snares hidden beneath the waters. Initially, their poles worked well, and they appeared to be making headway, but it soon became obvious to them all that they would miss the beach they aimed for. Suddenly, a crack rang out that was louder than the surging water; Ben's pole snapped. It had gotten caught on one of the rocks he was attempting to steer around. As the pole snapped, the raft hit the rock and abruptly stopped; it soon became wedged up on the rock.

The whole cart and raft teetered there, and the three were yelling at each other. I watched as Noah left the horse, leaped to where the raft was wedged, and used his own pole as a lever. When Caleb saw what he was doing, he rounded the cart and added his pole to Noah's. Inch by inch, they levered the raft off the rock and back into the river's flow. Caleb returned to the other side of the raft, and Noah continued to scan for more submerged rocks. Ben had taken Noah's place with the terrified horse at the front of the raft, but little he said calmed the horse.

The raft crashed into another outcrop of rocks not much further down the river. It did not wedge itself onto them, but the force of the hit dislodged one of the barrels on the cart and sent it tumbling into the river. There was nothing they could do to save the barrel; they were doing all they could save themselves. The force of the collision had turned the raft around, and everybody on the raft was thrown into confusion. Further, down the river, I could see a beach coming up fast. Ben had seen it and was frantically yelling at Caleb to join Noah on the other side of the raft and push the raft toward the beach.

With all of their strength and will, they drove the raft towards the river bank. After what seemed an eternity, the men landed on that beach. The three of them collapsed onto the sand, and if the horse had not still been strapped to the raft, I think they would have left the raft and not gone near the water again. Getting back to his feet, Noah untied the horse and did all he could to slowly lead the horse off the raft. The horse, however, did not want this to happen slowly, and Noah yelled for Caleb and Ben to help him. Once they finally got it and the cart from the raft, a celebration began that must have been heard far back in the valley they came from. They danced and hugged each other and yelled out in sheer exhilaration for surviving the Tigris River.

By the time their celebration was exhausted, they realized the day was gone, and it took no encouragement for them all to agree that this would be a great place to camp for the night. As Noah set up for the fire and started to cook the meal, he sent Ben and Caleb down the river to see if they could find the barrel that had fallen from the cart. I came and sat with Noah as he prepared the food. He turned to me and said, "Well, Eagle, have you ever seen anything like that?"

"No, my lord, I have not seen anything like this since Adam built a raft to cross the Euphrates River when he left Eden," I replied.

Mentioning Eden got Noah's attention, and he asked me, "Eagle, you have told me that story before."

"Yes, my lord," I replied.

"Remind me again of it."

I closed my eyes and allowed my imagination to take me back in time to a time when I did not know shame, talking lizards, or snakes. I could see Cain and Abel running through Eden, exploring every hiding place they could find. I could see Adam and Eve walking in the cool of the evening with the Designer. I could even hear His voice. Every word was love, and every word calmed my spirit. "My lord, it was the most extraordinary of times. No one worked the fields or made clothes, or even built homes. There was a freedom there that is difficult to explain; it is something that needs to be encountered. But when it came time for them to leave Eden, Adam built his first raft. The Euphrates River was not moving like this one, but Adam's first raft fell apart when he tested it. If the time had not been so sad, I am sure we would have all laughed. Adam learned quickly, and his second raft brought them all across the river."

"As you know, I often wonder what living in Eden, Eagle would have been like. If it is half of what your stories tell me, it would have been otherworldly."

"That is a good way of putting it, my lord. In the early days, no one knew what fear or shame was; they were not even words we spoke. It is strange how new experiences cause us to create new words to describe them. When the Designer made Eve, He created a word to describe their connection, and it was a word that sounded like 'ezer'. It is rarely used these days, if at all. The Designer said it means to be powerfully and dynamically connected and that the connection is so strong that Adam and Eve were no longer two people, but one combined person." Once again, my mind drifted back to that time. There was such purity in Eden. There were no lies, and there were no secrets. "As I said, my lord, it is difficult to understand if you have not been there; one must encounter it."

Noah was silent for a while before saying, "When I find my Eve, this is the word I will use as well. She will be my 'ezer'." At that, Noah could hear Ben and Caleb returning. They did not have the barrel, as it had broken open, but they were able to recover some of its contents; not all was lost.

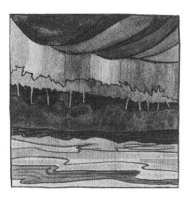

CHAPTER 22

By dawn, I was already again in the skies. The expectation within me to see Wisdom was again high. It was another day I hoped to find her up here. She knew how much I loved to be soaring when the sun was rising. Even as I spread my wings and lifted out of the tree, I could feel the change in the weather. Everything was quiet, the evening animals had all found their homes, and soon the forests would be alive with all manner of creatures. The trees surrounding the campsite were all old, as old as me. They had seen many seasons come and go, and yet they stood tall and strong. They would still be here for many more years.

I had silently left the three men sleeping by the river. The tension of yesterday's crossing meant they were asleep early and still sleeping soundly. It would take them some time to break camp and get moving. However, from up here, I began to see this was going to be a challenge; rain was coming, and by the looks of the approaching clouds, a lot of rain. Soon, the road would be slick with mud, and traveling would take great strength, a strength they did not have.

The clouds were gathering to the southeast, and most likely, it was already raining in the city of Enoch. The clouds were low, so the sunrise could not be seen from the ground. But what is unseen below is able to be seen above by the likes of me. As I flew through the clouds, I could feel the heaviness of the water that had already gathered in them. I always found this to be such a wonder, and each time I felt the water, I had another reason to marvel at the Designer's creation.

Through the breaks in the clouds, I could see Nashah and the people traveling with her. They would soon feel the full force of the Designer's creation in the rain. As I climbed higher, I could not see where the clouds finished; this would not be a passing shower. Higher again, I flew to see if I could find the edge of the clouds, but there was no end; it would rain for days.

I kept moving out in widening circles, and soon I could no longer see Nashah and her traveling party. Wisdom was not up here; she must have been below the clouds. There was an ache in my heart that her presence would only release, but the more I flew, the more I realized the ache would remain for another day. I turned back to where Noah was but quickly realized the clouds now hid even the Tigris River. I could still see the mighty mountains to the north, so I was not lost. But to find Noah meant I had to fly underneath the clouds. My only other option was to fly to the mountains, stay dry, and wait out the storm. But I already knew which I would choose; I was about to get soaked.

Unlike some birds, eagles can fly in the rain. Our design is such that my feathers can withstand heat, cold, and rain. While I can fly in the rain, it is not what I enjoy doing, particularly when it looks like the rain will be here for days.

Although it didn't take long to find them, I could see they were going nowhere. They, too, had seen the approaching clouds and rain. Staying under the trees would be their best chance of staying dry. Their tents would shelter them, but with this approaching rain, I wondered how long they would stay dry.

There is something exquisite about the rain. When it occurs, I find a place to shelter, and from there, I love to sit and watch it fall. It brings calm to my spirit, and it is, yet again, another part of the Designer's doing. He once took great delight in explaining how moisture from the ground gets drawn up into the sky to make clouds. Then, when the atmosphere in the heavens is just right, they release their storage tanks back upon the ground as rain, providing water to make all things grow. In this, I learned how the snow found its way to the mountains. This made sense to me with how cold it is up at those heights. When the snow melted, the water would etch pathways into the sides of the mountains and eventually flow into the most beautiful lakes. With wonder in His voice, He showed me every snowflake is uniquely different. At first, I could not believe it, I searched for two of the same design, but I did not find them. Again, I could only sit in awe and wonder at what He made. He loved to share His design with me, and I loved to listen to Him speak. I did not always understand it, but sometimes, understanding was not as important as knowing the Designer had made it all for me to enjoy.

He was not there to explain it to me. So, I sat, watched, and listened as the rain fell and replenished everything around me. Even the animals go silent when it rains. It is as if all of creation stops to witness something so beautiful and necessary to its existence.

While I was lost in my thoughts, I heard the wonderful, spine-tingling sound of Wisdom quietly flying up from behind me. She loved to surprise me, but I had become so familiar with her approach that I was smiling when she landed beside me.

"Good morning," I said to her.

"It is if you call this weather good," she exclaimed and then laughed, knowing how much I enjoyed the rain.

"What have you seen?" I asked her. It used to be the first question she would ask me. Long ago, I felt it was some kind of test to see if I could understand what I was seeing. We would often sit for hours sharing what we had seen and, hopefully, understood. Before she could answer, I said, "I did not see you this morning."

"You did not see me because I was not there," she responded. "I had flown further south, and then east to see how far these rain clouds had reached. They go back to Enoch and possibly much further, and it is moving slowly. Eagle, you will be able to sit in the rain you love so much for a few days at least."

While this made me happy to hear of the rain remaining, I knew it would frustrate Noah. All he wanted to do was get to Enoch and learn the trade he wanted to master. I could see the three of them busily building their camp further away from the river bank. The ground they had hastily built their tents on last night was too exposed to the rain and too close to the river. The last thing they wanted to do was to be washed back into it. They had spent enough time fighting it; they did not want to do that again. Ben had been sent out to find and stockpile dry firewood. Caleb had been sent to break up the raft for firewood and secure and shelter the horse as best he could. At the same time, Noah's task was to get the supplies off the wagon and into a place as dry as possible.

"Where is Nashah?" I asked. "Have they been able to find a place to shelter?"

"No," said Wisdom. "Last night, they camped on the open plain and are now making their way to the river. And if the Designer has anything to do with this, they will most likely come to this very clearing before the day is out. When they do, they will be tired, cold, and wet. It is a journey that would have taken two days, and they are trying to do it in one."

As we sat, suddenly we heard screaming; it was Ben. He burst into the clearing and was as white as the Designer's hair. Noah and

Caleb had run to him to see what the problem was, and it was not too long before they saw the cause of his panic. A huge animal had been grazing quietly in the trees, unbeknown to all of them, and hidden from Wisdom and me.

Adam had named these animals years ago, but their names were so long that I could not remember what he called them. There were also very few of them that still existed. Seeing them was very rare. They were easily the largest animal I had ever laid eyes on. It had a very long neck that could reach high into the canopies of trees and eat the leaves. They were not a danger to anyone unless they were frightened, and this one was. Which, in turn, rightfully had terrified Ben.

Noah desperately tried to calm Ben by holding him in place and begging him not to move. The panic in Ben was barely containable, and Noah held him with all of his might. Caleb, too, was paralyzed to the very spot he stood. The only sound that came from him was a whimper. The animal came to a shuddering halt as it saw the three of them. It became obvious it was just as afraid of them.

It was Wisdom that broke the moment of panic and paralysis. She had taken to the sky and distracted the animal with her loudest cry and caused it to flee north. They are timid creatures, but their sheer size would kill a person if one of those enormous feet landed on him.

Noah comforted Ben and Caleb as Wisdom landed again beside me. The men below were now shaking their heads and thanking the Designer that they were all safe. The day before, they were doing the same thing after crossing the river. They must have been wondering what the next day would bring.

Wisdom turned to me and said, "Those animals are being killed off by hoards of men further east of Enoch. They are not even using the animals for food, simply for sport. The bigger the animal, the greater the prize." I could hear the anger and contempt in her voice. I would not often hear her speak like this, but as she did, I could feel the same sense of foreboding when I smelled the smoke coming from the burning town only days ago.

"These men hunt them in packs. Once they isolate the animal, they throw many spears at them until they die. I can not fathom the level these people have turned away from the Designer and His design. Eagle, I watched as the Designer walked time and time again among the animals destroyed by these men, and His heart broke each time. He wept for the death and then released the life within each of them back into himself. I do not know how much more of this He will put up with. Creation has changed, Eagle, and I know we will change too if we let go of the Designer's words." We sat in silence for quite some time. Things were now happening in creation that could not be undone, nor could we stop. It felt as if we were hurtling toward a halt, but we did not know where or when that would be.

Below us, the men had returned to their chores. Ben refused to go back and look for firewood again; he did not want to find another of those animals. So Caleb hesitantly went out and searched for anything dry he could find. It was not long before he came crashing back through the trees, yelling as well. "Noah, Noah," he yelled. "A group of people is coming our way, and they will be here soon."

This startled Noah into action. "How many men do they have with them?"

"Not many, my lord, maybe five. But there are women with them as well."

Hearing that, Noah relaxed. I am sure he would have feared an attack if it had just been men. But traveling with women meant they were either travelers or people looking for a new home. They did not have to wait long before the five men cautiously came through the trees. They held axes, but they did not appear to be warriors. They were not looking for a fight but seeking a fire. All the while, Wisdom sat beside me and smiled.

CHAPTER 23

"My name is Cain," the biggest of the men said. At that, Noah's eyes widened, and he took a step toward them. "We are not seeking a fight, and we come as friends in need of shelter and a fire. Forgive us for coming into your camp with our axes, but we did not know what to expect. I understand travelers are becoming less and less frequent in these parts."

Noah stepped forward to greet them, "My name is Noah, and I greet you as a friend. Please, invite all of your people to our fire."

Cain turned and spoke quietly to one of his men; he hurried back through the trees and the rain. "I am traveling with my son and daughters to find the land of my ancestors. If I am not mistaken, they are on the other side of this river," Cain said.

"Where are you travelers from?" Noah asked.

"We have come from the city of Enoch. We have been traveling for many days."

As Cain spoke these words, the rest of his family came through the trees. There was an older woman, two young women, and a young boy. Instantly I could recognize Nashah; she indeed carried the mark of Cain and the glow I could see so easily in Noah. I turned to look at Noah, and he had seen the same mark, mercy, and glow.

Noah audibly gasped when he saw Nashah and said with wonder, "Could this be Nashah?" Cain was startled when he heard Noah speak his daughter's name. As was the older woman, who positioned herself between Noah and Nashah. Caleb and Ben also came forward when they heard her name. They must have wondered if this search for this woman could have been any easier. She had walked right into their campsite only a few days after leaving home!

Nashah was beautiful. She was tall and strong; nevertheless, she was young. Her hair was dark and long, and it had been tied, but the journey had made a mess of it. Her eyes, after she got over the shock of being named by a stranger, were dark and piercing. She would be a woman to be reckoned with, and as I looked closer, I could see she was the very image of Eve.

"You know my daughter?" Cain exclaimed. Cain's words broke Noah's gaze from Nashah and startled him back to Cain, who was obviously unsettled. There was a silence over the entire group as they waited to see what would happen next. All that could be heard was the rain beginning to fall and the sound of men uneasily shifting their feet beneath us.

Noah turned to Cain and asked, "Sir, your name is Cain. Can I ask you if you are indeed related to Cain, son of Adam?"

"Yes, my lord, I am," he said confidently, but there was also sadness in his voice.

"Cain, I have not met your daughter, but I have been told a great deal about her," Noah replied. At that, Nashah's eyes went wide. The shock on her face continued to be impossible to hide. The older woman had not moved from standing between Noah and Nashah, and Cain was fixed to where he was standing and lost for words. Noah then came back to his senses and, looking up, saw the rain was about to get heavier. "My lord, forgive me," Noah said. "Come, sit with us under what shelter we have and warm yourselves by the fire." Then, turning to Ben, he said, "Quickly, take Caleb and find as much firewood as you can. This rain looks to be lasting at least the night; we will need much and do not fear the animal returning." Caleb and Ben raced off into the trees to do as Noah had asked.

Cain turned to two of his men and said, "You two, do the same, but go in the other direction." As the four men set off to do their work, Noah began pulling logs to the fire for the rest of their group to come and sit by. All the while, his eyes barely left Nashah, and her eyes barely left his.

Wisdom turned to me and quietly laughed. She said, "The Designer told me this meeting would require no work of my own, but not even I could not have imagined this, even with the foresight I have."

"I was there when He told the same thing to Noah," I said, joining her in laughing. It was then I realized our laughter had Nashah's attention. She seemed to understand us.

Wisdom smiled at me and, as if reading my thoughts, said, "She is learning, Eagle. You should have seen her face the day when she realized an eagle was talking to her."

To keep himself from just staring at Nashah, Noah busied himself preparing food for Cain and his family. The older woman looked like she was lost for something to do. Everyone else had been given tasks, and hers must have usually been to prepare food for the family. She was fussing over Nashah and her sister when Noah asked her, "What is your name?"

Initially, she seemed shocked to be asked something like this so directly, but quickly recovered her composure and said, "My name is Baht." Then nervously, she said, "My lord, Cain, set me free from men who enslaved me many years ago, and this is now what he calls me. I have used my freedom to care for his family."

Noah smiled at her and said, "Baht, could you help me prepare a meal for your family?"

Baht took straight to the task and effectively moved Noah away from cooking the food altogether. We could all hear her say something under her breath when she realized Noah was no chef. She then set about correcting all his mistakes.

Noah joined Cain sitting on the log and said, "I am of the family of Seth, son of Adam." Noah allowed silence to fill the next moments. He wanted Cain to know the connection they shared was not just of a campfire on a rainy afternoon; they shared the same blood.

"The Designer asked me to go to Enoch to learn the trade of carpentry and to meet a young woman by the name of Nashah. He told me I would not need to find her, simply that we would be drawn to each other. When I asked Him how I would know it was her, He told me she bears the mark of Cain, the mark of His presence. I can clearly see she does, my lord." Cain was having trouble comprehending everything he was hearing. No words were coming from him; he had the look of a man who did not know whether to stay or run away. Noah continued, "I know this must shock you, but this is not my intention. I can see you are a man of honor, and I only wish to honor you by speaking the truth."

Cain stared at Noah for the longest time before he cleared his voice and said, "Nashah's mother died many years ago during the birth of our youngest son, Nacham. His name means to be comforted, but comfort is the last thing I received. The people of Enoch judged she was cursed and that the curse was now upon all the women of her family. Which means that Nashah and her sister, Deborah, are supposedly cursed." Then he continued, "I do not believe we are cursed, but staying in that city was the end of me. So, I packed up my family and my belongings to see whether I would be accepted in the land of my ancestors. All I have is what you can see: two daughters, a son, a woman I freed from slavery, and four of my apprentices who did not wish to stay in Enoch. When my Eve died, I lost all the joy of my existence. She was my everything, and now she is but dust in the ground."

"I have heard of women dying during childbirth as well," Noah said. "I am very sorry for your loss. If it helps, I also do not believe she or your family were cursed either. I know some people die before their time, and most people do not stop to ask or wonder why. Rather, they choose to find fault in the person who died."

"Thank you, Noah," Cain said, and then continued, "They have believed we are also cursed because of the mark of Cain on my family. I have grown to hate the mark, as it makes us stand out from everyone else when all I have ever wanted is to be the same." Noah's eyes widened when he heard this. He, too, carried the same mark and was going to the very city that mocked and ridiculed this family because of it.

Noah said, "My lord, once this rain clears in the morning, we will help you cross the river and get you on your way to our people. Once your men return with firewood, I will have them take turns being awake tonight to keep the fire going through the evening."

"And what about Nashah?" Cain asked.

Suddenly, Nashah came out of the darkness and into the light of the fire, and she looked angry. "How dare you decide my future without speaking with me about this. Am I just another one of your cows that you would barter me to some stranger?"

Wisdom smiled at me and whispered, "Eagle, I give you Nashah."

Both Noah and Cain were startled by Nashah's abrupt entrance; this was the first time Noah had heard her speak. "Father, I have followed you here. You know I wished to stay in Enoch, but you would not listen to me. Now, here we are again, and you are making decisions for the rest of my life. Would you give me away so quickly to a man you just met and know nothing about?"

With a rueful smile, Cain turned to Noah and whispered as well, "Noah, this is my Nashah."

Nashah stood glaring at both men from across the fire, daring either of them to challenge her. Noah glanced at Cain, and when he realized he would not say anything to Nashah, he cleared his throat to speak. "Nashah, daughter of Cain, and carrier of the mark of Cain. I would be the last person who would wish to claim you as one of your father's cows. I would never ask you to do something to which you could not say 'no'." Noah paused to see if he had fanned her anger even further into flame. When she did not respond, he kept going. "Nashah, I do not know what our futures hold, whether together or apart. But the last thing I would do to you is force you into a life you did not choose." Nashah exhaled deeply, but I could tell she was still very tense and seemed unsure of how to respond to Noah.

"My lady, if I may," Noah continued, "Please, come sit with us by the fire and allow the heat to dry your clothes and warm your spirit. This rain does not appear to be stopping, so let us not talk about futures or decisions; tonight, we eat and rest and will see if Baht is a better cook than I am."

Nashah's eyes went between Noah and her father. Where she stood, she was getting wetter by the moment. Once again, she exhaled audibly and cautiously came and sat on the opposite side of the fire from Noah and Cain and said no more. Soon, all the men returned with armloads of firewood. They quickly made a gigantic pile and covered it with green pine branches to keep the rain off it as best as they could. There was enough firewood there to last for a few days. Baht then called everyone to her cooking fire and served the meal. Each received their fill and was happy to have something warm to eat. At the end of the meal, Noah congratulated her and said, "Baht, truly, you are a better cook than I."

With the rain continuing, each of them left the fire and found a tent to shelter them and hopefully find some sleep as well. Only

Noah and Cain remained at the fire. Noah asked, "Why is she called Nashah?"

"After my Eve died, Nashah took on many of the roles of her mother with the younger two children. She even looks like her mother. Sometimes when I see her, my heart breaks all over again for the woman that I lost. No one will ever be able to take the place of my Eve in my life. I got lost in my grief, and Nashah got lost in being a parent. Then one day, she simply declared her name was now Nashah, for she had been forgotten. My heart broke all over again, hearing her say this. I had taken her for granted and became consumed by my grief. And that is how she became known as Nashah."

"She is courageous and cannot be tamed," Noah said as a statement, not as a question.

"What you say is correct. She is brilliant beyond compare, and at other times, she is hard-headed and stubborn," Cain said with a laugh to himself. "Many times, I have tried to find a man who would take her as his Eve, but each one quickly gave her right back."

"She is strong," Noah said. "Good night Cain; we will talk more in the morning. Hopefully, this rain will be done by then."

CHAPTER 24

Wisdom and I watched over them as they slept, and the rain continued through the night. It was not torrential rain but soaking rain. Creation would be blessed by it, but for travelers going in different directions, the rain would cause them to wait.

"Wisdom, what do you see?" I asked.

She smiled and said, "I see two powerful people in Noah and Nashah. They are equally matched, and I can see why the Designer wanted them to meet."

"What if either of them says 'no'?" I asked her.

"Then that would be the beginning of love, Eagle," she replied. I was just about to open my mouth and ask another question when Wisdom spoke again, "Remember, for love to be love, choice must always be given freely, with no added conditions. If both give each other the freedom to choose, we might see something very special."

I sat and pondered this long into the night. The Designer had spoken of a coming rest or judgment and a plan that included both Noah and Nashah. He also gave a time frame. A question was running through my mind, and finally, I blurted it out to Wisdom, "What would happen to the Designer's plan if either of them said 'no' to it?"

"Eagle, you have seen much, but yet there is much more for you to understand about the Designer," she laughed as she said this to me. "You seem to think the Designer only ever has one plan that happens exactly as He designed it to happen, but this is not how He works. Do you think it was His design for Eve to eat the fruit of the *Tree of Knowledge of Good and Bad*? Do you think it was His design for Cain to kill Abel?"

"No, I do not," I replied.

"But His plan is still happening, Eagle. His plan has not changed because of the choices these people made. It is still the same and will never change." She paused before continuing, "His plan is to love those He has created, and everything else is a work in progress. His character never changes, but His love is constantly changing His ideas for His creation and the love that returns to Him. So, whatever His ideas or desires are for Noah and Nashah, they can change any time they choose differently to what He sees."

I sat quietly, thinking through all Wisdom had said. She has seen much and understands the Designer in ways I have yet to grasp, and His love continues to be one of those ways. It does not matter how many years I have been soaring over His creation; it is always the talk of His love that continues to baffle me, grow me, confound me, and honor me. It matters not how much I know of His love; there is always more to comprehend. "Wisdom, I have seen some of what you speak of, but this love, His love, is bigger than my understanding. In my mind, I hear Him speak His plans to Noah, and I expect him to do exactly what He says. Surely Wisdom, it is love to just do what the Designer tells him to do?"

"Some would think so, Eagle," she said. "But this is not what I have encountered with Him. Even when I went to Enoch to watch over Nashah, He did not force me to do it; He asked me to do it. I knew I could say 'no' to Him and still be entirely loved."

"But surely, Wisdom, it would be better for us all if we just did what He said? If Eve had just done what He said, then we would not have been here today wondering if Noah and Nashah would join and become one," I replied.

"You cannot know that, Eagle," she said and then paused before continuing, "Eagle, how many times in Eden did Adam and Eve go close to the *Tree of Knowledge of Good and Bad*?"

"Many times," I replied.

"Every time that strange lizard tempted them and went to that *tree*, were they rejecting what the Designer asked them?" She asked.

"No," I exclaimed. "Each time they resisted, they did what the Designer asked of them."

"No, Eagle, you did not see clearly back then. What you witnessed was one mistake by Eve. But what you did not see were all the mistakes they made by choosing to listen to that strange lizard. All of those 'many times' you watched them being tempted were the slow undoing of the Designer's words and desires He had for their lives. They slowly let go of His words, desires, and plans. He did not let go of them, but the future began to change with each choice they made."

"So, you're saying the coming judgment can be changed?" I asked.

Wisdom smiled and said, "In a way, Eagle."

"In a way? Are you saying His plan is not dependent on Noah or Nashah?"

"I cannot see all things, Eagle. But I know the Designer will not take their choice from them." She paused as if in thought and then continued, "Yes, Eagle, what you say may well be true, but it is still His desire they become one. Maybe this is the difference between what He desires and what is His plan."

"What do you mean, Wisdom?"

"It is like you and me, Eagle. We both have desires that are not met. But His plan is different. It is not based on desire; it was birthed in love. His only plan is to love, and to understand this is to understand Him."

My mind needed more time to understand all Wisdom said to me. Sometimes I would look at her and wonder if she truly knew His love as well as she was explaining it. It all made sense to me at one level, but at another level, I could not comprehend the Designer giving those created in His image such freedom of choice. His creation was fast becoming a disaster in front of our very eyes. This freedom He gave had not resulted in many of these people loving Him as He loves them.

"Wisdom, what do you know of His love?"

She laughed and said, "Very little, Eagle. Each day is a new day to discover something of the wonder that He is. I live each day living in the wonder of what I have discovered and looking for the greater wonder that is His love."

"Wisdom, speak plainly. What do you mean?"

"Eagle, you long to understand something that must be encountered rather than taught. You have encountered His love many times, and each time, your life changed. Think about it this way, in the beginning, the Designer created all things, and He declared each of them good. Then, to each of them, He added His love. His love would be the very force that would keep creating in and through us. As we love, we grow, and as we love others, we grow. This is the sustaining power that every living thing holds, and through this love, we each have the ability to create." She said before pausing and then continuing, "But it does not end there, Eagle. Each time we love, the object of our love is invited to create and grow with us. They are invited into the creative process."

I felt like I was trying to drink water under a waterfall. I needed time to think through this. I had felt His love many times. I will never forget when He invited me to sit under the *Tree of Life* and let my talons dig deep into the ground when I reached past my fear and shame and into His love. It was the first time I had felt healing, and it surged through me with a warmth that changed me. But did I realize back then that I grew through that experience? As I thought through this experience, I realized the Designer told me of the change within me. He told me I had eyes to see more and was no longer a watcher but one who could see. Wisdom was right; I had grown.

"You see more clearly, Eagle, because His love has revealed much to you. Not everyone sees more when the Designer does this. Love is an invitation to see more of Him and all He has given you. Each time you have seen what His love has revealed, you have become an even greater expression of His creation and love." She said as if reading my mind.

"An even greater expression of His creation and love," I repeated to Wisdom. "But what does that even mean?"

"That is the question that will only be answered as love is chosen. It is impossible to answer what anything will look like when love does what it was created to do. Eagle, it is beyond what you can hope, dream, think, or even imagine. That is why it is so hard to understand, but yet it is so powerful to encounter."

"So, every expectation of the future can change when love operates in its design?"

"Expectations are always held loosely when love is operating as it was designed to operate," she replied.

"Wisdom, earlier, when I asked you what would happen if Noah or Nashah said 'no.' You responded with, 'Then that would be the beginning of love'." Wisdom simply nodded and let me continue. "That is still a confusing statement to me. I know you said it was tied to the freedom they have to choose, but I think I need more time to understand it. "

"Tonight, you heard Noah give Nashah that very choice. She has been given a gift, and she has been given something no man has ever given her before. If Noah gives her this choice freely, then she can make her own choices just as freely. If she says 'no' to Noah, this does not mean the relationship can not happen; it just means that it will not happen as we all want it to happen today. Let us watch and see, Eagle."

CHAPTER 25

The sun rose the next morning, but it could not be seen. The rain still fell, causing the river to rise and move faster. No one would be crossing the Tigris River on this day. During the night, a fog had formed amongst the trees that were only kept at bay by the fire the men had tended throughout it. Long tendrils of fog would reach out from the trees; they looked like long arms beckoning us away from the fire and into the mist.

Noah was up early and could quickly see that his desire to get moving would have to be waited on. He disappeared into the fog and soon returned to declare the road east had become a quagmire. There would be no traveling today. Cain found Noah standing under a tree, still peering into the fog. "If this rain does not stop soon, it will be impossible for us to go west, and from what I can see, impossible for you to go east."

"Yes, you are right, Cain. This rain does not look like stopping anytime soon."

"I do not want to stay here long, Noah. We need to keep moving; we do not have the supplies to last us many days. Maybe we should try to cross before it gets higher?"

Noah walked with Cain back to the river's edge and said, "The river has come up quickly. Crossing it when it was not flooding was hard enough. Cain, I know this river well, and it is dangerous. It is impossible to tell when the water level will drop to get you all safely across, especially if this rain keeps falling."

Cain looked up and down the river, looking for another place to cross. He then exhaled deeply and, as he turned away from the river, said, "And at the rate it is rising, we may need to find a new campsite soon."

"That is wise," said Noah. "Let us gather the men and have them search out another site. Maybe we can find one more protected from the rain as well."

Cain's men went north, and Noah's men went south. Ben and Caleb had not long gone when they came running back through the trees, and this time they were not being chased by an enormous animal. Ben said, "We have found caves not far from where we are. They are deep and dry and can house us all, including our horse."

"Well done," Noah replied. "Let us gather all our belongings and the firewood and make for the caves."

While packing up the camp, Cain's men returned, and one of them said, "My lord, the river has broken its banks further north. Soon, this campsite will be underwater, and we will need to move as soon as possible." With that news, everyone moved more quickly, and before long, the two groups of people were heading south to find the caves that Ben and Caleb found.

Noah was the last to leave the campsite, checking nothing had been left behind before heading off. During this, he saw Nashah coming back through the trees, her arms loaded with firewood. "Nashah, we are moving our campsite. We would have done so without you if you had returned any later. Did Cain know you were out there on your own?" Noah said and offered to take the load of firewood from her.

She pulled back from him and said abruptly, "I am more than capable of carrying this firewood. Maybe we would be better served if you found more of your own." Noah was taken aback by how direct she was, but he did not appear upset by this interaction at all.

"Do all women in Enoch speak like this?" Noah asked.

His question also shocked her, "I am sorry, my lord, I meant no disrespect. I will not become a burden to anyone; I will carry what needs to be carried and do what needs to be done."

"I took no offense, Nashah, but you intrigue me," he said. "Can I ask you a question?"

"That all depends on the question," she responded.

Noah stopped, smiled, and gently said, "You carry the mark of Cain and the glow of the Designer. Can you tell me how you received this mark?"

Noah's question caused her to relax, and she said, "I have carried it since I was a child. My mother carried it as well."

"Not your father? I thought he was the one related to Cain, the son of Adam," Noah exclaimed.

"I have found, my lord, that birthright alone does not mean the child carries the same mark as the parent. I have seen some of my ancestor's people do the most terrible things," she responded.

Noah nodded at this and said, "As have I."

Noah headed off through the trees and found an armload of firewood, and the two of them headed south together. As they walked, Noah asked, "Your mother carried the mark of Cain. Can you tell me about her?"

Nashah gave a sad smile and said, "She is the most magnificent woman I have ever known. Noah, she was brave and courageous. She knew who she was, and people would come far and wide to listen to the wisdom she carried. She taught me everything I know, but when she died, a piece of me died with her. I do not know why the Designer took her while giving birth to my brother. My father has not been the same either. He is a shell of the man he once was, and when people turned on us in Enoch, he just packed up and left. So, here we are." She took a few more steps in silence and said, "My only comfort during that time was meeting with the Designer in the cool of the evening, just like I had done with my mother most days. He brought me healing in a way that even if I told you about it, you would say I am being foolish."

Noah smiled and said, "Does it have anything to do with placing your hands on the ground and allowing your fingers to work their way into the soil?"

Nashah gasped and said, "My lord, that is exactly what He invited me to do."

"And what did you feel, Nashah?"

"You are going to think I am crazy, but I felt the pain and grief of losing my mother," she said. "It was an unbearable pain, so the Designer helped me bear it. He showed me His love and invited me to feel it. It took everything within me to hold on to His love when all I had was the pain of my loss. But Noah, and I am ashamed to say it; I did not want Him to bear the pain of loss. I wanted my mother." As she finished speaking, her tears flowed, and Noah could tell she had shared more than she intended.

"My mother still lives, but when I farewelled her only days ago, something within me revealed this would be the last time I saw her. She taught me many things, but what I remember most was the safety of her lap when I was a child. Whatever trouble I got myself into, I knew the safety and love she carried, and each time I sat there, I healed. If she passes before I return, I will know she is safe in the Designer's lap in Eden."

"In Eden?" Nashah asked.

"Ever since Abel died, we have been taught that those who die return to Eden," Noah said as he pointed to Eden across the river.

"The glow we carry, Nashah, is our spirit. The glow leaves our bodies when we die and returns to the Designer."

"Do you believe my mother is there?" She exclaimed. Nashah had halted and was looking through the rain into Eden. The rain and the river's roar made it impossible to concentrate on anything on the opposite side of the river, but it did not stop her from trying.

Noah walked beside her and asked, "What did the Designer tell you about where your mother is?"

Without breaking her gaze from Eden, she said, "He told me she was with Him now. But, all I could understand was she was not with me."

"The Eagle once told me that without grief, there was no love," Noah said.

These words broke Nashah's search of Eden. She smiled and even laughed before saying, "Wisdom told me the same thing." At that, they arrived at the new campsite. Everyone turned to see them walk out into the clearance, and everyone saw the glow that came from them both.

CHAPTER 26

"Eagle, let us fly above the clouds for a time," said Wisdom.

"There will not be much to see, but I would never pass up an opportunity to soar with you," I replied. At that, we took to the skies, and after flying through rain and clouds, we finally burst through the clouds and into brilliant sunshine. Still, as far as we could see to the east were clouds, and we knew immediately this rain would be with them for more days than they hoped. To the west, we could see the edge of the clouds, to where the rain had not yet reached.

Wisdom said, "I would have thought the clouds would be as far to the west as they are to the east. This sounds like the Designer's doing. Shall we go find Him?" That was all the encouragement I needed; we then flew north to the mountain He often met us at. We were high above the clouds, and the higher we flew, the more we could see of this cloud to the east. It stretched all the way from the direction of Enoch and back to where Noah had come from.

It would take most of the morning to get to the mountain, and we were in no rush. After spending a night in the soaking rain, it was refreshing to spread our wings and find those strong winds again that would take us higher and higher. No words passed between us; we simply shared the joy of being able to do what we were created to do.

The peak of the mountain stood proudly through the clouds. To us, it appeared as if the mountain was determined to stay in the sun's warmth. How different it was beneath the clouds to what was above. By the time we arrived at the mountain's peak, the Designer was waiting for us. Yet again, the smile on His face showed us how much He loved us. It never ceases to amaze me how much He can say without even speaking a word.

We landed on either side of Him, and as we did, He stretched His arms around us and drew us close to Him. These are the moments I never tire of when I can place my head on His chest, feel His heartbeat, and listen to His voice all at one time. "So, Eagle, what have you seen?" The Designer asked.

"I have seen a lot of rain, my Lord," I responded.

He laughed and said, "I'm guessing there is a question in there somewhere?"

"You know him well, my Lord," Wisdom said while joining His laughter.

"The clouds and rain are not behaving as I would normally think. Is this your doing?" I asked.

The Designer smiled at this as if giving Himself away, "Maybe," He replied.

"If I know you well, my Lord, I would say rain will be in their future," I replied.

The Designer paused before answering, and when He did, some of the joy had gone from His voice, "Many choices are ahead of them, but what you say is true, my friend. Rain is in their future." The silence grew after the Designer had spoken. All that could be heard was the wind now moving through the mountains.

It was cold up here, but it was the chill I felt from what He spoke that got beneath my feathers.

"As you both know and have seen, things are happening in my creation that I did not design. From the voice of the strange lizard to the talking snakes, the disease that has affected my design has grown. But it was not always the case," the Designer said. We could see that He paused and was thinking through His next words. "I know you have both wondered where this evil came from and why I have allowed it to go unabated for so long. Again, as you also both know, the spirits that entered the lizards, snakes, vultures, and the like, have now entered the sons of men."

He paused before continuing, "They have given their choices to what would control them and not to who would love them. They were lured, like Eve, with promises of a fantasy. They have left behind the truth and craved power. All that was once good in them has now become chaos. Kindness is rare, and my presence has been spurned. These evil spirits now occupy their spirits, affecting every choice and decision they make. Evil is now manifest where once it was love. The spirits of people are now becoming corrupted spirits. You have both witnessed the destruction caused to my creation because of this. Everything of my creation, every seed, plant, fruit, and even animals, can be reborn and restored. I can remake it all. But the spirits of people are eternal and irreplaceable. The time is coming when I will stand for it no more." Once again, the sound of the wind replaced the Designer's voice. We could feel the lament in His Spirit and the pain in His heart.

He continued, "These evil spirits were not always evil; they were like the angels you have seen guarding the *Tree of Life*. They were beautiful, and when I created them, I declared over them they were perfect. The fullness of my Spirit poured into them to make their spirits. They were not originally called 'angels' either. They were known by the names I created them with. You already know the names of those guarding the *Tree of Life;* Micheal and

Gabriel. I love them both dearly, and their faithfulness has been demonstrated time and time again. But more than that, their presence brings life to me."

"A time long ago, not measured by days, months, or years, there was an uprising within the ones now called 'angels.' I felt it long before most of them felt it. It started with one; his name was Lucifer. I called him that because of the light that shone from him at his creation. Every angel is different, just as every person is different, and Lucifer shone brightly; it was what made him unique. He always spoke the truth, always." The Designer was talking to himself and seemed lost in a memory; then, a sad laugh came from Him at the recollection of this memory.

"Yes, Eagle and Wisdom, he spoke the truth, and some angels grew to avoid him because he demanded they listen to him and him alone. Yes, he spoke the truth, but I have found that truth can be different depending upon the lens one looks through. So, Lucifer became everyone's truth, and this was where it all started." Once again, the wind filled the silence when the Designer paused.

"I spent time with him, much like the time I spent with Eve and Cain before they chose their own path. I spoke of my love and what it means to speak truth but to use love as your lens. There were times Lucifer would listen to me, but the times grew when he would not. And, as with the people today, I would never enforce my will upon him. I also gave him choice. His choices, though, became his weapons. He used his truth and voice to convince many other angels that this was all they would ever be, just my angels. He convinced them they would be my messengers and not my friends. Angels that would only ever serve and never live out the fullness of who they were. He convinced them I was holding back my love from them. They became convinced I was not who I was. He took the truth and made half-truths. The lies became convincing enough for the decaying seed of truth they held, but they held nothing but death."

So heavy were the words from the Designer I wept. The grief I felt was not for what I had lost or seen but for Him. I could feel the purity of His love in the words He spoke, and they were words that were breaking my heart. He continued, "They started making names up for themselves, and in doing so, it took them further from their design and further from me. Lucifer started calling himself the 'Accuser.' He called himself this because of the truth he thought he carried. He thought he could know all things and judge all things he saw. Each judgment he made brought more condemnation and control with it. He would judge the angels, and many of them became nameless; they were losing their identity."

Again, the Designer paused. Eventually, He inhaled deeply and said, "Here is something you both do not know: The two *trees* in Eden existed before the creation you see today. The *Tree of Life* was always the *Tree of Life*, but the *Tree of Knowledge of Good and Bad* was not always called that. It was simply known as the *Tree of Knowledge*. It became known as *Good and Bad* when Lucifer broke relationship with me. He took something perfect in the knowledge we shared and made it into something bad." The Designer bowed His head, and again we found ourselves swallowed up by the sounds of the creation around. Time passed up here; how much, I do not know.

"Knowledge is most often subjective, but for Lucifer, his knowledge became his absolute truth. He convinced many of the angels that knowledge was life, and its fruit was all they needed to live. So from that time, I called it the *Tree of Knowledge of Good and Bad*. All who ate from it came to think that their knowledge made them superior to all others." Another silence followed.

"Eagle, do you remember Cain being so fearful of losing my presence?" He said.

"Yes, my Lord, I do. That fear crippled him," I replied.

"Lucifer willingly led a third of the angels out of my presence. He led them away from the *Tree of Life* and away from my love.

They did not know what they had given up until they had left my presence. Before leaving, they tried to destroy the *Tree of Life*, but Gabriel and Michael stood guarding it back then as well. They were the ones who first sensed the chaos Lucifer was preparing for the *Tree of Life*. They were the ones that prepared all the angels for what would unfold in that chaos. Guess what Gabriel and Michael did, Eagle?" He asked me.

I spoke the first thought that came into my mind, "They drove their hands into the ground surrounding the *Tree of Life* and into your love?" I asked.

At that, the Designer laughed, and soon his laughter became so loud that the mountain shook. Wisdom and I looked at each other and drew ourselves even closer to the Designer. "Yes, Eagle! You see much," He declared. "Gabriel and Michael knew something of my love that Lucifer did not. You see, Eagle, their knowledge had become understanding to them both. What they understood of my love, Lucifer failed to grasp. He believed knowledge was the key, whereas Gabriel and Michael knew it to be love."

The Designer became lost in this memory again, and after a few moments of thought, He continued, "Lucifer and his followers came at the *Tree of Life* with weapons they had forged, but Michael and Gabriel had no such weapons. Michael's name means 'gift,' and Gabriel's name means 'strength.' The two of them combined means 'my gift is their strength.' As Lucifer threw all of his strength against them, they both reached for where their strength came from. They reached through the pain and chaos and into my love. It exposed Lucifer and all who followed him for what they had become. The glorious light that flowed from Lucifer had gone. He kept telling them all of the light he carried; he even told his followers to call him 'the Angel of Light.' But his light was counterfeit and was nothing compared to the light that flowed from the ground through Michael and Gabriel that day."

The Designer wept as he recalled these events. His heart broke all over again in the story's retelling.

"As they drove their hands into the ground and found my love, they released my love to do what it was designed to do. It drove Lucifer and his followers out of my presence. Their chaos, knowledge, and the fear they manifested would never overwhelm or defeat my love. They did not even get close to the *Tree of Life*. They dropped their weapons and fled. They feared my wrath more than they knew, my love. They could never again taste the fruit that would release them from their choices, so they fled and waited."

"I always knew where they were; nothing in all of creation can hide from me. There were other times they tried to attack the *Tree of Life*, but each time they got close, they felt the magnitude of the pain they had caused themselves. Each time, they would flee from my love and the *tree*. So, they learned to hide in their shame and adapted to living within it. It clothed them, and before long, it distorted how they looked and spoke. These are the voices you have heard. They sound horrific, but they mask their fear. They are scared and hollow forms of what they once were. What you are seeing today is another attempt they are making to reclaim the *Tree of Life* again. They think if they wipe out the last ones who love me, they will be able to finally feast on its fruit." Again, the Designer went silent.

"They have been gone from Eden for so long that they have forgotten Gabriel and Michael are still there. I did not place them there just to stop Adam and Eve from eating its fruit. I placed them there to remind all who are evil that my love will never be conquered. They now hold flaming swords, these you have seen. They are not swords of death, but swords of life. They will repel those who come seeking death, and they will crown those who seek life."

"I know it will not stop them from trying to destroy or claim the *tree*. They will also try to do the same for the *Tree of Knowledge of Good and Bad*. They believe if they hold this *tree*, they will have the seeds of knowledge to become like me. So, I have determined to do a work that will take the *trees* out of their sight. I will hide the *Tree of Life* until the appointed time when the seed of that *tree* is reborn, and when that *tree* is reborn, all of creation will change."

We sat in His presence for the rest of the afternoon. He had poured out His heart to us and allowed us to see and learn things we had not known. All of it was precious and challenging, but the longer He spoke, the more I sensed the hope within Him.

Later that evening, Wisdom and I flew back down to the caves where Noah, Nashah, and their people were gathered. When we got beneath the clouds, we could see it was still raining and had not stopped. We could also see the Tigris River had continued to rise. The Designer had given us much to think about, and once again, the mystery of the seed that would be reborn continued to intrigue me.

CHAPTER 21

We returned to find a hive of activity happening both inside and outside the caves. They were indeed big enough to house them all. Cain's men were busily clearing the largest of the caves. Old branches had either been left there or blown into it, and they were breaking them up and getting them ready for the fires they would need in the days ahead. A scattering of animal bones made everyone aware of the dangers of larger animals hidden in the trees. The shape of the cave looked as if it had been hollowed out by water from the Tigris River. But in my memory, I could not remember a time when the river had flooded to this extent. The rock the cave was made into was sandstone, and it had beautiful bands of different colored sand running horizontally through the rock. The cave's opening was high and wide but not deep. It was ideal for where they would all gather for meals.

Baht had a fire going at the cave entrance and was already preparing the evening meal. Wisdom and I could smell the meal long before we even saw it. Just watching her at work revealed her expertise in cooking. She needed no help and was perfectly at ease in preparing a meal for this many people. The smell of roasting garlic and peppers would soon draw all of them for supper.

The caves were far enough from the rising river, but with the rain continuing to fall, I knew Noah would be watching it like an eagle. The caves faced the river, which meant the rain was not being driven into them.

There were several smaller caves on either side of the one Baht was preparing the meal in. Noah's men were preparing to store all the provisions in a dry place deep in one of the caves. We could see the horse was pleased to be out of the rain, but it did not like the cave Ben was trying to lead it into. Its hesitation had given Caleb and Ben cause to proceed with caution. Caleb took a flaming torch and investigated to see what was causing the horse to panic, but then all too quickly, he came running out of the cave.

He was yelling, "A wolf. A wolf. A wolf is in the cave."

What happened next astonished me. Nashah simply, without fear, got up from her siblings and walked straight into the cave. She did not even take Caleb's torch. Ben exclaimed, "No, my lady. You can not go in there. The wolf will attack you."

She turned and said, "Ben, leave the wolf to me; just tend to the horse." Caleb was confused and did not know what to do, so he ran to find Noah.

Wisdom, though, turned to me and said, "Eagle, go in and watch what she does."

"But my presence might scare the wolf; I do not want to cause it to react and attack Nashah," I replied.

"It will not attack Nashah. Just go and watch," Wisdom replied.

So I flew down into the cave entrance, trying to make as little noise as I could. I knew the wolf would pick up my scent as soon as I arrived, but I did not want to scare it. What I saw astonished me even more. Nashah was sitting and talking with it like Noah would speak with me. She turned and saw me and said, "Eagle, the wolf is scared. She has been separated from her pups, and she does not know what has become of them. The last time she saw them was further downriver, and she fears the river has washed them away. Do you think you could have a look and see what you can find?"

I was shocked to hear this, she had not spoken to me before, but the authority in her voice made me take flight and begin a search. I closed my eyes and allowed the sounds of the rain, wind, and river to fade away. It was not long before I could hear the faint cries of wolf pups'. Honing in on the sound, I found they had sheltered in a hollowed tree. They were soaked and scared, and my presence drove them further into the tree.

I returned to the cave to find the wolf asleep on Nashah. She calmed the wolf in a way that again reminded me of Adam. I had seen him do this at the creation of all the animals. The Designer gave him dominion over them; I often saw him with a lion or a tiger asleep on his lap, just like I was now seeing with Nashah. The wolf was alert as soon as I landed, and Nashah said to me, "Eagle, you were not gone long. Did you find them?"

"Yes, my lady, they are not far downriver, hiding in a hollowed-out tree," I said.

Hearing my response, the wolf ran from the cave to find her pups. However, her fast exit from the cave then frightened the horse, and Ben could not control it. It bolted in the opposite direction of the wolf, and we lost sight of it through the rain and trees.

Nashah said to me, "This cave was not her den. She was here looking through all the caves for her pups when we arrived. She was scared and hid in this one. She will not return here." She smiled at me, got up, dusted herself off, and went back and sat with her siblings.

Cain and his men had been busy clearing out the caves when they saw the horse bolt past them and off into the trees. He came running to see what had happened, only to find Nashah sitting happily with his family, Baht cooking, and Ben standing in the rain, looking stunned. "What happened here?" He exclaimed. "I saw the horse disappear into the trees."

Nashah smiled at him and said, "Nothing you need to concern yourself with, father. Ben will eventually find his horse, and supper will be ready shortly."

Her younger brother, Nacham, was way more excited about the events that had just happened. He could not get his words out fast enough, and Cain could not follow the thread of what he was saying; something about a cave, a horse, a wolf, an eagle, and Nashah. He just shook his head and went back to his men to continue clearing out the cave they were in. At least there was one cave he did not need to worry about clearing.

But where was Noah? And then I realized it was the cool of the evening, and even the rain would not stop Noah from meeting with the Designer. I knew I would always be welcome in those conversations, so I flew along the river until I found the two of them sitting, deep in conversation, but their eyes were on the rising river. Noah looked up and said, "There you are, Eagle. The Designer was telling me about your day up on the mountain with Wisdom." I smiled at the thought of the Designer talking to Noah about me, and the joy only increased when I saw the joy flowing from the Designer as well.

"What have you seen, Eagle?" the Designer asked.

"My Lord, I have just witnessed Nashah sit with a wolf like Adam would sit with a lion," I exclaimed. Even as I said her name, I could see Noah's interest, but to hear she had been sitting with a wolf had him on his feet, and was about to run. He only stopped because he heard the Designer laughing. Noah was confused, and this made the Designer laugh all the more. It is a beautiful thing to hear Him laugh; to me, it feels as if all of creation reacts and responds to His voice and His joy. Everything, that is, except Noah; he had no idea of what was happening.

"Sit down, Noah. Nashah is perfectly safe, but your concern for her has me thinking you have already made up your mind about her," the Designer said. I watched as Noah blushed before he could respond. I saw this same reaction when the Designer talked to Noah about her back in the valley.

Words started, stopped, and stumbled out of Noah's mouth, which made the Designer laugh even more. Finally, he said, "I am just glad she is safe." At that, he sat back down beside the Designer.

Still, the Designer laughed, and when He finally stopped, He said, "There is much yet for you to discover about Nashah. You know she carries the mark I gave Cain, but there is so much more. When her mother died, she devoted herself to learning anything she could. It was the way she coped with the grief. Eve did this when Abel died. The difference between them was Eve devoted herself to people, whereas Nashah devoted herself to learning, particularly about animals. She still loved her family and became a mother to her sister and brother, but when she was not with them, she was with me or with people she could learn something from."

"When she was with me, our conversation would often turn back to animals. She found so much comfort in sitting with them, and to her, it did not matter the animal. The animals that scared most people were the ones she spent most of her time with. You are right, Eagle; not since the days of Adam have I found one who is as connected with my creation as she is."

The Designer went silent for a moment before He gathered His thoughts and continued, "Some of those she tried to learn from abused and mocked her. You have heard Cain speak of the curse many think her family has. She has heard many speak of it, even her own father. Now she finds it hard to trust men. When her mother died, her father withdrew from her and her siblings. He was not the father she needed. She looked for that father figure in other men. Her father also tried to give her to some of those men, but she would not be given away. Each time they hurt her, she would come and sit with me. She has learned much of the power of my love, and she knows where to discover healing. She now has a strength and resilience refined like gold in a fire. You have seen gold refined, Noah. The impurities rise to the top, and the goldsmith scrapes them off, leaving pure gold. This is Nashah." Again, the Designer paused before continuing, "She is still healing, Noah. One day she may share the pain and abuse in her story with you, but just know she is most definitely healing."

Noah responded, "She told me you invited her to place her hands into the ground to find your love and discover your healing. This alone speaks to me of her character and her willingness to cling to the words you have spoken to her."

The Designer responded, "She is your Eve, Noah. But do not take her, or this, for granted. For her to be your Eve, you will need to show that you can be her Adam."

The Designer looked at me and asked, "Do you agree, Eagle?"

"Yes, my Lord, Noah will need courage to be her Adam, and from what I have seen, a lot of it," I exclaimed. Both the Designer and I laughed, but Noah did not. He had gone back to staring into the river. I smiled as I watched him. He was rubbing his beard and lost in thought and action he would do when he had a choice to make or the future was unclear.

The Designer broke his thought and said, "Noah, Caleb is panicking and is searching for you. Ben has lost your horse and does not know where to find it. It is not far back upstream. Its reins have gotten tangled in a tree, and it cannot go any further, and your supper is nearly ready. Baht does not like to be kept waiting."

CHAPTER 28

Leaving the Designer back at the river, Noah and I set off to find the horse. Noah did not say a word. It was exactly where the Designer told us it would be, with its reins tangled in one of the trees, and we could see the horse was injured. There was a cut on its left front leg, and it was in pain.

When Noah got to the horse, its eyes were wide, ears were pinned to its head, and the sounds from it revealed its pain. Noah gently spoke to the horse and stroked its head with gentleness. Eventually, the horse calmed down, but it was clear that this would take longer than a day to heal. He continued to speak to the horse as he carefully untangled the reins from the tree. When it came free, the horse tried to stand again, but it was clearly favoring the right hind leg. Noah looked up at me and said, "Go get Nashah."

I spread my wings, and within moments, I was back at the campsite, but Nashah was not sitting where I had last seen her. Her two siblings were there, but she was not. I then looked for Wisdom, and she, too, was gone. So, I sat and listened carefully. The longer I sat, the more acutely I could hear. Back in the direction I had come from, I could hear someone walking through the trees, heading north. Immediately, I took off and found that Wisdom and Nashah were heading straight for where Noah was. I flew up beside Wisdom, who simply said, "She heard the horse's cry, got what she needed, and headed this way."

Noah was shocked and pleased to see Nashah arrive so quickly. She completely ignored him and what he was trying to say to her and went straight to the horse. She ran her hands gently along from the front of the horse to the back. I watched as the horse visibly relaxed by her touch. Its eyes returned to normal, and its ears were now facing Nashah. Her voice was like the Designer's voice when she spoke to it. Sounds were coming from the horse that she seemed to understand. She stepped back, reached into her bag, and pulled out two herbs that she chewed together. She made a paste of the two herbs in her mouth and applied it to the horse's wound. The horse flinched when she touched the wound but settled quickly as she spoke gently. When she was satisfied with what she had done and with the state of the horse, she took the reins out of Noah's hands and led the horse back to the campsite. It still favored the leg, but the distress had completely left it.

Noah walked up beside her and said, "That was amazing. I thought the horse had been permanently lamed, and I would have to kill it."

She replied, "That is the problem with so many men; they are too quick to destroy what could have easily been healed." Without another word, she walked ahead of Noah and straight back into the campsite. Finding Ben, she spoke to him about the injury and how to tend to the wound in the days ahead. Once that was done, she went back to find her siblings and got them ready for supper.

Wisdom and I landed back in a tree near where Nashah was

preparing her family for the meal. Wisdom turned and said, "Can you see more of Nashah, Eagle?"

"I can," I replied. "The ways of the distant past can be seen in her. Were you with her when she learned these things, Wisdom?"

"I was. It was when she spent time with the Designer. He taught her how to connect with all of His creation, from the smallest insect to the largest animal. She learned that His love was not just reserved for people but for all things. I think she has learned to connect better with animals than with people. She gleaned as much as she could from the farmers of Enoch, but it was always the Designer who helped her discover the cures you have seen today."

"Wisdom, I have not seen this since the time of Adam. What could it mean?" I asked.

"Only the Designer knows the answer to this, Eagle. Maybe this is available to anyone who wants to learn; we both know the Designer loves to share His secrets with those willing to share their hearts with Him. Or, it could be the very reason the Designer wants her to become Noah's Eve and for Noah to become her Adam."

"This is still a riddle, Wisdom, and at times, I feel I can nearly see the answer to it all. But then times when it all feels out of my grasp," I said.

"It can be like looking through a curtain, Eagle. Sometimes the shapes of what we are piecing together are clear, and we can nearly touch it, and at other times the shapes make no sense."

"Wisdom, you have foresight far stronger than mine. You have spoken of future events, seeds that need to die, and the greatest love story ever. Surely you can see what is ahead for Noah and Nashah?" I asked.

Wisdom smiled and laughed to herself before responding, "Sometimes, Eagle, this is true, but with this, I only see in part. Whatever the Designer plans, much depends on the relationship these two may have. To me, everything is in motion, but the only consistent thread through it all is His love for all of His creation. Today, Eagle, His attention is firmly fixed on Noah and Nashah." Our conversation was interrupted by Baht declaring the meal was now ready and everyone needed to gather around. No one needed another invitation. Everyone was eager to taste what she had been cooking. They filled their bowls and sat together in the great cave to eat.

Before they did, Noah stood and said, "Let us be grateful to the Designer. Today, He has revealed and given much to us. These caves will keep us dry for as long as He makes it rain. The food we eat has been harvested from the soil He created. And tonight, we join as distant parts of the same family He created. We are sharing the same meal He provided and Baht so wonderfully cooked. Let us be grateful." Noah then sat, and Wisdom and I heard the beautiful sounds of a family in conversation. There was laughter, shouting, talking, and, as the meal went on, even some singing. The rain continued to fall outside the cave, but inside it, they were warm, and they were becoming one.

CHAPTER 29

The rain continued to fall for the next seven days. Each time it would appear to be stopping, the clouds would darken again, and the rain would fall. The caves continued to provide the shelter they needed, and their supplies were sufficient for the time being, but their patience was dwindling. Baht would make the most out of every meal, and anything left over would become part of the meal the next day.

Noah and Cain would send their men out each day, looking for firewood and fruit from the trees surrounding them. They would also report on the level of the Tigris River. Worryingly, the distance between the river and the caves had halved in the past week.

Each day, Wisdom and I would take to the skies as well, and each of those seven days, we reported the same thing to Noah. The cloud still lingered, and the rain still fell as far as we could see. No one had ever seen anything like it.

On the seventh day, Cain's men returned with a fruit that Cain had not seen before. He brought it to Noah and said, "Noah, my men have found this fruit. Is this something that we can eat?"

Noah looked at it and exclaimed, "Avocadoes! Yes, Cain, you can eat them, and you will love them." Taking a knife, Noah sliced it open, got rid of the seed, and handed half to Cain. "Don't eat the skin of it, but scoop out the green flesh of the fruit."

Cain tasted it. His face lit up with delight, and he exclaimed, "This is delicious. This may well be the most delicious fruit I have tasted." Without looking up or sharing it, he devoured the rest of it.

Noah asked, "They do not have these in Enoch?"

"I've never seen the like of it, Noah," Cain exclaimed.

"They cannot be kept too long after they are picked. You must eat them when they are ripe."

"Noah, there is something about these lands. The trees here are so healthy, and I have hardly seen a tree that does not produce the fruit it was designed to produce. We could settle here for all eternity and not go without fruit. What makes the trees produce like this?" Cain asked.

Noah pointed across the river at Eden and said, "Eden is right there. Anything that grows in its shadow flourishes, and whether it be plant, animal, or person, everything flourishes." Cain took a few steps out into the rain and closer to Eden. I do not know if it was to get a better look or to get deeper into its shadow; either way, he was drawn to it. "Cain, tomorrow, come and meet the Designer with me. It is He you are drawn to, not the Eden you are seeing," Noah said.

Noah's voice broke Cain's thoughts, and he slowly turned back to Noah and said, "No, I cannot." And at that, he walked away, leaving Noah where he stood.

Wisdom then spoke, "Noah, not everyone who is drawn to Him has the courage to choose to sit with Him. To choose to sit with Him is to choose to feel His love."

Noah responded, "Why would anyone be fearful of doing that, Wisdom?"

She replied, "Because they do not know the power of His love or the freedom of His healing. They fear Him more than they love Him." She was silent for a moment before continuing, "He has not had the parents or grandparents you have had. His father did not love him as the Designer would love him. He feared his own father, and now he fears the Designer. His own father abandoned him, and I believe he fears the Designer would do the same."

Noah replied, "But surely he can feel the life and love here in the shadow of Eden?"

"He can, Noah, but he does not know he can trust it," Wisdom replied.

"I will share my stories with him and show him the Designer can be trusted," Noah said.

"Stories are helpful, Noah, but experiences of his own will change his perception. Think about the wonder of the avocado Cain just experienced. For you, it's another fruit; for him, it was an experience. This one experience can open the door for many others. Allow Cain to experience the love of the Designer, and you may see the awakening of his spirit to the Designer." Wisdom paused and then continued, "Remember also, Cain's wife died giving birth to their son. Part of Cain's belief in the Designer died that day. He carries many questions, Noah, and he may not be ready to ask them."

Noah replied, "In Cain, I see some of my father. He, too, carries a wound he will not bring before the Designer. He hides it from us and does not believe we all can see it. My grandfather is a great man, Wisdom. He has taught me many things, and I already miss him dearly. Through these lessons, he guided me, not with commands or riddles, but with his presence. He would sit and listen all day. Encouragement flowed easily from him, but my father, days and weeks would go by without an encouraging word.

I know he loves me, but I do not know if he can see the hurt this has caused. One day I hope to speak with him about it."

Wisdom replied, "And it is right that you carry this hope. You carry it, Noah, because you love him, and love is a costly gift. When given and returned, a bond of love is created that is not designed to break. Hearts are connected, and people become one through the love they share."

"I think I will be a learner of His love for all the days of my life, Wisdom," Noah said.

"Much of this you already know, even if you cannot find the words for it. You know it because you have experienced it. You agree with me because your spirit is testifying to the truth it has learned and experienced," she said.

"Thank you, Wisdom," Noah replied and then went off to meet with the Designer himself. Long after the cool of evening had become the cold of the night, Noah returned and went straight to the cave he slept in.

The next day, the rain stopped.

CHAPTER 30

As the sun rose, everyone came out of their caves, excited to see it again. The clouds had parted, and the sun was spilling through them and over creation. There was laughter, dancing, and a joy that had not been seen for days. The ground was still a quagmire, and the river was now closer and getting closer by the moment.

Noah was already out, but he was not laughing, singing, or dancing. He was standing, looking south towards Enoch. Whatever the Designer had told him last night had him focused on where he was going and not on where he had been. It would still take days before the road was firm enough to walk on, and his horse would need all of those days to heal properly.

Baht had been up early as well, preparing breakfast for everyone. She was enjoying the sunlight and sang as she prepared the meal. The avocados had made a welcome addition to the porridge they had now been eating for days. As they ate, they would look up at the clouds, half expecting they would darken again and the rain would return. But the rain did not return, and by the afternoon, there were no clouds at all.

Wisdom and I took to the skies. It was wonderful to no longer feel continuously wet and damp. We spread our wings and allowed all of our feathers to dry as we soared higher and higher. Moving out in ever-widening circles, we could see the clouds had moved far to the west overnight. We could also see the full extent of the flooding that occurred. As far as the east was from the west, we could see areas that used to be dry land were now inland rivers. It would take many days for the land to dry.

By the time we returned, we could see the river was getting closer to the caves. Although the rain had stopped through the night, much of the water was still cascading into the Tigris River, causing its banks to widen. No one was worried about it, but Cain had gone further upstream and was definitely keeping his eyes on it. That is where Noah found him, looking over the mighty river. "How many days do you think it will take before we can cross the river, Noah?"

"That I cannot tell you, Cain. If I had to guess, I would say many. I have never seen rain as we have just had. If we have any more, we will need to find higher ground. The river will keep rising over the next few days, but if we have no more rain, we should be safe and dry where we are."

"That long?" exclaimed Cain.

"At least, Cain. The river is treacherous to cross without all of this extra water. We barely survived our own crossing, and we even lost some of our supplies in doing so. We could not find a shallow point to cross, so we had to rely on the current and our strength to get across. To do so before this water recedes would be foolish. I think you will need to stay in the caves until it is safe to cross."

Cain stood and thought through all he had just heard. He was becoming desperate to get his family to the other side, but was he foolish enough to risk all their lives?

"When will you leave?" Cain asked Noah.

"As soon as the road is dry enough and my horse can walk freely. If the rain holds off and the wound heals, we should leave in seven to ten days."

"Will you help me build a raft?" Cain then asked Noah.

"We can help you build it, but I would not recommend you use it until the bank of this river has returned to its natural place."

"We have been here too long already, and if we are both here for another ten days, then our supplies will be gone. You will have nothing to take to Enoch, and I will have nothing to take across the river," replied Cain.

"You will not get across the river at all if you do not wait," said Noah.

"We will see," Cain retorted, walking off into the trees.

Noah stood at the river bank, deep in thought. He looked up and down the river, but all he could see were torrents of water flowing through the trees that used to be high on the river bank. Under his breath, he said, "It would be madness." Nashah had come up silently behind the two men while they talked. Cain's abrupt departure happened so quickly that he did not even see his daughter there, and she had heard most of what was said.

Approaching Noah, she said, "My father can be very stubborn. He was not like this before my mother died. He has always wanted to be busy, and these rains have frustrated him. Please do not judge him, my lord."

"I am not judging him; I just do not think it is wise to cross this river like this," Noah replied while motioning to the extent of the river. "Nashah, I could not guarantee your safety, and if you fell in, you would be washed away."

Nashah replied, "I do not need you to guarantee my safety, Noah. If I get on that raft, it will be my choice and my choice alone, so do not let that weigh heavily on your conscience." At that, Nashah left Noah and returned to the cave where her siblings were.

Noah stood shaking his head, and again, under his breath, he said, "I will need great courage to win this one over." Noah looked up at me and said with exasperation, "Eagle, can I speak with you without you getting upset with me?"

I smiled at him and said, "Of course, my lord, just do not ask me to help you build a raft." Noah laughed, and all the tension disappeared from him. He sat on a rock that overlooked the river and motioned for me to come and sit with him.

"Eagle, I am conflicted. It is still days before I can travel, but I know I must. My heart, though, is here, and it is here with Nashah." There was silence for a few moments before Noah erupted, "Eagle, she frustrates me more than I can express. Did you see the way she treated me when all I was doing was trying to keep her safe? Did you see the way she took over when the horse was injured? Did you hear her response to me when I asked how she had done that?" Again, there was silence. Noah was speaking, but he was not looking for a conversation. He was frustrated and simply needed me to witness his frustration. "Even so, Eagle, something about her makes me come alive when I am around her. It is so hard to explain. I have never felt this before, Eagle."

This time I replied, "I have."

He spun around to me and said, "You have?"

"Yes, my lord, with Wisdom. She can be the most infuriating, complex, and beautiful living being all at the same time."

Noah laughed at this and said, "Eagle, there is so much about you I do not know."

"My lord, if I may speak freely?"

"Of course, Eagle."

"Wisdom knew of the life I brought to her long before I had the courage to speak to her about it. When I did, she laughed." Noah stifled a laugh, but I continued, "When that happened, I wanted to disappear. I felt hurt, and at the time, I did not want to dig my talons into the ground and heal from it. However, after she finally stopped laughing, she simply said, 'I have been waiting for you to say this'." I smiled as the memory continued, "We have been one since that moment, and although we might be separated physically, we are never separated in our spirits. While she was in Enoch, I missed her terribly. There was not a day I did not think of her. But the pain I felt was my spirit's aching cry to be with her. Noah, your own spirit is aching right now because she has left you struggling to grasp the connection you want with her."

Noah smiled and said, "Eagle, you see much."

"Thank you, my lord. Could I add one more thing?"

"Of course, Eagle, you do not need to ask."

"You told Cain you would be here for seven to ten days. There is no need to put a limit on your time; another few days will not hamper yours or the Designer's plans. In the time you have with her, stop trying to be her rescuer. Stop watching her and start seeing her." I stopped to see if Noah would respond. When he did not, I kept going. "Try not to see her as a promise the Designer has given you. See her as the person she is. She is formidable, yes, but her strength is not in the way she tries to do everything herself. Her strength is in her identity. She even named herself Nashah. She thinks she is forgotten. So, when you try to parent her and tell her what to do, she believes you cannot see her." I paused again to see if he would respond, but he did not, so I continued, "Who is she, Noah? Who do you see? Look beneath the surface and see her heart. You will discover the true identity the Designer has given her there."

"Eagle, your words are honey to my soul, and I needed to hear them. Thank you, my dear friend. Thank you." Noah got up and left me sitting on the bank of the river. It was then my ears heard a familiar sound. Wisdom had been listening, and all I could hear was her laughing.

CHAPTER 31

The next day, the sun was shining in all of its fullness, and it was glorious to see and to feel. Even the trees looked happier as the sun hit their leaves, and they danced in the morning breeze. The ground was still very wet, but dry areas were now becoming more visible. The river had continued to rise, but not as quickly as the days prior.

Noah was up early with Ben and Caleb, and they were in deep discussion, much like when I found them on the other side of the Tigris River. They were trying to come up with an idea that would get them across this river. They had quickly concluded that a raft could easily be made, but to steer it through the trees alone would be very difficult. The river's edge was a long way from where it once was, and the flood waters had either washed away many trees or were now standing with rushing water around their bases. There was no clear path through them, and the water was moving so quickly. The only benefit they could see was that the water was so high the submerged rocks would pose no problem to them at all. By mid-morning, they were no closer to a solution when Cain found them.

"I have found a place far upriver where we can put a raft in, and if the Designer is with us, we should be able to use the river's current at one of the bends to drive us across the river and help us land on that beach we can see downstream."

Noah looked down at the beach Cain was motioning and then back at him, saying, "Do you mean that bend, the one just beyond the avocado trees?"

"Yes," Cain declared in a way that showed he was not as sure as he hoped to be.

"That bend is treacherous," Noah declared. "And you are counting on the current of the river to drive you onto the opposite bank. Do you understand how fast you will be traveling when you reach that point? If you reach it?"

"Yes," Cain said again. "If you can make us a raft sturdy enough, then I see no fault in my plan."

The men who arrived with Cain looked nervous and shifted from one foot to the other. Something not lost on Noah. Looking past Cain, he said, "Do you all agree with this plan?" There was silence as each of the men looked at each other but refused to look at Cain. It was obvious Cain was getting more frustrated by the moment.

Looking back at Cain, Noah said, "You would put all of your family at risk for this plan?" Noah did not give him a chance to respond and continued, "You and everyone on that raft would perish. You are trusting the raft to make its way across a river twice as wide as it once was. So fast is the river moving that even if you somehow navigated it through the trees, you would be fortunate if you were halfway across it. Then, once you got to the place you were hoping to land, and if you did get across, you would all be smashed against the rock walls. It is madness, Cain. I will not build you a raft that you all will perish on. We built a raft that barely got us across it. The beach we aimed for, we missed. But, fortunately, on this side, there are no rock cliffs for us to be smashed against."

Before Cain could storm off again, Nashah approached and said, "Father, please listen to Noah. This is not worth losing us all in; we have lost enough already. Father, we do not need to risk our lives this way to start a new life in a land we have never seen. There will be another way. Please, let us wait and see what the next seven days hold for us." Nashah's entrance into the conversation cooled Noah's anger; he even looked a little embarrassed to have spoken to her father in such a way.

Noah said, "I am sorry, my lord. I did not mean to offend you. I only meant to share with you what I thought would be wise."

Cain's anger, too, had been swallowed by Nashah's words, but his frustration remained evident. He gruffly said, "Let us talk no more of it this day. Let us see what the next few days bring us. Maybe, in that time, we could look for logs large enough to start building a raft."

Noah sighed and nodded at this and, calling Ben and Caleb to him, said, "Go see if you can find logs big enough for the raft we need." He then turned to Cain and said, "Maybe your men could do the same?" Cain exhaled as well and, nodding, gave his agreement to the plan. Turning to Cain's men, Noah said, "We need straight logs a hands' width in diameter. They will need to be twice the length of my cart, and we will also need long vines that will lash the timbers together. Bring back as much of it as you can find."

Once all the men left, only Noah and Nashah remained. She came to Noah and said, "Forgive my father, my lord; he does not know what he is doing. He needs something to do to stop him from going crazy. If you can find a task that makes him feel worthy, I am certain you will see the best of him."

"Your father is a good man, Nashah. I can see that within him. He seeks only to get you all into a new home as soon as possible. But I know this river well and have walked it many times; I cannot see how his plan will work."

"I believe he knows this as well, Noah. He just needs time to see it." There was a long silence between them. There was more on Noah's mind than building a raft. As the silence grew, the only things that could be heard were the sounds of the river and the insects now thriving in the sunlight.

Noah broke the silence and said, "Nashah, can I ask you something?"

"It depends on the question."

Noah smiled and said, "What do you want?"

"What do you mean, my lord?"

"What is it you want, Nashah? You have left your homeland and everything you know behind you to come to a new land. A land you do not know and to a people you have only ever heard about. Forget your father, your siblings, and all of this. What is it you want, Nashah?"

Nashah sat and thought through what she was being asked. "No one has ever asked me that, my lord. I do not know what I want. I have always served other people, and I have become lost in the needs of those people. I do not know what I want."

"Nashah, we still have several days before either of us makes our way in different directions. Think through what I have asked you. You have much to offer to all of us, but what you offer to yourself will become an even greater gift." Noah paused before continuing, "You have been through and overcome much, which shows to me you have great courage. There is little you cannot do for animals, and the way you care for them shows me your commitment and compassion. You love your family and have laid down your life for them, which shows me the devotion you carry. You have spent much time with the Designer, and He has shared much of His heart and creation with you, which shows me the desire you have to live with Him and be in His presence. From the moment I first saw you, I could see the glow of the Designer within you."

Noah went silent at that, and Nashah bowed her head; her tears started flowing. He had not meant to upset her, and I could see how uncomfortable he was becoming. I do not think he knew if she was sad or if she was about to yell at him and storm off. After a short while, she simply said, "Thank you, my lord. Nobody has ever seen me until this day."

Noah replied, "I feel like I am only scratching the surface of understanding who you are."

"There is not much to know, my lord."

Noah replied, "Your story is one of a person who has much resilience. Many more years are ahead of you, and your story will continue to grow. But, if I have learned anything in this life, my past is what I have learned, and the present is where I have the choice to use what I have learned. You have learned much, Nashah."

CHAPTER 32

The next few days were again marked by brilliant sunshine. The ground continued to dry out, and from it, all kinds of grasses and flowers popped out of the ground. The men brought fruit from all the trees, but the avocados seemed to be the most popular.

Noah's and Cain's men had found all the logs they needed to build the raft, and now they were gathering enough vines to make the straps to lash all the logs together. Noah had asked Cain to make the straps, and soon they would be ready to make the raft.

Noah and Cain would go down to the river each morning and assess its height. The rain was becoming a memory that the river would not let them forget. It had peaked three days after the rain ceased, and now they waited to see how quickly it would recede. It could not happen for Cain fast enough, but Noah seemed content to let it take as long as needed. Ever since his meeting with the Designer, all the urgency to leave had disappeared.

On the fourth day after the rain ceased, Cain insisted they start the raft construction; now they had all they needed, and the river was falling. His constant questions made Noah finally agree to do it. He put Ben and Caleb in charge of the building, and two of Cain's men would also help them with it. Noah trusted his two friends and knew they would do a good job and the raft would be sturdy. Initially, Cain only wanted his men to build the raft, but Noah would have none of it and convinced Cain they had no experience of doing so.

While they worked, Noah went back down to the river bank. He walked up and down the river to see what changed. He had even gone up to the place Cain wanted to put the raft in. Once he got there, he realized why Cain had spoken of this spot. It was on a bend newly formed by the river's raging waters. By putting the raft in there, they could all be firmly placed and then would use poles to push them into the river's current.

But it was the other end that bothered him. Cain's target beach was tucked between rock walls that stood high, steep, and sheer. It truly would be madness to think they could get across there safely. He could not see a solution. The river was too high and running too fast. I followed Noah throughout the day. He had not said a word to me; he was lost in thought. He sat on a rock through the entire afternoon overlooking the impossible bend, and there the Designer found him. "What are you doing, Noah?" the Designer asked.

His voice did not shock Noah; the smile that spread across his face showed he had expected the Designer to find him. "I am thinking, my Lord."

"What about?"

"You already know the answer to this, my Lord."

"Yes, I do, but I love to hear the sound of your voice, and I love to listen to the challenges you are facing. You have a way of bringing wisdom into each challenge."

"My Lord, a few days ago, you told me I had to go to Enoch. But to do so is to leave Nashah behind. And now it seems her father is willing to put her life at risk for a foolish crossing of this river."

"It would be very foolish to cross this river," the Designer said.

"Yes," Noah exclaimed, "But why can't Cain see this?"

"He is a proud man, Noah."

"I know, my Lord."

"He is intimidated by you, Noah. He even sees that Nashah has gone over to you." Noah nearly choked when the Designer said this. For the Designer to say she 'has gone over to you' meant she had truly gone over to him.

"But why would he be intimidated?" Noah asked, attempting to take the conversation away from Nashah and back to Cain.

"Some men crave leadership; other men just simply lead. You are the latter, Noah, and Cain is the former. Often when a man sees what he does not have, he schemes and plots ways to take what he lacks. Leadership cannot be taken; it is learned. Your grandfather and father are worthy leaders. They have learned well, and you have followed in their footsteps." The Designer continued, "Cain has tried to overrule you by attempting to intimidate you. Insecure men will always use control and manipulation to take what has been given to others as a gift. They do this because they do not know the gift they have been given. Where you are going, there are many who will try to intimidate you. It is what they know how to do, and they will do it well. They will seek to keep you under their control. They will even use words to say they are doing this for your protection and wellbeing." Again the Designer paused before He continued, "Noah, always look beneath the surface when you meet someone. Do not just look at what they do; look for their character. People can hide what they do, but they cannot hide their character." Noah sat silently as he pondered everything the Designer said.

Finally, he said, "My lord, can I ask a question?"

"Of course."

"When I get to Enoch, I will have no family around me. I cannot go to my father and grandfather for advice. Will you still meet with me in the cool of the evening?"

"You have asked me this before, and my answer is still the same. Nothing will ever keep me from meeting with you, Noah."

"My Lord, I greatly fear making the wrong decision or choice while I am there."

"I will tell you what I told your ancestor, Adam. When making decisions, think about it in this way, imagine the *two trees* in Eden. You know them by the stories you have heard; one is the *Tree of Knowledge*, and the other is the *Tree of Life*. They are both thriving in Eden, even as I speak to you. The temptation to eat from the *Tree of Knowledge* is strong, and its fruit will reveal to you right and wrong. But right and wrong are not the source of my love. The source of my love flows through all things, but its fruit comes from the *Tree of Life*. Life is not measured by right and wrong; rather, it is discovered in the embodiment of love. It is there that right and wrong are irrelevant. I know this is hard to comprehend, but let me give you an example. It is not right or wrong for you to become one with Nashah; rather, it is life. You are not doing the wrong thing if you do not choose her, much like it is not the right thing if you do. You told Eagle you feel alive when you are with her, but everything about her confounds you, and this confuses you. You are wrestling with right and wrong, but it is life that is drawing you to her. If you are sitting under the *Tree of Knowledge of Good and Bad*, you will continue to be confused. But if you are sitting under the *Tree of Life*, you are seeing her. Can you see what I mean?"

"I have never thought of it in these terms, my Lord. I have always sought to do what is right, and I dislike letting you down. Even my decision to go to Enoch was a decision to please you."

The Designer smiled at that and said, "Noah, you already please me. You were born pleasing me. Yes, there are times you make choices that would not, but it does not change how I feel about you or remove my pleasure from you. Whether you went to Enoch or not, you still would have pleased me. Whether you choose Nashah or not, you still please me."

"My Lord, you speak things that are too beautiful to comprehend. You honor me for no reason at all."

"Now you understand love, Noah, and here you will find the greatest love the world has ever known. Love was not designed to be comprehended by one person but to be encountered by all people. Here is the difference between the *two trees*. In one, you believe you will fully understand; in the other, you cannot. People will often choose what they can understand, but life is found when you step out beyond what you know and choose the greatest power the world has ever known. I am the definition of love, Noah, and in choosing the *Tree of Life*, you are choosing me. The fruit I carry holds the fullness of life that all people crave, but so few will step out beyond what they know and into what I know. Your parents and grandparents have done this, as have you, and as have Nashah."

Once again, Noah went silent. His mind was racing with what he had just been told. Finally, he said, "So much of this makes sense to me, and yet some of it is outside of my grasp."

The Designer smiled at this and said, "This is belief, Noah. This is the place of trust. This is the place of great courage, and this is the place of connection with me and all of creation."

The Designer continued, "There will be many decisions you must make in the days and years ahead of you. Sometimes you will choose wisely, and other times you will choose poorly. If you seek life, you will never make a choice that leads you away from me. By simply making a choice, you demonstrate your trust and love for me. So when you feel lost, just ask yourself, 'Am I sitting under the *Tree of Knowledge* or the *Tree of Life*?' and let that help you choose. When you feel you have failed me, just place your hands into the ground and remind yourself of the love we share. It is a love that always heals and restores."

Noah simply nodded at the Designer's words; he had been given much more to think about.

Once again, the Designer spoke, "Now let us talk more about Nashah and what choices you are making," and as He did, He laughed, and Noah blushed.

CHAPTER 33

The raft was completed three days later. Ben and Caleb could clearly see the dangers of crossing the river and were in no rush to finish it. The one they first built only took them a day; this one took longer. Noah and Cain stood on the raft, and both men jumped on it to test its sturdiness. They were both satisfied with its design, but the fast-moving river could reduce it to splinters in moments if it hit any of the submerged rocks that were starting to reappear. These dangers were obvious to everyone there except Cain.

Noah said to Ben and Caleb, "Well done, you two. You have both made me proud. The raft is sturdy, and when the river returns to its normal flow, it will be sturdy enough to make the crossing." Noah looked at Cain as he spoke those last words. Cain turned and walked away. He left his men on the bank with no thanks or appreciation for the work they had done. So, Noah said to them, "Well done, each of you. We could not have built this raft without the hard work you each have done."

They all climbed back onto the raft, and although they knew the raft to be strong, Cain's two men could not hide the anxiety they felt about making the trip across. They could see all the submerged rocks and tree trunks. The debris floating down the river from the flood was so thick in some places it looked like they could walk across it.

One of Cain's men said to Noah, "My lord, this river scares me, but what scares me even more is Cain will want to use this raft long before the river recedes."

Noah grasped the man on the shoulder and said, "I hope he soon sees the folly of even trying it, especially because his whole family will be on it. It is not just the rocks you will need to avoid; it is also everything that has been washed down the river." As Noah spoke the words, a dead cow floated past them. The animal was bloated and lifeless. Seeing the cow, Cain's two men stepped quickly off the raft and clambered up the embankment. Noah got off the raft and said, "We should station two men here at all times; that way, we will know the raft will not be taken either by the river or Cain." Noah looked each of Cain's men in the eye as he made this plan. After seeing the cow, I wondered if that would be a sign to these men about the death the river carried. Noah waited until each of them nodded their approval of the plan. Noah said, "One of the four of you will stay with either Ben or Caleb and if anything untoward happens, then the other will raise the alarm."

For the next two days, Cain started preparing supplies for the trip across the river. His own supplies were dwindling, and only a few barrels of wheat, oats, and rice remained. Their cooking equipment and belongings were still being used at the caves; these items would be packed last. There was no rain in those days, which everyone could see gladdened Cain's spirit. The rest of his men had become withdrawn as they obediently did all he asked of them.

The evening meal was shared with a strange sense of quiet. They all ate well and then retired to their caves for the night. Much later in the night, Wisdom and I were startled awake by distant screaming coming from the raft's direction. At once, we both spread our wings and took to the night sky, seeking the screaming voice. We first saw Nashah running as fast as she could through the trees, heading toward the caves. She was screaming, "Noah, Noah!" I turned back to the caves and saw Noah, too, had heard the screaming and was emerging from his cave. His was the one furthest south that the wolf had occupied. I could see he was trying to find the source of the screaming coming out of the dark. He did not have to wait long; Nashah suddenly appeared. Her dress was torn, and she was screaming and sobbing. Noah reached out to grab her, but she did not want to be held. She was yelling something that Noah could not comprehend. So he grabbed her by both arms and said, "Nashah, stop. Tell me, what has happened to you? Who has done this to you?"

Nashah's eyes blazed, and she all but screamed, "My father has killed Caleb and is taking the raft. Baht and my brother and sister are on the raft. Two of his men are with them; the other two refused to go. My father threw me from the raft. Noah, they have left! They are on the river." Noah was initially stunned by what he had heard. He had only just woken and must have thought it was a bad dream. So strong was the shock I could see him paralyzed. Nashah again yelled at him, "Noah, you must come; you must save them."

Noah shook off his shock and immediately turned to Ben and said, "Go get a long rope and meet me downstream from the bend that Cain wants to make a landing at. Let us hope we can get there before he does."

Noah and Nashah ran towards the river bank to see if they could spot the raft. It was then I saw Wisdom, and she was circling over what must have been the raft, but she was not moving with it. I screamed at Noah, "Wisdom is over the raft!"

He turned and yelled at Ben, "Ben, bring the rope to where you see Wisdom circling."

That night the moon was bright, and it gave them some hope of being able to see the raft, but the river was wide, and hope dwindled within me when I saw it. It had become jammed on a submerged rock. Some barrels had fallen off the raft and bobbed down the river. I could see the two children huddled at the back of the raft with Baht, but only two men were on it, and they were trying to lever it off with all their strength. By the time Noah got to the location, Cain's other two men had joined them, and they were yelling at Cain and all those on board.

Once I got to Wisdom, she said, "One man fell from the raft when it hit the rocks, and I have not seen him since." The sound of the river roaring made it so hard to hear, and Cain would need an eagle's hearing to have heard the people on the riverbank.

Noah had already realized they were too far into the river for them to swim to the riverbank. Anyone who fell in now would be lost. As soon as Ben arrived with the rope, Noah said, "Tie a log to its end and go upriver to the bend that is there." Noah pointed to the bend he wanted Ben to go to, "Throw the log into the river and hope that it gets taken by the current and gets near the raft."

Baht was watching the people on the riverbank; she looked terrified and held Nashah's sister, Deborah, and their brother, Nacham, as tightly as she could. She realized what they were attempting to do when Ben threw the log into the river and moved to the side she thought it would come close to. Cain and his man were oblivious to this and were desperately trying to lever the raft off the rocks, but the current was so strong it would not budge.

Baht had soon lost sight of the log; even though the moon gave some light for her to see it, she could not. The raging waters, the moon's reflections, and her panic had caused her to lose it. Ben's first attempt had failed. The log passed to the side of the raft, and Baht saw it too late and could not grab it. So, Ben pulled it in and ran back up to the bend in the river. This time he threw it with all of his might further into the river, and this time Baht could see and follow it. Cain and his man were still frantically working on levering the raft off the rock, and they did not see Baht grab the log. She untied it and secured it around the two children, yelling instructions at them both. Then she threw them into the river just as Cain spun around and saw them disappear under the water. "No," he screamed at Baht. "You fool. You have killed them." And at that, he pushed Baht off the raft and desperately tried to reach for his children, but he could not; they were out of his reach. He was screaming at them, but he could now do nothing for them.

Noah, Nashah, Ben, and the two other men pulled hard on the rope, but it became stuck. The lives of these two children were in their hands; they would not survive long in the river. Noah then screamed, "Designer, now is the time we need you." At that, the rope released its tension, and they all heaved as hard as they could. In just moments, the two children were pulled up onto the riverbank. Nacham was lying motionless, and Deborah was coughing up water beside him. Nashah let go of the rope, ran to Nacham, and pushed on his chest repeatedly. Then suddenly, he awoke to spew up what seemed to be a barrel of water in his lungs. He continued to cough and splutter, but the sheer terror in his eyes told the story of what they endured.

Noah had already pulled in all the rope and commanded Ben to find another log and do the same thing again. But as he spun around to see Cain and his man, we saw and heard the horrific moment of the raft breaking apart and the two men falling into the river. Noah wasted no time; he turned to me and commanded, "Eagle, follow them down the river."

Wisdom had already left; she was desperately trying to find Baht. Her search did not last long; by the time I had spread my wings and flown over the river, I could see her standing on a rocky outcrop. Baht was at the base of it, and she was not moving; she was dead.

As I flew over the river, I could only see one man, and even with my powerful eyes, I could not see if it was Cain. But I followed him and watched him disappear under the water, reappear, and then disappear again. Noah and Ben were running down the bank of the river, but it was moving faster than they could run. There was no way Noah could run fast enough to rescue him, and there was still no sign of the other man.

The man desperately tried to reach out to anything he passed, but the water was moving too quickly. Soon he was pulled into the current, and nothing was left to reach for. He was now at the mercy of the Tigris River. The bend ahead that Cain had hoped to traverse was coming up quickly. If the man knew it or not, I do not know, but I watched as Noah's prophecy was fulfilled. The speed at which he was going took him across the whole river, and the cliff that met him was the one that claimed his life. I did not see him again after that. I went up and down the river for the rest of the night with the smallest of hopes that I would find one of them, but I did not. So, as dawn broke, I returned to the caves, and finding Noah, I landed beside him. "Noah, I could not find the three men," I said.

Noah was visibly exhausted but said, "The one you followed was not Cain. We found him washed up on the shore further south, but he was already dead."

I looked around at the people gathered, and I could feel grief, relief, anger, and sadness, and over it all, I felt despair. I said to Noah, "How did this happen?"

He replied, "For that answer, you will need to ask Wisdom; I am too angry to have it repeated in my presence again."

Wisdom was sitting in a tree over Nashah, who was as still as a statue. She held her siblings in her arms, but her face was like stone, and there were no tears. I flew to Wisdom and asked, "What happened?"

"Cain had convinced two of his men his plan would work. One of them was with Caleb guarding the raft. After everyone went to sleep, they crept from their caves and murdered Caleb. His body now lies in one of the caves. The men then loaded all the supplies onto the raft and snuck back into the cave that had the children and Baht. The sound of the river hid all of their noises, and initially, they chose not to wake Nashah or the two other of Cain's men. They must have known Nashah would have resisted. Once everyone was on board, Cain returned, woke Nashah, and told her everyone was on the raft. She did not raise the alarm then because she feared for her siblings and thought she could convince her father not to do this. But she could not. Cain fought her, and he tore her dress as she tried to escape and get Noah. The last touch of her father was given in anger, and now he lies dead."

Below me, Nashah, Nacham, and Deborah wept. What words can comfort such loss?

CHAPTER 34

Five people who had sat around the fire the evening before were no longer alive. The sense of loss was heavy, and the conversation was very sparse. What could be heard over the sounds of the river were the cries of Deborah and Nacham. They had not stopped since they were fished from the river, and once they heard their father was dead, the crying only increased. The beauty of the day was lost by the immense sense of grief that flowed through every person. It was as if the dark storm clouds had come back over us all, and the rain had returned in force.

As the sun approached the day's highest point, Noah knew he had to do something with Caleb's and Cain's bodies. Cain was bloated and would need to be buried soon. Caleb, though, other than the terrible gash in his head, looked as if he was asleep. Noah went to Cain's remaining men and said, "We will need to bury Cain as soon as possible. Find a spot further from the river and dig a hole as deep as a man." The men were despondent and felt the shame of what had happened. Noah had assured them they would not be held responsible for Cain's actions and was free to leave or stay. They simply nodded at Noah, grabbed their digging tools, and looked for an appropriate spot.

Noah found Ben sitting with Caleb, and he, too, was despondent. Caleb had been his friend all his life, and now, he was dead. This journey to Enoch was an adventure for both of them; now Ben knew he would do it alone. Noah, too, had lost a lifelong friend and companion. I could see he was trying to find the words to say to Ben, but they would not come, so he went and sat beside him. He put his arm around him, and Ben collapsed into Noah's chest. His tears soon gave way to sobs, and before long, Noah joined him. Their grief was raw and unhidden as the anger, deep within them, was released. Everyone and every animal stopped to witness the pain these two men felt for their friend, who lay beside them as cold as the stone beneath him. Time passed; how much, I could not tell, but the tears and rage had long stopped, and the cool of the evening would be soon upon them.

Noah said, "Let us seal Caleb into this cave. Like we were told the Designer did for Abel all those years ago. Let us find rocks to do this, so man or animals will never disturb his bones." Ben did not say a word, but got up from beside Caleb, kissed his forehead, and went to find the stones. Noah helped him with this sad task. Not a word was shared between them as they sealed Caleb into his final resting place. They finished their task deep into the night. He was lying in the back of the cave where he first found the wolf hiding. As Ben and Noah sat in front of the stone wall, the Designer arrived and came in and sat with them. As He sat, I watched something I had seen many times before but never tired of seeing: Caleb's spirit came out of the cave. The glow of his spirit was strong, and all of us could see him. His spirit first came to Ben and kissed him on his forehead as well, and then went to Noah and placed his hands on his head. Noah said through tears, "I am so sorry, my friend. It should have been me who was there, not you. I am so sorry."

Caleb did not say a word, but I could sense the joy within him. He was not sad to have been taken from them; for now, he was free. After a few moments, he moved to the Designer, and we all watched as his spirit became one with Him. "He is with me now," the Designer said. "He is free from the constraints of this world and his physical body. Ben, you will see him again. You have only been separated for a short time."

Ben sat stunned at all he was witnessing. Noah had invited him to come and meet with the Designer before, but he had not taken up the invitation. Now, the Designer had come to him, and he had watched his closest friend go to Him. The Designer then said to Ben, "You are a good friend and a good man, Ben."

The Designer sat with the men in silence. Each looked to be lost in their thoughts and memories. Eventually, the Designer got up and walked from the cave. As He did, He turned to me and said, "Eagle, come walk with me."

He walked to where the two men had dug a hole for Cain's body to lie in. His body had been wrapped in linen, and his swollen and grotesque features could no longer be seen. The men were long gone, and we were there alone. So we sat in front of the hole and beside Cain's body. As the Designer sat, I watched the extraordinary moment happen with Cain's spirit. The spirit rushed to the Designer; the words that came from Cain I could hear in my mind, but I do not think they were heard by anyone other than the Designer and me. "Forgive me, my Lord, forgive me. I did not intend for my family to die. I only wanted to make a new home for them. I love them so much," Cain said.

"They live, Cain. Your actions have caused them great pain, but I know your actions were not evil. For the next part of their journey, they will do it without you. It is now time for you to come home, Cain." At that, Cain's spirit flowed into the Designer's. I felt honored to watch as His love reached beyond their poor choices and assured Cain of His love.

The Designer walked away from the gravesite and left me sitting with Cain's body and an empty hole. He did not invite me to go with Him, and I felt there was something else for me to discover here. As I sat and thought through all I had just seen, Wisdom came and landed beside me. She was quiet for a while before she spoke. "Eagle, what do you see?"

"I see an empty grave that needs to be filled, and I see lives shattered by the foolishness of one man's choice."

"You have seen this before, Eagle, and you will see it again."

"I have been alive for long enough to understand this, but I often tire of witnessing the choices of people leading them to destruction rather than life."

"As do I, Eagle, as do I."

"How are Nashah and her family?"

"Nashah has busied herself by making meals for them all, but she has said very little. Her siblings have stopped crying, but the loss they feel will live with them for the rest of their days." As we spoke, Ben and Noah walked up behind us. They were here to bury Cain, and Cain's men were trailing along behind them. Once all of them had arrived, they stood and waited; they were waiting for Nashah and her siblings. It was not long, but each moment they waited seemed an eternity to them as they looked down upon a man they had come to know and even loved; now, he was no more.

As the children approached, the two youngest started sobbing all over again. Seeing their father wrapped broke their hearts, and they all fell on him and let their tears soak the linen that bound him. Nobody said a word nor sought to pull the children off their father. Nashah stood silently watching it all, and eventually, she gently lifted her siblings away from him. Then, looking at Noah, she nodded her permission to bury him.

Noah gathered all the men around him and placed ropes under Cain. With such gentleness and honor, they lowered him into the hole. Once he was settled, Nashah came and dropped a gold ring into the hole and said, "May you meet our mother and be one again with her." At that, the men started moving the soil back into the hole. The children stood beside it and wept at the last images of seeing their linen-wrapped father. Nashah held them, but again, no tears fell from her eyes.

Everyone slowly departed and headed back toward the caves, and once again, Wisdom and I stayed and watched. That night we watched a wolf come and sniff around the freshly filled grave. After the wolf left, a most fierce-looking tiger with saber-like teeth came and did the same as the wolf. Then late in the night, a lion came through the trees and lay on the grave and slept.

Wisdom turned to me and said, "At one point, he thought he was a lone wolf; at another, he thought of himself as a fierce tiger. However, he was made to be a lion in this life, and he will remain so in the Designer. Eagle, do not let his poor choices determine who he was in your eyes. Now he rests."

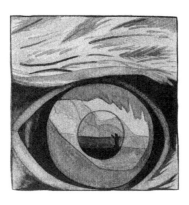

CHAPTER 35

Before the sun rose, Wisdom left to go and be with Nashah. Nashah had said little since the disaster of the river crossing. She only shed tears when Noah told her they could not retrieve Baht's body. The river had claimed it, and Wisdom could not find her once it had.

The lion had stayed on Cain's grave until the break of the day and then disappeared into the forest as quietly as he had come. All was quiet as I sat and pondered all that had changed. Then deep within myself, I longed to sit where the lion had sat and to feel what the lion had felt.

Silently, I flew to the ground, allowing my talons to sink into the soft soil. I could still feel the warmth lingering on the ground from the lion. It would never know the warmth it left was the warmth I now shared. Moments like these continue to speak to me of the Designer and all He has done for us. I closed my eyes and allowed my spirit to listen and see.

Usually, I would have felt through whatever the pain was, and on this day, I expected that pain to take my breath away. Often,

I would allow my talons to reach far into the soil, through the pain, into the love, and then to a dead tree that was returning to life. This time, I went straight to another tree, and it was dead. It had been burned and charred beyond what I could recognize. I could feel the fear rising within me, and if I had not known the Designer's love, I would have released my hold.

My mind surged with emotion and confusion. This could not be the tree I saw returning to life. I searched my vision looking for another tree, but there was none. What I saw was a land devoid of life and hope; nothing grew there. My vision was marked with red dirt and a red sky. The sun had been obscured, and I could only see its faint glow. As far as I could see, it was this red dirt. The horizon shimmered with the heat coming from the ground, but it gave me no understanding of where I was. I allowed my senses to heighten; all I could feel was a hot and dry wind coming from the East. In the wind was a putrid smell that offended all of my senses. I could taste and feel the smell it carried. Nothing was right about this vision; again, I told myself I needed to go deeper. I knew the Designer would only have allowed me to see these things if there was something for me to experience. It was then I heard an old familiar voice ...

"Eagle, you have seen what I am bringing creation to."

Even as I turned, I already knew who owned that voice, "Lucifer."

"That is not my name," he responded. "You came here thinking you would find someone else. You came here believing the dead tree would live once again. Look, Eagle, and see for yourself; it is dead and will live no more. Look around you. Will anything thrive in a land so barren? Where is your Designer now, Eagle? He has abandoned you, and He has abandoned creation. He knows I have won. He knows I am the lord of his creation. He cannot take from me what I have taken. Look to the East, Eagle. What do you see? Can you count my horde of servants? Look at the dust that goes ahead and behind them. Soon, all of creation will be destroyed, and I will rule."

"And just what will you rule, Lucifer?"

"That is not my name," he growled. "All that you see, I will rule."

"What I see is devastation. If that is the mark of your kingdom, then the Designer will be wise to take His people home."

"None will escape," he growled again. "Like Cain, who lies dead beneath you, everyone will join him."

"Lucifer, I care not if you use this name or not, but it is how I know you. Lucifer, you cannot even reach out and take my life. I stand fixed to the ground. I am vulnerable and alone, and still, you cannot take my life. You come to me with threats and fear, but I see nothing but fear within you. It is not you who has shown me this tree or the stark land that surrounds me; it is the Designer. And if He has given it to me, He has also allowed you to be here. He has no fear of you and has no fear that you can hurt even one feather on me. He knows your power, and He knows how powerless you are. You can feel it, but to admit it will destroy you."

He spat at me as he turned his back, and soon his voice and presence I could feel no more. I turned back and, in my vision, went closer to the tree. It was indeed black and had been burned beyond what it could recover from. There are trees that recover from fire, and many of them need it to crack open the seeds they carry. But this tree, there was no longer any life in it. Whatever fire had consumed, it was hotter than any fire I had known. I looked back to where Lucifer had disappeared, but he was gone. I do not think he would have the power to create a fire that could do this.

Slowly I came out of the vision and, once again, found myself sitting on Cain's grave. The sun had risen, and the new day had begun.

CHAPTER 36

I flew back to the caves with much now on my mind. The new day had brought with it more than a vision; new decisions needed to be made. The sun had now been shining for enough days for much of the ground to become firm underfoot, and Noah wanted to be away from this place. He called Nashah, Ben, and the men to meet with him after they had a meal. He spoke to Cain's men first, "Today, you are free to do as you wish. You no longer owe anything to Cain, nor do you owe it to me. You are free to come with me, or free to do whatever you choose. I will set out for Enoch as soon as I can."

The men looked at each other and quickly responded, "We will travel back with you to Enoch and to our families, my lord."

Noah nodded and said, "Go pack up all of your belongings; I hope to leave first thing tomorrow morning." Next, he asked Ben, "Do you still want to come to Enoch, Ben? I would understand if you wanted to head back home."

Ben replied, "My lord, I will travel with you to Enoch and see what the Designer has in store for me there."

"Get all of our belongings together, Ben, and see to the horse as well."

Nashah had said nothing, and after all the men left, it was just her and Noah. Noah let the silence grow between them, and when he finally spoke, it felt awkward. "Nashah, we have come together in the most unusual of circumstances." He paused before continuing, "I would never seek to control you or tell you what you should or should not do. The events of these past two days have most likely scarred you and your siblings for the rest of your lives."

Before Noah could get another word out of his mouth, Nashah interrupted him. "I wish to go with you, my lord. My sister and brother will come too if you allow it."

Her swift answer took Noah aback, and once he got over the shock, he said, "Of course I allow it. It is what I would have wished."

What followed was another long and awkward silence before Nashah spoke. "He was a good man, Noah. He just made foolish decisions. But I will miss him; he is the only father I have known. He made many mistakes and had many flaws, but I loved him."

Noah's awkwardness found even greater depths as Nashah cried. He did not know whether to hold, speak to, or comfort her. He had not seen her cry before; she had always been so strong. But here, the strong facade had crumbled, and he was seeing the little girl who was all alone. He gently guided her to sit with him on a large rock. She did not resist or throw off his gentle touch on her shoulders. She allowed him to lead her, and when she sat, she was closer to Noah than she had been before. Noah did not speak at all; he allowed his presence to be a reassurance that he would not leave her there in her grief.

Nashah whispered, "We will leave with you, my lord. I will go prepare my siblings and gather all we have left of our supplies and equipment."

As she got up to go, Noah spoke again. "Nashah, do you believe the horse is strong enough to pull the cart?"

"Yes, my lord, the wound has now healed."

Another awkward pause followed this before Noah said, "Nashah, there is a time ahead where I would like you to no longer call me 'my lord.' I would like you to call me by my name." Her eyes widened at what she had heard; it could not be misunderstood. She turned fully toward him and leaned into Noah's arms, and he held her tight. It was only a moment, but the most profound event occurred. I watched as the glow between them grew. They both could see it, and they both took comfort in it. Noah had become her Adam, and Nashah had become his Eve. Noah whispered to her, "From this day forward, we will no longer be separate; we will be one. Our bond has been forged in the fires of our losses, a flood, a river, in grief, and in joy. I am no longer your lord, Nashah, and you are not beneath me. We walk together as one. Whatever the Designer has prepared for us, we will meet it and with Him together."

Nashah had buried her head into Noah's shoulder, and tears that fell earlier in grief were now falling in joy. Her mourning, although unfinished, was now being tempered with love, joy, and a future.

Wisdom and I watched all of this unfold right in front of us. The glow they both carried continued to grow until we both had to look away from them. It was as if we had witnessed the mark of the Designer seal them both. His glory and His love were manifest. We took to the sky to soar together. We both knew and had seen His glory and His mark many times before, but this moment was sacred and precious. As we lifted higher, we saw the most beautiful thing; many angels were there in the skies with us, and they were celebrating this moment. The unity of Noah and Nashah had caused the heavens to rejoice. We could see the Designer's joy and design in its fullness again.

Wisdom let out a cry as loud as she could, and the angels responded with a song only sung in the Designer's presence. It was so pure and filled with such love and honor. Every sense of mine was completely overwhelmed by what I was witnessing. As their voices grew, so did the radiance of the sun, and then it was as if all of creation joined in with the angels' song.

Well, everyone except Noah and Nashah; they were singing a different kind of song.

CHAPTER 37

The next day, the sun shone brightly, and everyone was prepared for the journey east. The days and days of rain were now becoming a memory. There was still water on the ground, but the memories the ground held would take far longer to heal. The road was dry and hard enough to get started, and Noah wanted to leave the Tigris River and the memories behind them.

No one commented on the lingering glow still seen between Noah and Nashah. It was as obvious as the sun in the sky, but each person was still dealing with the emotions of the past two days. The two young siblings were only aware of the hole their father's passing had left in their spirits. Tears continued to flow from them, and even if they stopped, we could see they were continually on the verge of tears falling again. Cain's men kept to themselves and looked as if they hoped no one would ask anything of them, their shame still plain to see.

Ben, I could tell he had noticed the glow, but his grief was still too raw for him to be able to speak. He had already packed up all the supplies, cooking equipment, and personal items and spent his remaining moments at the cave Caleb's body was sealed into.

Wisdom and I were soaring again as the smaller group started out for Enoch. We moved out in ever-widening circles, and as far as we could see, the sun was doing the work of drying the land. Thanks to Nashah, the horse's injury had healed well. Whatever provisions they still had were now all loaded onto the cart, along with a whole barrel of avocados picked that morning. Noah carefully picked his pathway through the remaining pools of standing water, holes, and soft ground on the road. He could not afford to lose the cart on this journey. Nashah's siblings rode on the cart, and as much as Noah tried to persuade Nashah to ride with them, she flatly refused. She might well be his Eve, but she was still Nashah.

Nacham and Deborah's faces were fixed on the road behind them; they were leaving their father behind. The wounds caused by his foolish attempt at crossing the river would affect them for the rest of their lives. So much of their world had changed since leaving Enoch for this new land, and now it was a new land they would only see from across a river that claimed their father's life. Now they were headed back to the city he desperately wanted them gone from.

Nashah, though, had her face firmly fixed on the road ahead of them. It was as if she was defying her grief and holding onto the love she shared with the man she now walked alongside. It was an act of will for Noah to look ahead as well; although he proudly walked beside his Eve, we could all still feel his grief. Conflicting emotions and a land he knew little about were ahead of him. He did not know how long it would take them to get to Enoch, and he did not know what he would find when he got there.

I had seen these moments in the lives of people before. Some had fled from them, but others chose courage in the midst of such fear and uncertainty. Noah was the latter, and whatever happened next, we all could see that Nashah's presence had changed something within him. What the Designer had planned was now what Noah now realized he had longed for. Nashah was his Eve, and he was her Adam. Noah looked at her and said, "You are my ezer, and I am yours."

"What does that mean?" Nashah asked.

"The Designer told me of this word when He told me of you. He spoke of the relationship Adam and Eve shared, and this is the word He used. It means a powerful, dynamic, and helpful connection. I do not yet know what this means for us, but I believe we will discover its meaning."

Wisdom smiled at me as we listened to them talk. She motioned for us to head to the skies, and soon we were high above them. "What do you see, Wisdom?"

"I see possibility, Eagle. But it is what I feel I am noticing more than what I am seeing. Eagle, I feel hope again."

"Yes," I declared. "I feel it too."

"Shall we go find the Designer, Eagle?"

"Yes," I declared and then turned toward that familiar mountain. But as I turned, I could hear Wisdom laughing.

"He is not there, Eagle," she laughed.

"Where is He, Wisdom?"

"He is waiting for us in Enoch."

At that, she took off to find one of those powerful winds that would take her high into the sky. Watching her soar was one of the joys of my existence. Every part of her body became an arrow that shot through the skies, and then when her wings stretched out, I could see the magnitude of her strength and grace. It was everything within me to keep up with her, but that is exactly what I did. To us, it was like a game, and it was a game we loved to play.

It took us two days to get to Enoch, and as we approached, the joy of the flight was replaced with the sadness we could sense in the city. It was as if we were approaching a cloud that was unseen to our eyes but felt by our spirits. When Cain established this city many years ago, it was known for its training and discipline. Now, it seemed, the city had lost its identity.

We found the Designer sitting on a hill overlooking the city. He smiled at us to acknowledge our arrival, but the sadness within Him was felt by us both. We sat by Him as the sun set; the cool of the evening had arrived.

"What have the two of you seen?" He asked.

"We have seen a man and a woman become one," Wisdom said. "A likeness to Adam and Eve that I have not seen since they walked the earth."

"And what have you seen, Eagle?" The Designer asked me.

"I have seen hopelessness replaced with hope, and now I see that same hope replaced with another kind of hopelessness," I replied.

"Then you have not seen all there is to see, Eagle," The Designer said. I cast my eyes over the city and longed to see what He had seen, but maybe it was I who longed to feel what He was feeling. "You have thought me to be sad, Eagle. But that is not all that I see. To only see sadness is only to see what you know. To see hope, you must look into the hearts of those who carry it."

"This sounds like a riddle, my Lord," I replied.

"It is not, Eagle. What did you feel when you saw Noah and Nashah?" He asked.

"I felt hope while I was with them, and I could feel their future and all the possibilities it carried," I replied.

"So you felt something you could not properly describe?" He asked.

"Only you know the future, my Lord."

"Yes, and has not Wisdom told you that the future is a love story?"

"Yes, she did. But here, I see no such thing. I see people walking about a city without hope."

"Eagle, there are three things that will always be present. The first is love, the second is hope, and finally, there is belief." I had heard the Designer talk like this before, but instead of reminding Him, I remained silent and listened to Him speak.

"What you feel here is what the strange lizard wants you to feel. He wants you to be devoid of belief, hope, and love. This has always been his plan, and it is not a new plan. If anything, he is very predictable. He always wants to steal, kill, and destroy. If he can keep you fixed on what you have lost, you will no longer be looking at what you have." The Designer paused before continuing, "He did this to Eve and Adam, and you watched him do this to their son, Cain. Like a cheap magician, he sucks people into his deception with a distraction. As you look out upon this city, you are being distracted by the lies he has woven here, and those lies are here. They are all around us, and each lie attempts to steal the hope you felt this morning. But here is a truth, he cannot take what you do not give. The sadness I feel here is not for what he has stolen but for what the people have given him. Do not give away your hope, Eagle."

"Yes, my Lord," I said, and I felt the shame of having given my hope away so easily again.

"Eagle, Noah will bring with him a light that strange lizards or talking snakes cannot fathom, but they will try to hide it from all the people. We are about to witness something quite exceptional, something Enoch has not seen for many years. Enoch will be invited to fulfill its name, and we will see if it receives the invitation."

"What would you have us do?" Wisdom asked the Designer.

He smiled and said, "Noah and Nashah will be returning to Nashah's family home. It has been abandoned since they left, and no one has gone near it. The people here have been fooled into thinking it is cursed. It is another lie, and it is one that controls anyone who comes near the home. These people fear what they do not understand, so the talking snakes have made it clear to them that death lives in that home. I want you both to prepare their home for them."

Wisdom smiled as well and took to the sky. She knew where Nashah's family home was, and she apparently also knew what we had to do to prepare the home for Noah and his new family. I followed her closely, and when we circled the house, I immediately saw what the Designer meant; the house was full of talking snakes. There were more there than I could count. Wisdom looked at me, and with a nod to the ground, we both flew towards the house. There were times when I would have felt rage to see talking snakes, but as I came close, I could feel their fear. As we landed, a wonderful phenomenon occurred; the snakes fled from the home. They left cursing us, but none of their words affected Wisdom or me. They claimed they would return, and they claimed Nashah was theirs. They also claimed the city was theirs, but they did not know who walked with Nashah.

CHAPTER 38

It took weeks for Nashah and Noah to arrive, and when they did, all the people of the city came out to stare. Wisdom and I saw them coming from a long way out, and we circled them as they entered the city and made for Nashah's old home. We could hear people whispering under their breath, wondering who Noah was and what had become of Cain. We even heard a few wondering if Noah killed Cain and took Nashah for himself.

I was not sure Noah could hear them, but it was obvious he felt their fear and their hatred. He drew Nashah close himself and had Ben walk closely behind the cart. Deborah and Nacham were seated on the cart and looked scared of all the people staring at them. No one would touch them or speak directly to them. Noah and Nashah carried the mark the Designer had placed on them, the same one He placed long ago on Cain. The Designer had told them they were safe here, but could feel they were not welcome.

If Nashah was embarrassed by her people's attitude towards them, she did not show it. This was not a place that held many good memories for her with these people, but her face was resolute, and she was set on leading Noah to her home.

Wisdom knew of all that had happened to Nashah, but I did not. I could tell the strength that she displayed covered the hurt she had carried. Gone was the grief she hid from Noah at her father's death. Gone was the joy she had displayed in becoming Noah's Eve. Her guard was up, and no one from Enoch was going to get to her.

Noah was acutely aware of the people and their disdain for his Eve. He now saw himself as Nashah's protector, and we could see his anger growing the further they ventured into Enoch. His patience was wearing thin, and like Nashah, he wanted nothing more than to get to their destination and close the door behind him. Once they finally got to Nashah's home, she released a shout of joy. "Noah, my Adam, this house is now your home," she said as she wrapped her arms around him.

"Nashah, let me secure the home and ensure we are safe," Noah replied.

Nashah laughed and said, "The Designer brought us here, Noah. He knows what He is doing. Tonight we will rest, and then tomorrow, we will plan for what comes next."

Noah was not as convinced by Nashah's assurances, but he knew the Designer well. "My Eve, tonight we will rest," he said as he released himself from Nashah's embrace and walked the perimeter of the house that would become his home.

Later that evening, Noah came looking for me. "Eagle, tell me all that you have seen."

"I have seen much, my lord."

Noah laughed and said, "Tell me what you found when you arrived here."

"We found a house full of talking snakes. They all left as soon as we landed but claimed that they would return and take what was rightfully theirs."

Noah laughed at that as well. "Rightfully theirs," he repeated. "They must have been here for a while then."

"Nashah would be the person to ask, my lord."

Noah then changed the topic and said, "Eagle, Enoch was once known for its training and discipline. Have you seen any of it in your weeks here?"

"No, my lord, I have not. I have seen chaos, depravity, deception, and all manner of evil that a person is capable of doing. What was here in the days of Cain is long gone. You are seeing the crumbs of a society that built itself on the reputation of a man whose body is now dust."

"Why then would the Designer have brought me here to train in a trade that no longer exists?"

"My lord, you misunderstand me. I did not say the city lacked good tradespeople, just good people."

Noah nodded and said, "This will be harder than I had hoped."

"Harder, my lord?"

"Yes, Eagle, harder. I thought I would come here to learn how to be a carpenter, but now I see I must get them to trust me."

"I understand, my lord."

"Come, Eagle, let us find the Designer." At that, Noah stepped out of the home and walked to the same hill where we met the Designer. Somehow, like Wisdom, Noah always seemed to know where He was. But when we arrived, Noah was surprised to see that he was not the only one to seek out the Designer; Nashah was already there beside Him.

"Welcome, Noah. It is so good to see you," the Designer said. "Come and sit with us. Nashah was just telling me of the wonderful reception the city gave to you."

Noah laughed and exclaimed, "Wonderful reception. You mean awful reception."

The Designer smiled at him and said, "Noah, learn a lesson from Nashah today. She knew this would be her home as soon as she realized you would become her Adam. She also knew I would not abandon her, even when her people had abandoned her. She has clung to my words, even through the most difficult times of her life. She has lived in a home with many talking snakes, an absent father, and no mother, and yet she continued to listen for my voice." The Designer turned to me and asked, "Eagle, were the snakes in every room of the house?"

"No, my lord. They were in every room but one."

"Whose room do you think that was, Noah?" He asked.

"My Eve's room, my Lord."

"Eagle, what did you feel when you were in that room?"

"I felt belief and hope, but what I felt the most was love. It was unmistakable, my Lord." The tough exterior that Nashah had shown on the journey through Enoch had now disappeared; now, her tears fell.

"Noah, your Eve did not have your father, or your grandfather, to teach her of my love. But she is curious, and her curiosity led her to me. When I found her, she was not the woman you see today. As I have told you before, she had been beaten by her father and abused at the hands of the men of this city. Her friends were the animals I drew to her. She learned empathy through the horses. She learned to nurture through the sheep. She learned faithfulness through the lowly dogs that most people scorn. Who you see today is a woman healed and healing. She is resilient, she is strong, and she should never be underestimated. She knows my presence and has felt the power of my love that surges through every living thing." The Designer paused before continuing, "She does not need your protection; she needs your love as you need hers."

Noah had become silent as he listened to everything the Designer said. He had been corrected but not humiliated. That night, we watched and listened as the Designer spoke to them long into the evening; the more He spoke, the greater the light that flowed from Noah and Nashah again. By the time they returned to their home, the city had become strangely quiet. The previous nights had been loud and chaotic, but not tonight. It was as if the city was holding its breath and waiting to see what would happen next.

CHAPTER 39

The strange quiet in the city greeted the sunrise the next morning. I would have been in the skies by now if I was anywhere else, but something kept me from being up there. The sunrise was still just as stunning, and its colors would always be an invitation to spread my wings and fly. Even the breeze I felt would have beckoned me to soar upon it, but the strange quiet had unsettled my spirit. Wisdom and I sat on the roof of Nashah's home, taking in the sunrise.

"You have been watching Nashah for many years. What did you see?"

"Some of what the Designer spoke of I had not seen. Her early years were already behind her when I arrived. When the Designer gave me this charge, He warned me of what I would see and witness. Some things I have witnessed have horrified me; others have saddened me, but others have inspired me. When I arrived, I saw Nashah protecting her brother and sister from all she endured. They cannot comprehend what she went through for them both to be safe, and I doubt she will ever tell them. To do so would traumatize them and give them a wound that was not theirs to carry. They now have their own to heal from."

"Nashah did not look back on her father's grave," I said.

"No, she did not," Wisdom replied before continuing, "Deep down, Cain was not an evil man, but he was a broken man who lost who he was."

"Wisdom, will she grieve the loss of her father?"

"She has been grieving that loss for many years, Eagle. When her mother died, she became the mother of the home, and she was alone in this. As you know, that is when Cain also gave away his role as a father to her; he was lost in his grief, and Nashah had to create a home where her siblings were safe. I believe his death has become closure for her in two ways: she no longer fears him and can now live her life. For her, this is not like the suddenness of Abel's murder; she has been losing him ever since her mother died. His grief stole the opportunity to love his children. I think they will discover something they had not dreamed possible in Noah: a man who loves well."

I sat and pondered all that Wisdom had said; there was much for me to see and learn here. The city was awakening, and with it, a familiar sense of hopelessness crept around my spirit. But this time, I recognized it and would not let it corrupt my thoughts. There was love here, and it is always here. I just needed to see it. "Wisdom, the Designer spoke of three things that would always endure, which means they are all present in front of us. Can you see them?"

"You do not need to see them to know they are here, dear Eagle. You just need to trust what the Designer has told you. As you trust, more will be revealed, and as more is revealed, you will see more of the Designer than you have ever seen before. This you already know."

"Yes, I do," I replied. "I have just not become used to seeing so much evil. Even all those years ago, when I saw Abel lying lifeless on the ground, I could still see the love in Miriam and his parents. Here, there is so little."

"What you say is true, Eagle. But look beneath all you are seeing. There is a love here that evil cannot touch."

"Is this how you coped being here for so long, Wisdom?"

"I coped by spending time with the Designer and with Nashah. Without them, I would have no place to land here and no place to rest. With them, though, I discovered all the love, hope, and belief to trust in the Designer, even when I could not see them." She continued, "When I arrived, I was much like you are today. I was overwhelmed by all I saw. Nashah's curiosity inspired me to search deeper than I had seen before. She had endured so much, but there was a part of her that could not be extinguished. The glow of her spirit was like a flicker of a flame that refused to go out. The flame would become a blaze, and she would often talk of my presence and what I brought to her. She spoke of the safe place I was for her. She spoke of the love she felt from me, and she spoke of the hope I carried." A long silence followed before she spoke again. "Eagle, back when I arrived, my hope dwindled. But it was her hope that brought me back to life. Somehow, we were stronger together, and together we discovered more of what the Designer had sown long ago into the ground here. The same love that flows through Eden is in the ground here, but as you can see, there is a lot of filth on the ground surrounding us; it will take courage to press through the filth to discover His love."

I sat and looked at all the filth—the city stank of it. Human waste was everywhere; it would have been impossible for anyone to walk on the streets below us and not get it on themselves. I became very thankful for the wings the Designer had created me with. But, here, the people had become used to the filth, and they appeared to put up with it. The longer I sat, the more I realized what I had to do. "Wisdom, will you join me and place our talons into the ground?"

Wisdom was initially startled by my request, but soon she agreed. We both flew to the ground in front of Noah and Nashah's home. Our landing caused a commotion among the people walking on the road. Some yelled at us but soon walked around us like we were another obstacle in the road they needed to avoid.

I sank my talons in through the reeking filth that covered the road. Every instinct in my body declared this to be foolish, and my mind felt emotions it had never experienced. There was more than apathy here; there was disappointment, perversion, fear, and hatred, all within the surface of the soil. These emotions raged through my mind, and I wondered if I would ever be truly clean again. It was then I feared what diseases lurked in this filth and what scurrying rodents carried that plagued this city. I even feared the people who walked past us.

As I let my talons sink deeper, new feelings surged through me. It took me a few moments to understand what I was feeling, but soon I realized I could feel so many lost ambitions and dreams. These emotions then shifted as I went deeper still, and I could feel a loss of gigantic proportions; this was the layer where hope was being replaced with hopelessness. A little deeper again, and I felt the searing pain of abuse and death. The ground had witnessed and held so much evil.

I looked across at Wisdom and saw tears rolling down her face. For one who is known for the wisdom she carried, I wondered if any of this made sense to her. But, like me, she had learned that healing is found only in the love of the Designer, so she dug even deeper into the ground beneath us.

It was there a blazing vision came into my sight. Cain, not Nashah's father but Adam's son, sat right where we sat and placed his fingers into the ground. I could hear him talking with the Designer. He said, "My Lord, you have given me this land, and I have built a new home here. This home will always house your presence and be a place where your love is discovered. May all who are forgotten find a safe place here."

I could even see Cain's tears as clearly as Wisdom's. An age ago, a conversation with the Designer happened in this very place, and today I can see the fulfillment and heartbreak of Cain's words. Nashah, whose name means forgotten, has made her home right here. I closed my eyes again and soon realized my talons had discovered the Designer's love, and with it, the realization, all the fear I had initially felt had gone. In this place, and at this depth, I was at one with the Designer and His design. My talons were deep in the mire of the city's filth, but I felt the cleansing power of His love, and the filth had lost its grip on me.

Once again, I opened my eyes, and this time, I saw Wisdom fully aglow. People had stopped to look and wonder, and then I realized they were not just looking at Wisdom; they were also looking at me. My feathers were glowing, and I could feel the love spreading from me and into Wisdom and from Wisdom back into me.

She looked at me and said, "I think it is time to soar." We spread our wings and left the people standing there with their mouths wide open and staring into the skies as they watched us take off. "What did you see, Eagle?" She shouted at me as we flew higher and higher.

"I saw Cain," I exclaimed.

"I saw him too," she responded.

"Wisdom, what happened to Cain's body when he died?"

"The Designer took him back to Eden. He lies in the same cave as his brother."

"Today, I saw Cain do what he would not do when the Designer sat with him all those years ago; he placed his fingers into the soil and did not let go this time. I heard a prayer he prayed that is still as powerful today as it was when he spoke it."

"His words and presence were still felt today, Eagle."

CHAPTER 40

Noah had farewelled Cain's other two men the previous evening, and they were happy to be back with their families again. This morning, Noah and Ben went out into the city to find work. But it was no easy task, as all the city's people were wary of Nashah being back among them, and none of them knew who Noah was. He wore the cloak of his father, hoping someone would recognize it, but I did not feel the same hope he carried.

Noah looked specifically for a carpenter who would take them both on, but each door they knocked on was met with a firm rejection. This would become the pattern for the next few days; no one would risk employing either of them.

Each evening, Noah and Nashah went out to spend time with the Designer, and His response to them was to keep knocking on doors until he found one that would be open to them. After a week, Noah wondered if this was the right place to learn this trade. "My Lord, I've knocked on more doors than I thought there were doors in this city, but every single one is closed," Noah said to the Designer.

"Maybe you're knocking on the wrong doors," the Designer replied.

"If one does not open soon, we will run out of supplies. No one in this city will give us any credit to buy what we will soon need."

"Noah, do you trust me?" The Designer asked.

"Yes, my Lord, I do."

"Where in the city have you not knocked on doors yet?"

Noah sat and thought about this, and as his mind scanned the entire city, he said, "The only place I can think of is the docks, but surely these people will not teach me how to build homes with timber?"

"Maybe I do not want you to learn how to build homes," the Designer replied.

"You want me to learn how to build boats?" Noah exclaimed.

The Designer got up from where He was sitting, looked down at Noah, and said, "Maybe." He walked off, leaving Noah to sit and think of all he had just heard. Nashah sat beside him, firmly gripping his hand. She did not look as concerned as Noah; each day, she encouraged him as the Designer had just encouraged him.

The next morning, Ben and Noah set off to the docks. This was an area of the city most people avoided. It was filthy, even more filthy than the streets of Enoch. Not only did it carry the stench of human waste, but it also carried the stench of rotting fish. To every one of my senses, it was a repulsive place to be, but to Noah, desperation was driving his needs. Ben asked, "Are you sure this is where we should look for work?"

"No, Ben, I am not, but these are the only doors I have not knocked on in this city."

They saw a crowd gathering around two men as they approached the docks. The closer they got, the more they realized what was happening; a younger man was beating an older man, and the younger man was clearly winning this fight. The men surrounding them were yelling at them both, and no one was intervening. The cheers from the crowd showed they were not about to stop what was entertaining them. With each punch, the older man would be flung to the ground; his face was bloodied and messy with the dirt and filth he was lying in. The younger of the men was reveling in the attention he was getting. The old man continued to rise to his feet, only to be met with another devastating blow. The crowd would cheer, and the younger man would throw up his arms in triumph. Then, with one final hit, the old man could not get back up. The younger man stood over him and yelled, "Today you die, old man."

Noah reacted instantly and, pushing his way through the crowd, pushed the young man away from the older man. The older man tried to return to his feet, but his blood now flowed freely from his nose and from a gash to the back of his head. The younger man was shocked by Noah and soon lunged back at him, only to be stopped by Noah's huge hand in his chest. "Stop," yelled Noah.

The younger man soon realized who stood before him, and regaining his composure and menace, he turned his mockery to Noah. "You are the one who killed Cain and took his daughter. Who do you think you are to tell me what to do? We all know you are looking for work, but you will find no one here who will employ you."

Noah was unmoved and silent. His eyes were locked upon the younger man, and he refused to look away. It was not long ago I saw Noah looking at Cain with the same stare. The younger man moved from side to side; Noah's silence made him visibly uncomfortable. Each taunt was met with the same stony silence, and at no point did Noah look to engage him with words.

Behind Noah, Ben had helped the older man away from the commotion. Settling him on a bench, he returned and stood shoulder-to-shoulder with Noah. Ben was much taller than Noah, and his size alone changed the younger man's demeanor even further. The crowd, who were cheering for the younger man moments before, was now taunting him and yelling for him to kill Noah.

The rage and mockery there moments before was rapidly changing, and fear soon filled his eyes. Slowly, he edged away from them, still cursing, spitting, and muttering threats at them. Once he disappeared, the crowd was at a loss. As they realized no one would fight, and one by one, they, too, edged away from Noah and Ben.

Noah turned and saw that the older man was still sitting, watching all that was happening. Blood was still flowing from the wound on the back of his head, but the blood from his nose had stopped. His head was bruised, and one of his eyes was swelling and soon be difficult to see from.

"What is your name?" The older man asked.

"My name is Noah, and this is my friend, Ben."

"Noah, is it?" The old man said, and then continued, "I had a dream last night that a man by your name would meet me today."

Under his breath, Noah said to Ben, "I think a door might have just opened."

"What are you two doing down here by the docks?"

"We are here looking for work. I have come to Enoch to be trained in carpentry."

"Turns out, young Noah, I am a carpenter of sorts."

"Of sorts?" Noah asked.

"Yes, of sorts, that's what I said." There was a pause as the older man gingerly regained his feet. He was battered and bruised but would not let Noah or Ben help him walk. "Come with me and sit at my table; we can share some food and talk there." Noah and Ben looked at each other, and with a nod from Noah, they walked with the man. He lived in a shack beside a large shed at the end of the docks. He invited them to come and sit as he brought out three roughly hewn cups, some cheese, and some bread. Noah and

Ben watched as the old man settled himself at the table, broke the bread, and poured each a cup of wine.

"Thank you for stepping in when you did. I do not know how much longer I could have survived before that fool of a boy fed me to the sharks."

"Why was he trying to kill you?" Ben asked.

"He is a jealous fool," the older man said. "We both build boats, and people seem to like my boats better than his boats," he laughed as he spoke. "He used to be my apprentice until he thought he could build boats faster and better than I could. So, he left and started his own business."

"So, he was getting rid of the competition," Ben said.

"He was trying to. It is not the first time he tried to do it. He tried to burn down my warehouse not long ago, but the fool could not light the fire by the time I caught him."

"What is your name?" Noah asked.

The older man looked Noah in the eye and said, "My name is Banay. I am a master builder, but that does not count for much in this city anymore. You saw what the mob did when that young fool tried to kill me. They cheered him on! They are more intent on seeing death than learning a craft that will die with me."

Noah replied, "So, a carpenter of sorts. By that, you mean you are a carpenter that builds boats."

"At your service, young Noah."

"And you have a vacancy for an apprentice or two?"

"I have boats to build. If you learn fast, I can employ two of you. If you learn slowly, then I can only employ one."

Noah thought on this for a few moments and then replied, "Let us both work for you for the next three weeks at no charge. At the end of that, if you believe we are fast learners, then take us both. If not, then choose the one you would have as an apprentice. Throughout this time, one of us will stay here with you, and maybe that young man will think twice before he attacks you again."

Banay looked them both over, nodded his head, and said, "Agreed. Let us start today."

The three of them sat at the table, eating Banay's food and drinking his wine. Wisdom and I sat outside the small shed and saw the Designer's plans take shape; they had knocked on the right door.

CHAPTER 41

Noah was back at the dock at first light the next morning. Ben had remained with Banay and was already being ordered around by him. I could feel the excitement in Noah, and it was as if he had just been with the Designer and given permission to come here to Enoch. I smiled and thought of how much had changed since that moment for Noah.

When Banay saw them together, he said, "So, what do you two know about building boats?"

Ben answered, "The closest we have come is building rafts."

Banay laughed and said, "Well, you are already building boats better than that young fool from yesterday. Here, I build boats out of cypress. It is beautiful timber, and you can smell it in the air. Take a deep breath and remember its scent. Nobody else here builds with it; it is more expensive to build with, but my boats never sink." Noah and Ben both inhaled deeply and allowed the strong scent of the cypress tree to be imprinted in their memory. There were great trunks of it lined around the warehouse walls, and Banay loved each log. They watched as he walked around the warehouse, running his hand along the logs. To each, he would stop and gently speak of all it would become and the seas it would sail. "Cypress is not just a great timber for making boats. Its resin can be made into a tar that waterproofs the boat," he said before continuing, "Something that young fool could never master, and now half his boats have more leaks than he has buckets for." The older man shook his head and laughed at his own joke.

"In the next three weeks, I will teach you how to listen to the timber you are building with." Noah and Ben looked at each other as if they thought Banay was losing his mind, but they did not dare say it. Instead, they both nodded and listened intently. "I will teach you how to split the logs with such accuracy that very little of the tree will be wasted. I will teach you how to bend the timbers to whatever shape you need, and I will teach you how to build a boat without using a nail." Banay stopped to make sure they both were listening and then continued, "I will teach you how to design a boat that will sail the oceans or a boat that will never leave the harbor. I will teach you all my secrets from the smallest wedge to the great masts of ships at anchor."

"How many years have you been building boats?" Ben asked Banay.

He stopped, thought, rubbed his chin, and replied, "Honestly, I do not know the answer. More years than I have counted. I have outlived my wife and my two sons. They worked with me for many years, but both have been dead for more years than I have counted." Banay paused before continuing, "To be honest, I thought I would join them in death yesterday, and I was ready to. I am tired, and soon I will put my tools down for the last time." He exhaled, looked up at Wisdom and me, and said, "But first, tell me why those eagles follow you."

Noah smiled, looked at us both, and said, "They are our friends. The Designer has given them to us, and they watch over all we do. They bring comfort wherever they go; you will find healing while they are here with you, Banay. Have you not already noticed how the swelling on your face has nearly disappeared? Like us, they carry the Designer's presence; you will be surprised how much will change now."

Banay looked at us both and back to Noah. After doing that several times, he shrugged and said, "Let us see if you are fast learners then." Banay then picked up wedges and hammers, and their first lesson commenced.

Noah and Ben returned home that night tired but happy. Nashah had prepared a meal for them, and she heard every detail of their day and all they had learned. Nashah's curiosity asked question after question, and Noah and Ben were willing to answer every one they could. Some of her questions they could not answer, and Noah noted them all down to ask Banay when he returned to the port later that evening.

Nashah would have loved to be down at the docks learning everything they did, but she was now back in charge of raising her sister and brother. It was a task she knew was hers alone now. They had no one else in Enoch prepared to help her, so she took to caring for both Deborah and Nacham. Her learning about boats would happen by asking questions and using her imagination to do the things that Noah and Ben do each day.

The three weeks with Banay moved by quickly, and soon Noah and Ben were back sitting at his table, drinking his wine and eating his cheese. They were both excited for this day to come. They had enjoyed working with Banay, and both hoped he felt the same. Banay was never in a rush; slowly, he gathered the cups, then the bread, cheese, and then finally the wine. He took his time pouring the wine for each of them, and then after breaking the bread, they ate together. Throughout the meal, the two men wanted nothing more than for Banay to tell them of his decision, but Banay resisted and allowed their nervousness to become more and more visible. He shared stories of his youth, wife, and children. He told them of some boats he had built and then stopped to point to them out in the harbor. Noah and Ben had finished their wine and bread long before Banay finally put the last bite into his mouth. He chewed on it excruciatingly slowly, then he cleared his throat and said, "I will take you both."

Noah and Ben let out a collective sigh, which quickly turned to joy and laughter. Wisdom, and I could feel the relief flowing through them. "But," Banay interrupted them both, "We will continue to assess this arrangement each month. We have two boats to build this year, and neither of them is small. It will take a lot of hard work, and you still have much to learn. We will need to work together, but I think if you continue to learn, we will fulfill each of the orders."

"Thank you," Noah said. "This means more to us than you can know."

"Well, if my dream about you three weeks ago has anything to do with it, then I am sure whatever you are here to learn will last for generations after you." Banay paused before continuing, "Noah, I saw three sons that would come from you, and one will carry the same glow as you do. But he carries something more, and it looks like a seed, but it is not a tree he will plant. That seed will bring such a big harvest many years from now; the world will have never seen its like."

Wisdom and I looked at each other as we heard this. Wisdom smiled, and I knew the seed that Banay spoke of was the same seed that Wisdom had spoken to me way back when Eve chose to eat from the *Tree of Knowledge of Good and Bad*. "Others have seen the Designer's plan," I said quietly to Wisdom.

Wisdom nodded and said, "The Designer is readying His creation for events that have never happened before."

As she said this, I could feel both the sadness and yet hope in her voice, but our attention was drawn back to the men. "Those eagles that follow you around are a part of all of this, are they not?" Banay asked.

Noah responded, "They have been with my family since before I was born. As I said earlier, the Designer has given them to us to watch over us, and it may sound crazy to you, but we can talk with them, and they understand what we are saying."

Banay said, "I have seen many things that others would consider crazy. You do not get to live as long as I have and not see things that people cannot understand. The eagle with the white head, though, I have seen her many times here in Enoch, and she was always with Cain's daughter."

"Nashah can talk with her, as I do. She has had a connection with animals ever since she was a little girl," Noah responded.

"And that would be true, young Noah. Her father would often be found wandering the docks after his wife died. When she was young, she was never far behind him, and every dog, cat, and animal would be drawn to her. Some said it was witchcraft, and some said her mother died because of a curse, and then somehow they thought the curse meant she could talk with animals. But, as I said, I have been here for long enough to know grief when I see it. I have also been here for long enough to know the Designer's hand when I see it."

Noah was shocked to hear Banay speak of the Designer and said, "You know the Designer?"

"I did not say I know Him. I just know of Him. It has been many generations since the Designer was welcomed in these parts. I guess I am old enough to know that one day soon, I will meet Him."

Noah said, "I can take you to Him today if you like."

The old man smiled and said, "Not today, young Noah. I have much to fix in my life before I meet Him, and I have done many things I am ashamed of. Maybe training you two will go some way to correcting many of the wrongs I have done."

Noah smiled back at him and said, "That is not how it works, Banay. Have you not heard the story of Cain, Adam's son?"

"That story has become a myth here, young Noah, and it has been many years since I heard it, and that was Cain."

"Let me remind you then," Noah said before continuing, "the Designer found Cain in his shame. He had murdered his brother and, in doing so, betrayed his family. Like you, he had done something he thought was beyond healing. But also, like you, it was not, and it never would be beyond the love the Designer had for him. He went searching for the one who had wandered away, and those two eagles watched every part of his story. The Designer restored him and came with him as he built this city."

Banay sat and listened to every word Noah spoke and finally said, "Then, yes, one day I will go with you and meet with Him." Banay stood, picked up his toolbelt, and then said, "Come on, you two, there are boats to be built. And they will not get built if you are always eating my cheese and drinking my wine," he laughed as he spoke these words.

"Can I ask you one more question?" Noah asked.

"You can ask, but whether I answer it, that's another question," Banay chuckled as he spoke.

"Everyone in this city fears Nashah and me. Why don't you?"

"Maybe, I am too old to be scared? Maybe, I see a young man and woman needing a friend. Maybe, your help three weeks ago restored some of my belief in people. Or, maybe, I just like you. I do not know the answer to this question, but when you are around, I feel safe. Now come, let me show you how to make a mast."

Wisdom and I watched all of this unfold. We watched a man whose heart had just given birth to hope.

CHAPTER 42

The weeks started becoming months; before they knew it, the months became years. Noah and Ben became master shipbuilders in their own right. Banay's business thrived, and the orders for the boats kept coming in. What started in a shack, eating cheese and bread, and drinking wine, had now become multiple warehouses, many employees, and the entire shipyard became a center for fine boats.

Ben and Nashah's younger sister, Deborah, became more than friends; she was now his Eve. Then one day, they announced they were having their first child. Nine months later, a beautiful baby boy was born, and they called him Abishai; for he was their gift from the Designer. Noah and Nashah celebrated with them; this was the first child born to their family since coming to Enoch. Nashah cherished this child and became a mother figure to him as well. She had not conceived a child of her own yet, so she poured all of her love and attention into Abishai. Ben had asked Noah if he could move his young family to another part of the city and start his own home. Noah had seen this day coming, and through tears, he willingly gave his blessing to them.

Nashah's younger brother, Nacham, had also become an apprentice in the shipyard and was making a name for himself as a sailmaker. Before long, he also asked Noah if he would bless him, release him from their home, and begin his life abroad. He wanted to travel and see the world. His trade and skill meant he could find work wherever he went as long as it was by the water. Again, Noah willingly and happily released Nacham as well.

Throughout these years, Nashah continued to learn all she could about building boats. She no longer had her siblings to look after, so she busied herself with the knowledge of boats and continued to spend as much of the day as possible with animals. Women were rarely seen at the shipyard, and some men still feared that she was cursed. I would come to learn that many of those who believed she was cursed were the ones who caused her so much pain. They fed the lie of a curse to hide their own shame.

Nashah ignored their mockery and their accusation of curses. She had learned their words only gained power if she allowed herself to listen to them. She carried Eve's story of the strange lizard in her heart. She determined not to make the same mistake and learned to listen for those voices that would tempt her to become someone else. Even when these men would condemn her, she continued to find ways to love them, which, in turn, would make them uncomfortable to be around her. Shame and love do not go well together. It was always odd to see grown men avoiding her, even hiding from her at times.

She never stopped meeting with the Designer, and from a young age, she had learned so much of His love and restoration. Like Noah, she would often spend entire nights with the Designer, never tiring of sitting in His presence. He would often draw many of the wild animals of the forest to her as she sat at His fire. It reminded me of Adam when He drew them to him to name each of them. As the years went by, the connection she shared with them grew. She was a woman at peace with all of creation. There was only one ache in her heart, and that was to have a child. As the years slipped by, it would be the one question she would continue to ask of the Designer.

Wisdom continued to be Nashah's constant companion, and I would be Noah's. We cherished our time together and would often be seen circling the city. People came to know us and were no longer scared of us, but none could understand us. Often children would run after us as we flew over the city. Their squeals of laughter were life-giving and drew more children to their chase of us. We watched as the atmosphere in the city slowly changed through this time. The stench that greeted us all those years ago was fading. The streets were becoming cleaner and safer. People became more friendly to each other, and even the young man who tried to kill Banay all those years ago became a friend to Noah.

Then one of those days, of one of those weeks, of one of those months, of one of those years, Noah returned home and found Nashah beaming. She said, "I have some news for you." Her smiling face would often greet him each time he walked through the door, but this time there was more. He could sense the news behind the beaming face was about to bring him so much joy. "I am pregnant," she squealed as she spoke. Noah lifted her in his arms as if she was as light as a feather. His joy overflowed, and they both cried tears of happiness. I had not seen Noah as happy as he was that day, and I am sure everyone on their street could feel and hear the joy they shared.

Wisdom and I sat together, and she leaned across and said, "The Designer's plan has become more seen today."

"When will I be a father?" He asked through his tears.

"In the season between winter and summer, we will be parents, Noah," she exclaimed.

Noah replied, "If it is a boy, we will call him Shem; for he will carry our names. If it is a girl, we will call her whatever your heart desires, my love."

Nashah smiled at Noah, and holding her stomach, she said, "Noah, I am excited, but I am also terrified. I have longed for this day, but I cannot get the memory out of my mind of my mother dying when she gave birth to Nacham. I want to give you a child, but I am so scared."

Noah held her. He knew everything about building boats, but he knew nothing about childbirth. Everything about it had scared him too, but he would not share that with Nashah. Instead, he said, "The Designer has brought us this far, my love. Each of the things He's asked us to believe of His plan has happened, and this will be no different." The last phrase sounded more like a hope than a statement.

As Nashah progressed through her pregnancy, even the women who had avoided her all those years softened to her. They would often stop to see how she was doing and also to see if there was anything they could do. They would share their own stories of childbirth. Some of them horrified Nashah, and some of them comforted her. Each woman had their own unique concoction to drink to make them go into labor or settle the discomfort of pregnancy. They all meant well, and she relished the friendship and acceptance they gave her.

Winter came and went, and the days got longer and warmer. The child's arrival would soon be upon them. Noah had become like a little puppy to Nashah, always wanting to be by her side. He would offer to do everything he could for her, but she was still Nashah and refused to let him wait on her. She would scold him each time, saying she could look after herself. But as the time crept ever closer to the birth, Nashah realized she could not do as much as she used to. Deborah had returned home for the birth and offered to do all she could. She had born her own children, was well-educated in childbirth, and had a way of calming Nashah's fears. One evening, Deborah said, "Your child will be here soon after the new moon."

"And not soon enough," Nashah responded. "I am not sure I can even do this."

"You can and you will, sister. It is hard, but you are strong, and so is the life that grows within you. I was too young to remember our mother's death, but it was in my mind and my thoughts when I had each of my children. I know you are afraid, but I will be right here beside you through it all."

"Deborah, I am scared," Nashah replied.

"Do not fear the birthing process. In peace will you labor well, for this is living in your design. Ask the Designer for a birthing promise and let that hold your gaze throughout every moment. Your child carries a great seed, and the Designer's Kingdom will celebrate as your child enters this world. He has everything you need to love and raise this child. He loves helping us." Deborah paused before continuing, "Nashah, how often did you tell me to listen for the Designer's voice? Now, it is my turn to remind you: hear His voice as the child is born, and then you will find Him in this child and then the everyday moments of motherhood. Pay attention to your child; I often see Him speaking the loudest in children. When you feel overwhelmed, remember the best gift to your child is your love and connection. He has chosen you to be the mother of this precious child, and that is no accident. Love yourself well, and you will love your child well. Learn to receive the gift of child-like belief through your child. From this child's first moments, the Designer will be present and known. Honor, encourage, and embrace what they see and imagine. This tiny life will unlock the Designer's mysteries that He has prepared for this little one to find."

"Thank you," Nashah said, then closing her eyes, she allowed sleep to overtake her. Deborah excused herself from Noah's company and headed home, leaving him to watch over his Eve. He would sit throughout the evening and do this until he could not keep his eyes open. He loved her so dearly.

"Eagle, what do you see?" Wisdom asked.

"I see a man at one with his Eve."

Noah opened his eyes, smiled, and said, "Yes, Eagle, I feel it even more than I see it. I also feel the Designer's hand in all of this. He has spoken to us many times about this time, but now that we are here, His words have proved true again."

"I have often found that, my lord. There have been times when I have felt He has spoken in riddles to me, but then one day, I see the riddle all of a sudden make sense. What I could not see before is now as plain as day. It is then I can look back and see how each of these words spoken makes perfect sense. I saw this in Eden when Eve ate from the wrong *tree*. I could not have comprehended or guessed what the Designer would do, but He told me it was all part of a greater love story. Then, I saw it with Cain after he had murdered his brother. His action changed many people's lives, but it did not change the way the Designer loved him. The riddle of the love story became the wonder of His great plan. Riddles, promises, seeds, and a dead tree are all combining to show us something that I am yet to understand."

"It's both beautiful and maddening at the same time," Noah chuckled as he spoke.

"It is Noah."

"What have you seen of my child, Eagle? Do you hold the same foresight that Wisdom does?"

"I can see much, my lord, but Wisdom can see more of what you call foresight. What I see is a child that carries the same glow you and Nashah carry. The words of Banay ring in my ears as I say this. The child carries a seed that will be sown from one generation to another. I see that seed like a star in the heavens.

It is impossible for me to comprehend, yet it is still so beautiful to watch. Your child will bring change to all of creation, and many will discover the Designer through him."

"Him," Noah exclaimed. "You have seen a boy?"

"I may have already said too much, my lord. Whether it is this child or another, a great lineage of generations will come from you. Look up at the stars, Noah. If you can count them, you will discover how many people this life will bless."

"You are talking like the Designer now, Eagle. You are talking in riddles," he laughed.

"Maybe I am," I said and laughed as well. After the laughter finished, I continued, "I have seen many things through my long years, and I have spent much time with the Designer to know and see Him at work. Like you, there have been times I have wondered if His promises would come true, and also, like you, I have doubted His promises as well. Learn a lesson from an old eagle. There will be times ahead of you when you second-guess yourself and wonder if all you have heard from Him is true. In times like these, you need to remind yourself of His love and faithfulness. You have seen them both, and you can testify to their truth. But not everything you have heard from Him has happened the way you expected. When you look back, you are using your hindsight. It is a gift He has given to you to show you His love and faithfulness."

"Yes, Eagle, sometimes my expectations of His plans and words are not even close to the outcomes I see. Could I have imagined that Nashah would arrive at my campsite? Could I have imagined the city of Enoch before I came here? Could I have imagined I would build boats? Could I have imagined we would take years to conceive a child?" Noah paused before chuckling, "I have learned that my expectations need to be held lightly with Him."

I responded, "I have learned He is less interested in our expectations than He is in the way we love. I have learned that relationships are the centerpiece of His design, and everything else is secondary. I have learned that we are eternal; life here is merely a moment of our eternity. I have learned that love and life are the essence of who He is."

"What you say is true, Eagle. I have just not heard it this way before. I have tried to understand my life through the time we are given here in creation, not the eternity we inhabit. This is an impossible thought to hold for too long by myself, but when I am with Him, it all gets a little clearer for me. There is no place I would rather be when I am with Him. It is there I feel safe. When I am with Him, I feel the love and life you speak of."

"Yes, Noah. What you are seeing and feeling are powerful truths of His creation. When we are away from Him for too long, we become lost, and our thoughts become too difficult to understand, and we get confused so easily."

"There are times when I can see the whole city of Enoch slowly turn towards Him. I know that Nashah and my coming here have turned a tide, but what will happen when we leave? Will Enoch sink back into the cesspit it was?"

"That is for the people of Enoch to decide. It is not your responsibility what they do after you leave. You have loved them well and allowed them to encounter the Designer's love. Banay has felt this, and so have many others."

"Sometimes, Eagle, I wonder if I have done enough or done the right things here or could have done more."

I smiled as he spoke and said, "Noah, as I have said, surely you must know by now the Designer is far more interested in the love you give than whether you have done things right or wrong. When you arrived here, you discovered a city that traded in right and wrong, and good and bad, and look where it got them. You and Nashah coming here showed them something new. When you arrived, the people thought Nashah was cursed and you a murderer. They shunned and rejected you. They gossiped and slandered you. Banay risked everything in taking you and Ben on. You were unskilled and unproven, but he saw something he thought was worth the risk in you. That was many years ago, and now you are welcome. Now, you are sought for your wisdom and expertise. Now, Nashah is honored and not cursed. How many right or wrong things did you do to make this happen?"

Noah smiled and said, "You are correct, Eagle. All of the rights and wrongs would never bring change to this city. It would only ever be love."

"Good night, Noah. May your child be born with the Designer's glow seeded deeply within him."

CHAPTER 43

"Eagle, you have been dreaming," I heard the Designer say. It took me a moment to realize where I was and who it was speaking to me. I had fallen into the deepest of sleep, and the things I had seen there were beyond what I could imagine. "Eagle, you are safe. You are with me," I heard the Designer again. It took a choice to come out of all I was seeing and open my eyes to see Him. Any other time, I would have eagerly come into His presence and cherished the sound of His voice. But I had seen the Designer in my dream, but he looked different.

"Eagle, what did you see?"

"My Lord, you were in my dream; do you know what I saw?"

"Yes, I know what you witnessed, but I want to know what you have seen," He said with an emphasis on 'you.'

"My Lord, I saw so many things, but none of it makes sense to me."

"Tell them to me as they come to you. Do not worry about the sequence or even understanding them."

"My Lord, I saw a person who looks like you, but he was starving. It looked like he had not eaten for weeks. He wandered the wilderness with the glow I can see in you now. To me, it looked as if he wanted to find something, but the one who found him was Lucifer."

"It was Lucifer, Eagle."

"My Lord, the dream changed, and I saw a sea split in two. I watched as many who carried your mark walked between the waters. But then the dream changed again, and I saw many people washed away in those same waters. I could not tell who was saved and who was protected. My Lord, I witnessed so much death, and I do not know who that starving man was."

As I shared the dream, I could feel anxiety rise within me. I had never had a dream like this, and everything I was recalling was grieving my spirit. Breaking my thoughts, the Designer asked, "What else did you see, Eagle?"

"My Lord, I saw Noah with his head in his hands, and he was grieving. I could feel the weight of his grief like a stone inside of my spirit. I do not know what he was grieving, but I could not see Nashah. Did she die, my Lord?"

"One day, all living things will die, Eagle."

"My Lord, I need to know, is Noah grieving Nashah?"

"Eagle, there is more to the dream than you have seen. All will be made clear to you in the days ahead, but there is more yet to the dream. What else did you see?" I closed my eyes again and started recalling it. All the events I had spoken about were there, but I knew there was more. Then I recalled I had been in Eden and was sitting outside Adam's tomb. I knew there was something here for me to remember, so I breathed deeply and allowed my talons to find their way into the soil beneath me. As I did, I noticed I could hear the Designer's breathing, and the more I concentrated on it, I noticed my breathing matched His. Then, suddenly, I realized

I was hearing His heartbeat. It was rhythmic to my ears, drawing me deeper into my dream and His presence.

I do not know how much time had passed, but I realized I was sitting closer to Adam's tomb than when I closed my eyes. Into my vision walked the great angels, Michael and Gabriel. They took hold of the stone that sealed his tomb and easily moved it aside. It would have taken many people to do this, but to these two angels, they moved it as easily as if it were a bag of wheat.

I sat in awe of what I was seeing. I could not remember if this was in my dream or if I saw it in my vision. The next thing I noticed was what I heard and not what I saw. I could hear a person within the tomb wrestling with something. All of my senses had come alive, and I thought this must have been a dream; I felt I was about to see Adam rise from his grave and come out. My mind was racing; I wanted to rush in and see Adam, but something in my spirit was causing me to wait. It felt like an age to me as I waited to see who would emerge from the tomb. But when the person finally did, it was not Adam at all ... It was Nashah.

CHAPTER 44

Soon after the new moon, the day finally arrived for Nashah to give birth. Noah paced around like a lion stalking its prey. So many women perished in these moments, and with them, the child they carried. My dream repeated continually in my mind. Only the Designer knew of my dream; I had not even spoken of it to Wisdom.

Early in the morning, Nashah had screamed herself awake as a pain tore through her. It lasted moments, but it was long enough for her to know this was no pain or experience she had felt before. Deborah had told her this would be the case, and when her waters finally broke, all of Deborah's words came back to her, and she knew she was about to birth a child.

People scattered everywhere, and each was assigned to their appointed tasks. One of the women had run to fetch Deborah, and once she arrived, she ordered everyone around the room. Noah's task was to wait, which he showed very little aptitude for. As the day progressed, each time he heard Nashah cry out, his own spirit cried out to fix the pain she was feeling. Every problem and difficulty in building a boat had a solution, and he was so good at finding solutions that would baffle other men, but this problem was one he had no solution to.

Each time one of the women helping Nashah would appear, they would inform Noah all was going well and it would not be much longer. But as the day passed, Nashah's cries increasingly unsettled Noah whenever he heard them. Silently, he begged the Designer to release the child from her, but as each new cry came from the room, disappointment and frustration surged through his body.

At one point, one of the women came from the room, and Noah caught hold of her and exclaimed, "Surely this is not right. The child should have come by now."

"My lord, we encourage women to cry out in childbirth. Strangely enough, it helps the mother relax and allows the body to ready itself for the delivery." As Noah released her from his grip, she raced off to get what Nashah needed.

After what seemed an eternity to Noah, a shrieking cry from Nashah chilled him to the bone. He stopped pacing and moved towards the room she was in, but as he arrived at the door, he was greeted with shrieks of happiness. Deborah was holding a child out for Nashah to embrace. Nothing would prevent Noah from getting to Nashah now, even the feeble protests of some of the women in the room saying, "We need more time."

"My love, I have given you a son," Nashah said through tears and pain. She held the child to her chest and listened silently to its first sounds and cries.

Deborah handed Noah a knife and said, "Cut the cord which has brought life to the child for these past months, my lord. When that is done, we will need just a few more moments with Nashah." Noah cut the cord and was ushered from the room one more time. As he left, he heard Nashah cry out again, and then she was silent. He waited a moment more to hear her voice and know she lived.

Relief flooded into his spirit as he heard her speak again. He then listened as the women tended to his Eve. They spoke tender and kind words to her, and each of them encouraged Nashah to rest and now to heal.

Looking up at me, with relief on his face, he said, "Eagle, I remember when we entered Enoch, and not one woman would come near her. Now, she has many who will help her in these most precious and vulnerable moments." Relief flooded my spirit as well. I could not get the dream from my mind; hearing her speaking was a gift to my spirit.

"Much has changed, my lord."

After a short while, Deborah came out and said, "Nashah is ready for you. Your son is strong and healthy; she has already told us his name is Shem. It is a good name, Noah."

Noah looked at her and smiled as he walked into the room to see his Eve. Shem was being encouraged to nurse, and Nashah was trying to listen to one of the women giving her advice while trying to get him to feed. Noah exhaled and said, "My Eve and my son. The Designer has given us a gift beyond value." As he came to the bed, Nashah gave up on feeding and handed Shem to Noah. As he took him from her, he leaned over, kissed her, and said, "My love for you has never been as great as it is this day."

Nashah leaned back and fell asleep as she watched Noah with Shem. She was smiling, even though she was sleeping. She was exhausted and in pain, but she was happy.

It was late in the afternoon, and all the waiting of the day seemed to disappear to nothing to Noah as he sat staring at his newborn son. Shem was squirming and wanted to be fed, but none of it bothered Noah. Noah did not realize the cool of the evening had arrived and, with it, a visitor.

Wisdom and I had been watching all of this unfold in front of us. The beauty, wonder, and pain of childbirth were an extraordinary part of the Designer's plan. No two births would be the same, and every child was unique.

As the Designer entered the room, Nashah stirred and awoke to see Him with Noah and Shem. Wisdom and I could see the joy that flooded from her spirit, and with it, the most extraordinary moment happened, and these are moments I will never tire of seeing. The glow of the Designer was joined with the glow of Nashah's joy and love. This was then joined with the glow of Noah's spirit, and all of it was centered on Shem, a child who not only carried a name but he also carried a seed.

The Designer stayed with them till long into the night. To Nashah, He spoke quiet words of healing. With Noah, He just sat and listened to the words and joy overflowing from his heart. When it came time to leave, He asked, "Noah, can I hold Shem?" Noah was embarrassed that he had not placed Shem into His arms earlier and quickly handed Shem to Him.

Then the Designer breathed upon him, saying, "You, my son, carry the same life I breathed into Adam. Generations will come from you, and the light within you will never be extinguished. Kings and queens will bow before the generations that come from your offspring. One day, the seed within you will give birth to the greatest king the world will ever know. A harvest will begin that will not be measured by achievements but rather by my love. You, my son, are marked by my love." The Designer gave Shem to Nashah. This time, Shem quickly attached to Nashah and drank himself to sleep. As the Designer was about to leave, He turned and said to them both, "Soon, I will invite you to leave this place and return to your home." Noah and Nashah sat in the silence of that moment. All they could hear was Shem quietly drinking his fill. The Designer's plan was about to open a new door for them.

Wisdom looked at me and said, "It is time for us to soar."

Silently, I thanked the Designer that my dream had not come true. Relief continued to flood through my spirit as I listened to Wisdom's invitation.

CHAPTER 45

As we lifted into the night sky, we both knew our lives were taking a new twist. Each time we were invited to see, and as we did, we always saw new things about the Designer and His plans.

"Eagle, my foresight has been strange these past days. I was able to see the birth of Shem, but things past that are not so certain. I have the sense there are still years before Noah and Nashah make the trip home, but what happens when they get there has been hidden from me."

"Whenever this has happened, it usually means the Designer is waiting for those created in His image to make choices. It is these choices He never rushes, but the sense of it all coming to a head is growing within me," I replied.

"Banay spoke of two more sons to be born. I believe that both will happen here in Enoch."

"How do you know that, Wisdom?"

"Because the Designer gave it to Banay in a dream. I think Banay will lay down his tools for the last time and join the Designer soon after the third son is born."

"I fear for this city once they return home, Wisdom. I know I have said this before, but the fear I feel is like a foreboding foresight, and I fear it will be overrun with evil once they leave."

"I have felt that too, Eagle."

As we flew higher and wider, we found ourselves far north of Enoch. At first, we noticed a strange smell in the wind, but as we turned to face it, the strange smell turned into a familiar stench, something I had not experienced in years. A long way ahead of us, the darkness hid the cause of the smoke. It was the smell that had turned my stomach; it was the appalling stench of a town that had been set alight.

As we flew north, the stench grew, but the smoke gave way, and we could see the red and orange flames of many fires. The closer we came, the more our horror increased. No one was putting out the fires or tending to the people on the ground. We heard no shouts for help nor any sounds of battle. The fires were out of control and quickly spread from house to house. The thatched roofs ignited as soon as the fire came near them, and then the house would quickly become a cauldron of fire and smoke. The stench was nearly unbearable, and I could feel it leeching into my feathers. Every piece of me wanted to flee from this scene of devastation.

"Eagle, look north; what do you see?" Wisdom asked me.

"I see people carrying torches," I replied. "They must be the survivors; let us go and see."

To escape the city, away from the smoke and stench, was a mercy, but what we found broke our hearts. As we flew, we saw that the people carrying the torches were on horseback. There were many of them, but amongst them were people chained together and being led by them. There were children, women, and aged people among them all. No one had been spared this horror, and all we could hear were the wails of the children and their parents.

Looking back on the size of the city and how few people there were below us, I soon realized how few had survived this attack. I had been to this town before and remembered many more than those walking below me. Reading my thoughts, Wisdom said, "The rest are dead, Eagle. Surely you saw that no one was alive as we flew over the town?"

"I saw that, Wisdom, but some must be hiding?"

"I believe these are the ones below us now."

I felt so helpless in witnessing all the death in front of me. We followed silently; I did not know what I could have said. We watched as some of the aged people fell, and instead of helping them up, the horsemen struck them down right where they lay. A trail of death was snaking its way through the valley.

There was no rush by any of the captors; they feared no one. Anyone who raised their voice against them was struck down as well. Soon, cries of anger and complaint went silent, and everyone marched in line. The parents still tried to stop their children from crying and drawing the horse riders' attention to them.

Then another familiar sound came to my ears: the sound of evil. Wisdom and I could see them coming from a long way off, but I recognized their voices; the vultures and crows had come to gloat. There were many of them, and there was only Wisdom and I. I turned and looked at Wisdom; her eyes burned with fire, and I could see the anger rising within her. "Come, Wisdom; their day is coming. Let us return to the town and see if anyone has survived."

We turned with mocking voices in our ears. They taunted us to turn and fight them, but to do so would be to play into their talons. We knew we could destroy many of them, but we were not commissioned to destroy; ours was to watch. Crows tried to land on our backs as we flew, but this had happened before, and Wisdom and I knew what to do. We just had to fly higher. Crows cannot breathe where we can fly. So, we headed to the heavens, away from their claws and the hideous voices that occupied their bodies. It did not take us long to return to the town, and Wisdom was right; nothing was alive, not even an animal. Everything was dead.

That morning we saw Shem being born, and tonight we see nothing but death. It was hard to believe we had witnessed the wonder of love and creation, producing the most precious and vulnerable form of life. Now we are witnessing the evil of hatred and death. Somehow Enoch, so far, had been spared this horror. Again, reading my mind, Wisdom said, "Enoch was not just spared this horror, Eagle. Enoch was protected from it."

"Why did the Designer protect Enoch and not this town?" I asked.

"It has nothing to do with the Designer protecting one and leaving another for destruction."

"Then, what is it?"

"Love, Eagle. It is love. Evil things have still happened in Enoch, this you know. It is not devoid of hatred or death. But love has changed the city. Love has created community. Love has driven fear away. Think about Banay and the young man who tried to take his life all those years ago. They now sit at the same table and eat. Banay does not even call him a 'fool' anymore. This is what love does. Love creates unity. Love creates strong relationships. Love instills forgiveness, and love heals. The unity of this city has gained it a reputation of strength. These weak-minded people who seek to destroy look for cities that are not unified and cities that are fraught with fear. Today they found one."

We were about to turn back to Enoch when we noticed the Designer walk out of the trees north of the town. But then, we saw something else moving in the shadows behind Him. My first instinct was to cry out and alert the Designer, but Wisdom held me back. She whispered, "Just watch."

I strained my eyes into the forest behind the Designer and could see flickers of flames. They were the torches we had seen earlier being held by the evil horsemen, but now they were being held by those walking, not riding. The Designer was leading the captives' home. They broke into a run, and I could tell they, too, had returned looking for survivors, but they would find none. Their freedom had been won, but their bondage to death and despair would need far greater healing.

We watched as the Designer did what He did so many years before; He slowly and intentionally went to every man, woman, and child lying lifeless and scattered around the town. He reached down to each one and whispered words we could not hear. As He did, we watched as their spirit was released from their body and returned into His. It is always a sacred moment to watch as the Designer releases them from the torment and pain of death and into His freedom. We could see the sadness He carried for the pain they had endured, but we could also feel the relief of restoring their spirits into His. Long into the night, He continued His grief-filled work.

Just before dawn, the Designer came and sat with us on the outskirts of the town. We were upwind and out of the terrible stench. The quietness of the morning had overtaken the violence of the day before, and if I closed my eyes, I could pretend that an undisturbed town was in front of me, and soon it would come to life. The morning was cool, but it was not cold. The gentle breeze moved all the trees around us, but what was absent was the sound of the birds and the animals of the forest. The longer we sat there, the more unnatural the quietness became.

"What have you two seen?" He asked.

"I have a question rather than an observation, my Lord," I said.

"Ask, my friend."

"How much more of this can you put up with, my Lord?"

The Designer exhaled loudly and said, "Soon, the evil of this generation will have run its course. Then there will be a great gathering of the spirits of people, and I will take them where evil cannot touch them. Then evil will be exposed for what it is and how powerless it is compared to my love."

Wisdom and I looked at each other before Wisdom spoke, "The gathering of the spirits, my Lord?"

"Yes, Wisdom, that is what I said," He said with a sigh and a heavy heart.

"My Lord, my foresight is not clear. Normally I could see what is ahead, but now something has prevented me from seeing. When you speak of a 'great gathering of the spirits,' I would hope I could see what you mean, but I can not."

"Much is changing, Wisdom. It will become clear to you soon, but I just ask you to trust me for now. Still, much rests on Noah and the days ahead of him."

"What will become of this town, my Lord?" I asked.

"This town is becoming like many others, Eagle. You have seen this once before, whereas I have seen this now many times. The evil working inside of people has far exceeded greed and envy. Nothing was even stolen from this town. It was just destroyed. This town will return to the dust and will soon be known as cursed."

"Cursed?" I responded. "Have you cursed it, my Lord?"

"Not by me, Eagle. Can blessing and curse come from the same mouth?"

His question startled me, "No, my Lord, that is why I was so shocked that you would call it cursed."

"I did not and will not call it cursed. Others will do that when they see the magnitude of the death here. People will say that I have forsaken this town, but I have not. I have returned to save all those who strayed away from me. If anything, this place is now a place where its people met with me. Long ago, I named this town

Jericho. Its people used to meet with me, and their words were like a sweet fragrance to me."

"There are so many conflicting feelings here, my Lord. The grief and sadness are nearly unbearable, but releasing these people from death into life gives birth to hope."

"I am sad too, but my sadness is because each of these people suffered at the hands of hatred. I am sad because of my love for them and because many hopes and dreams were crushed here. Think about it, Eagle, would you not be sad to be taken from creation? Would you not be sad to no longer soar with Wisdom here among the mountains?"

"Very sad," I replied.

"Then you understand some of the grief I feel. Eagle, each of these people I created and designed uniquely, forming them with my love. So many dreams died today, dreams I spoke into their lives."

"My Lord, can I ask another question?" The Designer smiled and nodded. "When you walked among the bodies, there were three that you did not stop at. Why was that? What happened to their spirits?"

"You see much, Eagle," He said, but there was such grief in His words. "These were of the men that attacked this town, and now there are others lying dead north of this town. These men had given their lives over to the evil voices that inhabited them. They no longer fought them; they welcomed them in and became the very essence of the evil that possessed them. There was a time when I knew each of them by name, but for these, their names they no longer remembered. They have long ignored me and chosen the path that led them to their death, and their death is not just the physical life you see. Their death is an eternal one." He paused before He continued, "Do you remember when you dreamed of the one called Lucifer?"

"Yes, my Lord, I do."

"He no longer remembers his name. If I called him by it, he would not recognize it, for the corruption of evil within him is complete. He has shipwrecked his design, and along with it, he has rejected my love." He paused before continuing, "As I told you before, in the same way, Cain feared losing my presence. Do you remember this?"

"How could I forget it, my Lord?"

"There was a time when Lucifer feared the same, but that was back before time is now measured. Now, he calls himself the Accuser and can no longer access my presence; his hatred has driven him away. So he wanders, bereft of home, and he has abandoned my love. These three men you speak of have done the same. These are the spirits he is gathering together. One day, there will be a reckoning for them all, and I separate them from my creation like a farmer separates the wheat from the chaff. Eagle, one day the chaff will be burned away."

"But where do they go?" I asked.

"For this time they seek hosts in my creation. You saw the very first one in Eden. That strange lizard, as you liked to call it, was the first. But you have now seen it many more times in animals, and now you have seen it in the ones created in my image. They wander, Eagle. When they are cast out of the host they have, they go search for another."

"Why do you not stop them from finding another?" I asked.

He smiled and looked at me, and with tears in His eyes, He said, "It is a love story, Eagle. For it to be real, love must be chosen. Those created in my image have the power to withstand these evil spirits; more than enough power."

"And you never make a person choose you," I said.

"You have heard me say that many times, my friend. It is not only choice I give, it is also permission. Freedom exists where permission empowers choice, where they make their choices free of my control. In the times to come, people will scoff at this and believe I have abandoned them or no longer care." He paused before continuing, "People now realize they do not have to know me to live. They are beginning to see where their choices are taking them and that there are other powers in this world. These other powers do not care as I do, and nor do they give choice or permission to do anything that does not serve their purposes. But I will never withdraw my love from them. It always stands ready and always invites them to return. Their choices, combined with my love, will overthrow any evil power. I will never remove choice from them, and because of this, there will be some who will not return to me. It is for those that my heart breaks."

Silence again enveloped us. Still, there were no animals to be heard. The sunrise was breathtaking to behold, but only we would see it from this town on this day. Eventually, Wisdom and I stretched out our wings and went to the skies again. We spoke no words. We just had the sound of the wind in our ears and the stain of death in front of our eyes. The only words running through my mind were the Designer's 'the great gathering of spirits'.

The flood of evil had begun.

To be continued in *Three Floods: The Chaos of Rest*

AUTHOR NOTE

This is a two-part story. In dividing it into two books, I've wanted to build a backstory for Noah of all that brought him to build an ark and do the things the Bible has given us. The Bible gives us the names of Noah's ancestral line but very little story to accompany them. We all know him from the ark he built, but I believe there is an extraordinary story that built the man who built the ark. His story, to this point in the book, has taken hundreds of years, and if our lives are anything to go by, so much would have happened to him. There would have been many choices, actions, relationships, lives, and death that occurred in his own lifetime.

Three Floods follows the narrative of Genesis, with what I call the flood of evil in Genesis 6:1–7. These verses have always been somewhat of a mystery to me, and to be honest, I have found them hard to understand. So, when I came to write this story, I allowed myself to sit in a time where I've seen evil sweep across the world like a flood. Being in Lebanon in 2019 gave me a window of what it looked like for evil to sweep across the land of Syria and see firsthand the impact of this on the people who are now living as displaced people in Lebanon.

It was a joy to spend a chapter with Enoch, the man, not the city. He might be a character I someday return to and create a story for. His life is recorded in an extraordinary couple of verses in the Bible (Genesis 5:18–24), and I think it would be fascinating to work with a story of a man who "walked with God." Being that he was Noah's great-grandfather, I wanted to create a story about the generational character traits and belief systems that get passed down through every ancestral line. These generational traits have been something that has fascinated me about my own family line, and I wanted to demonstrate that we are often living with much of what has been carried by our forebears.

We know even less about Methuselah, and his son, Lamech (Noah's dad). We know they lived, had children, and died at an extremely old age. But, as with every character I write about, I love exploring their names' meanings. I believe they give us a window into history and the character of the people in the Bible. You will notice I do that with all the characters in this story. Names in the Old Testament give us a beautiful lens into who these people were. This was a very cultural thing to do in history, and I wanted to share that with today's readers. There's something profound in everyone's name, and these days, I do not think we spend enough time discovering who a person is; rather, we seem to focus on what a person can do rather than who a person is.

There are no women named in the Bible for these men. So, every woman in the story is also a work of fiction. I would have loved the Bible to have recorded this information, but it does not. So, I sort to place women in the story who would become partners (Eve's) with their men (Adam's). I used this to create an understanding of the relationships that were, hopefully, real for you as the reader as you walk out of some of your own relationships.

If you have read *Three Trees*, you will know that Wisdom and Eagle are eternal creatures through which the story flows. I thought about giving them offspring that would take their roles as they went from one generation to another. But, I decided not to do that and keep the voice of Eagle and Wisdom as you have read them. This way, I hope to give you a lens into my curiosity and growth. This also allows me to build their knowledge rather than start afresh with another character who will need to learn all that has gone before.

The city of Enoch is one that has fascinated me. In my research, I have not found a reliable source of its location. All we know of it is what the Bible has given us its reputation for; tradespeople and instrument makers. This gave me a natural city for Noah to learn his trade and discover the art of shipbuilding. I also loved the aspect that musicians would be drawn here, and it fascinates me to explore what that might mean and what instruments they would have produced. Again, this is something that has been lost to history.

The location of Eden is also a point of contention. We know from the Bible that the Tigris and Euphrates Rivers bordered it, and those two rivers are still known by the same names today. Experts, archaeologists, and biblical scholars all argue whether this is true. I have placed it somewhere in modern-day Iraq and Syria. From there, I have attempted to place cities, seas, and directions from that location.

As I said above, *Three Floods* is a work of fiction in which I have attempted to place much of my own story. That means I've tapped into my own experiences of pain, grief, shame, guilt, love, compassion, healing, and life to write. This has allowed me to place real emotions into such famous characters and, hopefully, help you be able to connect with them as well. Much of the way I interact with God is written on every page, and I hope it will be helpful for you as you navigate your own relationship with God.

This method of writing has become a powerful way for me to understand God. By putting Him in the story, gives away my own belief that God is a present God. Often in our world, and at times in our churches, we live as if He is a distant God, where we hope He hears and we hope He turns up. For me, He is always with us and always wants us to be with Him. It's a promise that Jesus gave when He told the disciples He would never leave them, and it's also an Old Testament concept where David expresses there is no place he can go to escape from Him. In this, I've used creation, community, and relationships to highlight how I connect with Him. He is my Designer and my friend.

ARTIST NOTE

I don't know if I have ever been more captivated by a form of storytelling than I was when reading through these pages for the first time. To return as the illustrator and accompany Matt in the creative process once again has been an experience I will treasure all of my life.

Matt has a talent for immersing his readers into a world that calls to life our senses and awakens our hearts as we dig our fingers into the soil of our stories. We go deeper into ourselves, creation, and the Designer with each turn of the page. I found my mind drawn to the very real people and places I experienced throughout the text, often forgetting this was a fictional story. The characters became so familiar they began to feel like family. Their real-life experiences of trials and triumphs were relatable in every way, so much so it was hard not to see myself within each one of them. This made it a very exciting place for me to dream about which parts would come to life through my paintbrush.

When it came time to begin the illustrating process, I wanted to push beyond where I had gone before with these characters and the world they are a part of. In *Three Trees*, I wanted to capture the simplicity of creation within its original design. I did this by stripping back form and realism to focus on lines and the continuity they create together. This time, in *Three Floods*, I had a desire to allow space between the lines, to discover more texture, depth, and layers. In the same way, we see more of the Designer as we return to His presence; I wanted my paintings to capture different ways of seeing and imagining the landscape, the characters, and the 'glow' that is ever-present in this story.

How does one capture a glow that radiates from within? A glow from the seeds that are carried in the hearts of God's people. What does it look like when we shine a light into the world, and how do our lights transform when they come together? These were the questions I started to ask myself as I imagined the history and lineage of the descendants of Adam and Eve and the mark they carried. The way this translated through my work was inspired by the rings of a tree. For me, this took the idea of light and embedded within it a story, represented through lines that appear as ripples around the characters seen throughout the illustrations. There is a generational inheritance present within each line that flows outwards and inwards.

There are several moments I have brought to life where the Designer and others are portrayed through a silhouette. This has become a way for me to balance how much I'm revealing and how much I'm concealing. There are parts of the relationship between the Designer and His design that I want to keep hidden and sacred but also reveal enough of it that can be a tangible encounter. Something visual that can accompany the story in such a way that it is an extension of what we are experiencing uniquely as we read. But not in such a way that I suggest too much that takes away from the moment we are invited into through the narrator. This style feels timeless as I could see any one generation, from the beginning of the age to the end, within these illustrations.

In the beginning, there is a portrait of Noah as a young boy riding on the shoulders of what could be his father, his grandfather, or the Designer Himself. At the same time, it could be any one of us in that tender moment within our own stories. It was my intention to make these scenes come to life in such a way we feel like we belong there as well.

There is a scene in the book where Noah and Nashah share a glow for the first time as their lives come together. Instead of this glow becoming two distinct patterns that collide as they walk side by side, this union becomes a circle as a mark of eternity. It's the love and the seed that they carry into the new creation they will become a part of. The circular glow lines emanate through the ground and mark the path they are on. Meanwhile, the vertical rainlines pour down before them to signify what lies ahead.

At the end of the book, we read about new life coming through Noah and Nashah as they welcome their firstborn son. The Designer enters the room after his birth, and we see the joining of the glow they each carry to His. This powerful interaction highlights the oneness that flows through us all, and I wanted to show His wrap-around-presence and breath of life filling the atmosphere in this painting. The very breath that traces back to Adam and the light that he carried within "that will never be extinguished." Each ripple I've placed around the two silhouettes symbolizes the journey of the seed that each generation carries. All part of His big love story.

Three Floods is rich with landscapes from mountain tops to the valley lows, from glittering star-filled skies to fish-filled rivers. Eagle is our guide and our eyes through it all. He has been given a gift of sight, but seeing also means he knows both dark and light. There is a flood of evil taking place, and I wanted the moment I captured of fear and uncertainty to come through his eyes and his tears as they 'mingle' with the Designers. Eagle also has visions and dreams in this book that unlock a door of hope and another flood. Though the future is full of unknowns, Eagle sees there is more to the story, and his eye is fixed not solely on the storm but the tree that carries the promise.

Lastly, I wanted to share the love between Eagle and Wisdom that soars weightlessly to the highest height and breaks through the hardest ground. These two characters carry such love and faithfulness that I yearned to see them together in an image time and time again. Their love captures the heart of the Designer and what it is to be beloved.

In this series of artworks, my prayer is for the audience to find a connection to creation, to love, to hope, and to each other. Thank you to Matt Beckenham for allowing me to come, once again, to soar with Eagle and Wisdom, to sit with the Designer, and to find my hands deep into the soil of His love.

Jessie DeCorsey
www.jessiedecorsey.com

ABOUT THE AUTHOR

Matt is an author, speaker, and teacher whose desire is to help people discover their identity and design. His work stretches out beyond the four walls of the church and is an invitation to explore the narrative of how a relationship with God moves and unfolds in our daily lives.

Matt, along with his wife, Trish, are the founders of Greater Things International, which draws people together from all over the world to deepen their relationship with God. With their 30 years of ministry and counseling, they are committed to seeing people live in the freedom of their original design through community and connection.

His desire is that everyone would discover the immense love of the Designer, and live from His design for us. Over the years, Matt has done this through each of his books, online courses, mentoring and the Greater Things International podcasts.

Matt was born in Australia where he and Trish currently live and have three adult children. Before stepping into Greater Things International, he was in pastoral ministry for 19 years.

Prior to this, he worked in structural and civil engineering as a draftsperson and IT Manager.

If he and Trish are not in Sydney, you'll often find them exploring New Zealand, a place that has captured their hearts. To be a part of this movement, you can find Matt at:

greaterthingsinternational.com

Winifred DeCorsey (age 7)

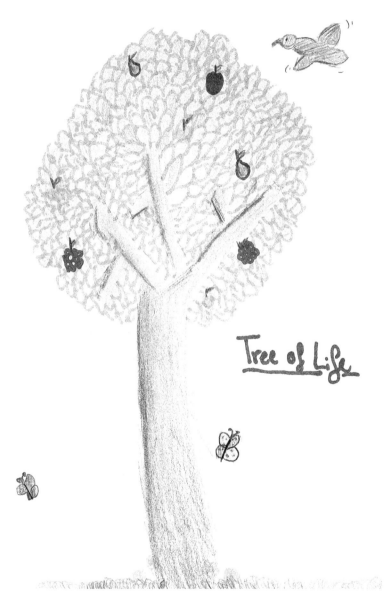

Willow Gamble (age 11)

Zoey Engelbrecht (age 10)

COMING SOON

An extract from Matt's next book

THREE FLOODS: THE CHAOS OF REST

CHAPTER 1

Jericho is a name that will live long in my memory, but not for the fragrance the Designer knew it by. There was no sweet fragrance in Jericho that day. All I could smell was evil and death. The Designer had told us that long ago, people met with Him here, and their conversation with Him was like a sweet-smelling fragrance to Him. Now, it lies in smoking ruins.

The flood of evil has begun, and this town, below Wisdom and I, was a stark reminder of what evil was doing to the Designer's creation. Two days ago, this sleepy town would not have known what was about to befall it. They would have watched a sunrise similar to what we were seeing today. They would have seen the striking mountains to the north that are being lit up with the first rays of the sunrise. Maybe they have grown used to seeing such beautiful sunrises and were just going about their morning routines, unchanged by the generations before them. The chill in the air told them of a season that was slowly changing, and soon, the warmth of the day would be upon them.

But, for now, Wisdom and I are soaring above clouds that will soon be burned away by the sun's warmth. A day that breaks as beautifully as this should be remembered for the wonder of creation, not the scar of death we see below. It is not just the town this evil has affected; the regions surrounding this town will feel the power of evil. Even now, we can see herds of animals to the east and west of Jericho that have lost their shepherds, and they will wander until someone finds them. Much has changed in two days.

The few survivors of Jericho were now choosing whether they would stay or follow us to Enoch. The Designer would stay with them until they made their choices. Moments, such as these, He would never rush. Most of them had just lost everything and everyone; there was nothing left for them here, except to grieve all they have lost. While they were with Him, they were safe and no one would harm them. Could they understand that while they were with Him, they would heal and flourish again?

I watched as some just sat on the ground and wailed. Others were digging holes to bury the dead. Some walked through the smokey ruins in the desperate hope of finding someone still alive. There were so few survivors.

The Designer rescued them from the evil men who attacked their village. They had been chained together and forcefully led back to be sold as slaves. Wisdom and I had seen them being led away, but we did not see the Designer rescue them. That night was dark, and after we found the lines of prisoners, we searched for the Designer.

Today, in the light of the new day, we can see where the evil men lay dead, no longer on horseback and no longer fierce and evil. They looked to be sleeping and would soon awaken with the sun's rising to wreak more evil on creation. But there would be no rising for these men. They had made their choices and now lay dead in those choices.

As one day passed into the next, some survivors came to the Designer and chose to stay in Jericho, but for what purpose, I could not tell. They spoke of rebuilding their town, but this time with a wall to surround it. The rest accepted the Designer's invitation to return to Enoch. Each of them had witnessed His rescue, and now each was bringing their choices to Him.

Each evening, Wisdom and I listened to the stories of the survivors as they gathered around cooking fires. Each person's recollection was different from the next, and by the time they reached Enoch, it would most likely be a different story again. Some spoke of a blinding light, while others said it was a great voice from heaven. Some were so traumatized they had not yet spoken, and some just cried.

But the main point we gathered from them all was that the Designer simply stood in the middle of the road. As the horsemen approached, their horses stopped in front of Him, unwilling to go another step forward. It did not matter how much they cursed or beat their animals; they would not move. Each of the survivors told of how the evil men could not see the Designer, but they, and the horses, all could. The Designer then approached each of the horses, and as He did, the horse would settle, but the evil man on it writhed to the point they fell from their horse. The Designer would then go to the writhing man and say something to them that the survivors could not hear. Each responded with a blood-curdling scream and then died. No one knew what had occurred, but all could see the result. As the evil men saw what was happening to their own men, they dropped the chains that bound their prisoners and beat their horses to make them flee; even so, none of the horses moved. As each man was unhorsed and died, something was released from the horse. The Designer would then reach out to the horse, heal its wounds, and then set the animal free.

The evening before we set off for Enoch, Wisdom and I sat with the Designer at His fire. Ever since He returned with the survivors, His demeanor had changed; we could all feel His sadness.

"My, Lord. Can I ask a question?" I asked.

"Of course, my friend," He responded.

"The survivors all spoke of the evil men not being able to see you, where they, and their horses, could see you perfectly well. Why were the evil men not able to see you?"

The Designer sat silently for a few moments before He exhaled and said, "When a man's spirit has given itself to evil, it can no longer discern good from bad and right from wrong. These men only had eyes for evil."

"But you were still there. Everyone saw you," I responded.

"Yes, Eagle, I was there, as I am with you today. Let me put it another way: When you are with me, you can no longer feel evil, can you?"

"No, my Lord, when I am with you, I feel more alive than I have ever been."

"So it is with these men, except I am not their Designer anymore. Their designer is Lucifer, and he is all they can see; they can no longer see me until I reveal myself to them."

"Is that what you did when the survivors told us of you speaking to each of the evil men on the ground?"

"Yes, Eagle. Even then, I invited them to return to me, but none did. My invitation was the revelation of who I am, but they still chose to reject me. To each, I spoke the name I gave them, but none of them recognized it. Now they are gone."

"Gone, where?"

"They are no longer in my presence, Eagle. They carry another mark now, and it is not one you will recognize, for it is not of my doing. But they can no longer harm you, or anyone else, ever again."

Once again, I felt the weight of the Designer's voice and words. Each one felt like another weight had been added to all I was witnessing. My comfort and presence were all I could offer him; I had no words.

Days had passed since these events, and life was slowly returning. The animals that were all absent in the surrounding forests were returning. Many of the farm animals had come into the ruined town looking for food and care, and each day, a few bedraggled survivors returned to their destroyed homes.

Wisdom then said, "My Lord, would you have us return to Enoch and tell Noah all that has happened here and expect the survivors in a few days?"

"Yes, Wisdom, that would be wise. I will walk with them, but I will not walk with them alone. I have called another eagle, Joy, to come to me. Each of these survivors will need her to travel with us. She will be here in the morning. Once she has come, you are free to return to Enoch."

To be continued …

Other books by Matt Beckenham

EDEN'S BLUEPRINT

Eden's Blueprint is an invitation to feast on the divine revelations the Father has entrusted Matt to share. You will find yourself drawn into sacred places that you were designed to walk in. As you journey through these pages, your heart will be moved by the language of the Kingdom, a language that began in the Garden, a place that will bring healing to your heart and draw you back to Eden, back to home.

ISBN: 9798985346725 (paperback)

THREE TREES

As the sun rose on their first day outside of Eden, Adam and Eve stood at the edge of their paradise, uncertain of what lay ahead. Eagle, their watchman, soared above them, his keen eyes scanning the horizon. Much had changed, but some things would never change. The Designer's love can provide hope and restoration, even in the darkest moments.

ISBN: 9780645786804 (paperback)

Printed in the USA
CPSIA information can be obtained
at www.ICGtesting.com
JSHW081045061123
51404JS00004B/15